THE
SISTERS

JANET KAY

World Castle Publishing, LLC
Pensacola, Florida
Copyright © Janet Kay 2018
Hardback ISBN: 9781629899145
Paperback ISBN: 9781629899152
eBook ISBN: 9781629899169
First Edition World Castle Publishing, LLC, April 30, 2018
http://www.worldcastlepublishing.com
Cover: Karen Fuller
Editor: Maxine Bringenberg

DEDICATED
WITH LOTS OF LOVE
TO MY TEN AMAZING
GRANDCHILDREN:

Derek Jenson

Madelaine Graber

Malachi Jenson

William Graber

Abigail Graber

Audrey McLochlin

Andrew Graber

Milton Jenson

Jared McLochlin

George Jenson

ACKNOWLEDGEMENTS

This book would not have been possible without the valuable assistance of a number of individuals, groups and resources.

I wish to thank my first readers and reviewers for their insight and feedback: Agnes Kennard, Shane Jenson, and Peggy Roeder; also my content experts: Eric Christopher, Past Life Regression Therapist; Renee Tallent of the Galveston Historical Foundation; and Dash Beardsley, "The Ghost Man of Galveston."

I would like to acknowledge the Rosenberg Library of Galveston, Texas and the Duluth, Minnesota Public Library for their assistance with my historical research. Other resources that were very helpful to me included books by Dr. Ian Stevenson, Dr. Michael Newton, Brian Weiss, James Van Praagh and Sylvia Browne. I would encourage you to explore their work for more information on past lives, life on the other side, and reincarnation.

A special thank-you to the St. Croix Writers of Solon Springs, Wisconsin for their ongoing support, encouragement and feedback – and to Anna Martineau Merritt for my author's bio photo.

To my agent, Faye Swetky Literary Agency; my publisher

World Castle Publishing (Karen Fuller, Publisher; and Maxine Bringenberg, Editor) – thanks for all you've done and continue to do to promote this novel.

Many thanks to my readers – to all who have enjoyed my previous novels, *Waters of The Dancing Sky* and *Amelia 1868*, and have been anxiously awaiting publication of *The Sisters.*

Last, but certainly not least, thank you to my children – Shannon & Will Graber, Shane & Sandi Jenson, Sherry Jenson; and my grandchildren – Derek, Madelaine, Malachi, William, Abby, Audrey, Andrew, Milton, Jared and George. Thank you for your love, support and encouragement - and for your understanding when I am pre-occupied, living in the world I've created for my characters!

ONE
BELLA

"Goodbyes are only for those who love with their eyes. For those who love with heart and soul, there is no such thing as separation."
Rumi

Shivers slithered up and down my spine as I huddled beside the ruins of a tilting Gothic Revival mausoleum covered with moss and ancient sprawling vines. I was trying to hide, trying to protect myself from the devastating reality that my soul mate's ashes were being interred here today...and the fact that I was essentially nobody in the life he had lived upon this earth.

I was alone, as I'd been most of my life. Sixty years old, never married, having spent my life in love with a man I could not have. Alone. The unwed mother of an adorable little boy who had been called home to Heaven many years ago when he was just three years of age.

My tears threatened to erupt into uncontrollable, gut-wrenching sobs — tears that would give away the secret I'd carried for so long. As ominous clouds and layers of fog drifted in from the Gulf of Mexico, hovering over the Old City Cemetery in my hometown of Galveston, Texas, the wind picked up. Ancient trees danced in the breeze, their leaves rustling across the old, weather-beaten cemetery and its moss-covered tombstones.

Evergreen wreaths, in honor of the coming Christmas season, surrounded me. Christmas was the worst possible time of the year for anyone to die, I lamented. Why couldn't he have waited…for me, for us?

I stood alone in the shaded recesses of the cemetery, watching my older sister, Veronica, one of Galveston's prominent socialites, as she almost seemed to be weeping over her husband's grave. She leaned against her three grown children, as if she needed their support to survive the death of a husband she never really knew. Her grandchildren surrounded her.

Veronica and her family were all appropriately dressed in funeral black — unlike me, their eccentric Aunt Bella. I wore a long flowing red skirt, one of my Goodwill purchases, colorful dangling jewelry I'd made myself, and a vintage red straw hat adorned by a white oleander flower. Jimmy would have been pleased. He was the one who gave me that hat years ago. I'd worn it as we'd explored the beaches of West Galveston together, the Stewart Mansion, and other haunted locations. Memories I will treasure forever.…

The lonely sound of "Taps" echoed from the distance, followed by the traditional military gun salute. Finally, twelve white doves were released into the heavens, one for each member of my sister's family. I did not count.

I had to escape soon, although a wave of guilt suddenly washed over me. I *should* be there for my only sister at a time like this, I reprimanded myself. What kind of a sister was I? One who had betrayed her, I must admit, but one who had also been wronged by her. She'd taken from me that which should have been mine, the most important person in my life.

My sister and I had fought for years, about anything and everything, although we'd never come close to acknowledging or discussing the real reason we could barely tolerate each other. Did she know? Did she suspect?

Should I, could I, just slip away quietly as if I hadn't been there?

Sa Bella, my dear Sa Bella, Jimmy's voice suddenly whispered into my mind as I felt a chill pass through me, then the reassuring warmth of his arms holding me close. Of course he wasn't really there—nor would he ever be again.

He was the only one who had ever called me "Sa Bella" instead of Bella or Isabella, my given name.

"Oh Jimmy, it's you," I whispered into the mist that now swirled through the cemetery. Finally, after many long and lonely years, he held me once more. All those years that I'd tried to be content with a "friends only" relationship. All those years of hoping with all my heart and soul that we would find a way to be together someday, the way we were meant to be.

Jimmy Caldwell had been the perfect picture of health, a true Texas cowboy and prominent businessman; until he'd dropped of a heart attack several days ago at the age of sixty-nine.

I'll always be here for you. Someday we will be together again, the way we were meant to be, he assured me. *But you need to do the right thing for your sister. She is also grieving, whether you know that or not.*

With that, he tipped his Stetson hat in my direction, flashed that big Texas grin of his, and suddenly disappeared. A lingering chill filled the air, leaving me with a warm glow spreading throughout my heavy heart.

"Aunt Bella." My niece Maria's voice suddenly broke through my reverie as she descended upon me. A beautiful young woman dressed elegantly in a long black dress, she was Veronica and Jimmy's eldest daughter, and a respected psychiatrist. Maria was the one who had tried over the years to calm the angry seas and bickering between her mother and aunt.

No two sisters could possibly have been more different than Veronica and me. We were like black and white, like fire and ice.

I was the family's black sheep, the spinster sister with fire running through her veins. The one who had scandalized the town by having a baby out of wedlock. Yes, I was the one people whispered and wondered about. A free spirit who had difficulty conforming to the rules that the rest of the world seemed to live by.

Even down here in Galveston—where most islanders these days enjoyed the freedom of dressing in casual Hawaiian shirts, shorts, and scandals as they drove their golf carts along the beach and partied at the hot spots along the Seawall—I still stood out as being eccentric. I danced on the beach late at night by myself, talking to spirits. I refused to attend many of the family and social functions that the rest of my family felt were essential. I spoke my mind, whether others wanted to hear my opinions or not. I was a recluse at times, holed up in my cottage, creating my art and ignoring the rest of the world. I marched to my own drummer, so to speak, and did not care what the rest of the world thought of me.

I'd spent my life lurking in the shadow of my "perfect" older sister, Veronica. She was the proper one, one of Galveston's finest citizens—and the wife adorned in sheets of frosty ice. She was so much like our mother, Olivia—formal, politically correct, always dressed fashionably and properly, always doing what was expected of her, and never expressing her true feelings about anything. She lived her life pretty much as our ancestors had half a century ago, carrying on the old traditions instead of letting her hair down and enjoying modern life.

I turned my attention back to Maria, reaching out to give her a big hug. I'd always liked Maria, and sometimes felt bad for refusing her invitations to family gatherings that included

Veronica. "I'm so sorry, Maria. So sorry for your terrible loss."
My loss, too, I shouted silently, wondering if Jimmy was still
hanging around watching his funeral proceedings and perhaps
listening to my thoughts.

Wiping tears from her eyes with a delicate lace handkerchief
that had once belonged to her grandmother, Maria smiled sadly.
"Dad was larger than life and we all miss him—including my
mom, you know…." She waited for the response that I was
unable to give her.

Sighing, Maria continued more firmly. "I am asking you
to come over to the house this evening for a family gathering
to honor Dad. He would want you to be there, you know. He
always had a special place in his heart for you."

I was taken aback. What did she know? What did she
suspect? Could she see right through me, analyzing everything I
said and did? Composing myself, I replied, "And he was always
very special to me." I spoke softly, trying to absorb her words.
More special than any of you will ever know!

"We've put together a slide show of his life that we will show
tonight for family only," Maria continued. "You need to be there,
Bella…."

"Why is that?"

"Because you are still family, despite the differences between
you and my mom. She even wants you to come."

"Really? Why?"

"You are family, Aunt Bella, and we love you. So did my
dad. He was the one who urged us all to include you in family
gatherings, despite your frequent refusals to attend. He was the
one who loved spending time with you taking photos on the
beach, even chasing those Galveston ghosts! Things my mother
had no interest in doing."

"I don't know, Maria…." *How could I control my grief in front*

10

of them all without breaking down and revealing myself?

"Please come. For Dad's sake. You and my mother need to put your differences aside, at least for one day, as he would want you to. Eight o'clock tonight at Ashton Villa, Bella. It's still your family home, too, you know. I personally will be upset if you do not show up. Do it for Dad, for Mom, for all of us."

I felt a nudge from beyond the grave, a wink in the eye of the cowboy I'd always loved, as I found myself agreeing to attend this memorial event at Ashton Villa, my childhood home.

I glanced back one more time at Jimmy's fresh grave. Veronica stood there alone, staring at the wreath of red poinsettia flowers and evergreen branches that marked her husband's grave. Her slumped shoulders were shaking as though she were actually crying.

Go to her. The thought flashed through my mind and propelled me forward. I could almost feel her pain. As Jimmy had reminded me, I wasn't the only one grieving, after all. Approaching her from behind, I gently touched her shoulder. She startled, then turned around to face me, obviously surprised to see me. Her eyes were puffy, streaks of mascara dripping down her face.

My arms opened to her automatically and she fell into them. We cried together, our tears mingling, holding on to each other. Neither of us spoke. Words were not required. Jimmy had brought us together in our pain, at least for today. We both knew deep down that this truce probably would not last. We'd be back to our bickering someday soon. For now, this was the right thing to do, for both of us.

As her children approached, gathering around her once again, I left, promising to be there for the family celebration of Jimmy's life that evening.

Emotionally exhausted, I slipped away to find my battered old Honda and begin the drive home to my little cottage on the

West End of Galveston Island. I'd have time for a nap before driving back to Ashton Villa this evening. If I could possibly sleep….

As always, the drive along the Gulf Coast was therapeutic. The waves were wild today, pounding and splashing against the seawall. Surfers were out riding the waves. I opened the windows to feel the breeze, my long dark hair whipping around my tear-streaked face.

As I breathed in the soothing scent of the sea, images flooded my mind—images of times Jimmy and I had spent together walking these beaches, capturing stunning photos of the changing moods of the sea, of sunrises and sunsets.

Stolen moments perhaps, I sighed. Still, "stolen" wasn't exactly the right word to describe our time together. We didn't do anything wrong; not then, not after he married my sister.

I'd also spent many lonely hours by myself over the years, walking barefoot in the surf as I mourned the loss of my baby son so long ago. It would be forty years this week since my three-year old pride and joy was snatched from my life. He simply did not wake up one morning. How I missed my Little Jonathan.

How I hoped that he and Jimmy were together in Heaven, the way I always wanted them to be on Earth. Thankfully, Jimmy had enjoyed visiting and playing with Jonathan during those years.

My baby, born out of wedlock, needed a father figure in his life, Veronica and Olivia had decided. I suspected they didn't trust me, free spirit that I was, to be a good enough parent on my own. Of course they, and the rest of my family, had been thoroughly humiliated that I'd gotten myself pregnant and disgraced our prominent born-on-the-island Galveston family. Instead of identifying and marrying the father of my child, I'd refused to reveal his identity. It was none of their business. And no, marriage was not an option, I told them repeatedly.

So, pregnant at twenty, I'd moved out of Ashton Villa, our Italianate Villa mansion that had been built before the Civil War and passed down through many generations of the Brown family.

I had to get away from them all for a number of reasons, including the burning shame they'd inflicted upon me—and their insistence that I go away to have my baby and put him or her up for adoption. I could never do that. I wanted this baby desperately. This innocent little child was probably all I'd have left to remember his father by.

I'd found and moved into my little cottage on a narrow spit of land on the west end of the island, sandwiched between the Gulf of Mexico on one side and Galveston Bay on the other. Thankfully, I was able to purchase the place with some of the trust fund money that had been set aside for me when I was a baby.

That was the only time I'd dipped into my trust fund over all these years. I refused to draw my funds down, not even to buy myself a more respectable car or designer clothes like the rest of my family wore. Instead, I clipped discount coupons and used them extensively all around the island, and I did most of my shopping at Goodwill, to the embarrassment of my prominent family. To be honest, I relished the look of horror on my sister's face when she saw me coming out of Goodwill with another bag full of slightly-used vintage clothing.

Beyond the side benefit of humiliating my family, my real purpose was to support myself through my art, photography, and writing so I could leave the bulk of my trust fund to a local foundation for the benefit of orphans and abused children. I was doing this in memory of my dear little Jonathan. Jimmy was the only one who knew about this fund. He had helped me to set it up.

13

My tiny cottage sat on a point that jutted out into Galveston Bay. From the old-fashioned Victorian gazebo overlooking the bay, I could watch the sun set every evening. It was painted a faded aqua color and was perched on stilts, as many houses on the island were to protect them from storms and flooding. Surrounded by overgrown gardens and massive twisted palm trees, the cottage seemed to be hidden away from the world, which was exactly what I wanted at that time—and still craved today.

Over the years, I'd turned my hideaway into a colorful artist's and writer's studio. This was where I worked researching and writing my books, developing and framing photos, painting, and designing jewelry, all of which I sold at local stores and on my website.

Today as I pulled into my narrow driveway, I could hear my wind chimes clanging in the ocean breeze. Midnight, my favorite black cat, and her six playful kittens came out to greet me. Midnight purred and rubbed against my leg while the kittens tumbled playfully at my feet. They were my children now.

It felt good to be home in my own place, away from the world, and hopefully, from some of the pain that seemed to surround and haunt me. The bright colors of my walls, full of my paintings, always cheered me up. Vases of wild flowers, framed photographs, and lots of books were scattered about the open living room and kitchen, which featured a window wall overlooking the sea. One long shelf wrapping around the nook in the corner was full of sea shells and pieces of driftwood I'd collected on my walks beside the ocean.

Below the shelf were several paint-splattered tables overflowing with paint tubes, artist and jewelry supplies—and a partially completed sketch. I'd been in the middle of sketching an image of Jimmy as I remembered him in the early days...walking

14

on the beach, laughing, with a gleam in his eyes. Picking up the sketch, holding it over my heart, the tears began to flow once more.

"Oh Jimmy," I cried out. "I miss you so."

Replacing the sketch, I made my way to my cluttered davenport. Shoving a stack of unread newspapers onto the floor, I collapsed. Shivering, I wrapped a blanket around me as Midnight jumped up onto my lap. Maybe I could rest a bit.

But first, I had to pick up the old photo album that had spent forty years prominently displayed on my dust-covered second-hand coffee table.

Little Jonathan—I'd stenciled the words across the wood cover. It was filled with photos of the three short years of his life. I still liked to page through that album, remembering the good times, the funny times.

He'd been such a smart little guy, curious about everything, so loving and happy. As I paged through the album once again, I rubbed my index finger over one special photo, trying to absorb the energy of the two people I'd loved most in my life. It was a photo of Jonathan, Jimmy, and me laughing and playing together on the beach. Jonathan had died so unexpectedly, two weeks later. And now, Jimmy was also gone.

Tears filled my eyes once again. Would they never end? Gently shoving the purring cat off my lap, I decided to indulge in a glass of wine. Maybe that would dull the pain—and also provide some instant courage to help me through the event at Ashton Villa tonight.

15

TWO
BELLA

*"The leaves of memory seemed to make
a mournful rustling in the dark."*
Henry Wadsworth Longfellow

A full moon glowed over Ashton Villa as I arrived and parked my rusty car with the dented fender on Broadway Street amongst a Lexus, Porsche, Jaguar, vintage Lincoln Town Car, and other gleaming cars, the kinds of cars everyone in my family had always driven. Everybody except me.

I hadn't even bothered to get a car wash. Perhaps I was just making a statement. Sure, I could have afforded a somewhat respectable vehicle, but I was determined not to dip into my trust fund any farther. I was determined to live a life totally different from the lives my family lived. Jimmy had been the only one who understood that. And now Jimmy was gone.

Still, I was not immune to the charms of the classic mansion I'd once called home. The red brick three-story structure featured cast iron scrollwork, bracketed eaves, and iron lintels over the tall slender windows. Candlelight glowed through the windows across the beautifully landscaped lawns and gardens. Majestic palm trees and ancient oak trees swayed in the ocean breeze.

As waves of nostalgia washed over me, I took a deep breath and rang the doorbell. How long had it been since I'd paid my sister's family a visit? It will be OK, I tried to reassure myself. This wasn't about me, after all. It was about paying my respects to Jimmy.

Edward, the aging butler, answered the door, nodding stiffly as if he didn't remember me, the allegedly "crazy" daughter who grew up here. I could still hear him muttering to himself, "somethin' wrong with that child." He'd just shake his head whenever I'd insist that he acknowledge my imaginary friends, invite them along for a drive, or serve them all individual plates of cookies in the parlor.

Old Edward wore several hats these days, including chauffeur. He'd have been the one who'd picked up my eighty-three-year old mother, Olivia, from the nursing home where she now resided.

Although our mother was suffering from Alzheimer's disease and needed around-the-clock care, the family tried to get her out as much as they could handle. I tried to visit her as often as I could, although the visits were sometimes strained and painful as she'd scold me like I was a rebellious child. Other times, she didn't know who I was.

"Good evening, Edward." I attempted a smile to counteract his sour demeanor.

He merely nodded sternly, gesturing at me to enter, and escorted me into the Gold Room. It was beautifully decorated for a Christmas that would now take on an entirely different form and shape.

The family had gathered around a cozy fire in the elegant white fireplace with gold leafing. It was dwarfed by a massive Christmas tree decorated with ornaments that had been passed down through the family for more than a century.

I glanced around the elegant mirrored room, where little had changed over hundreds of years. One of my nieces was softly playing the baby grand piano, her image reflected in the French mirrors with their gold-scrolled gilded frames. The ornate gold chandelier hanging from the fourteen-foot ceiling was surrounded with frescos of cherubs.

I'd always loved the daring paintings still hanging on the walls, some of which Bettie Brown, former owner and, perhaps, our most popular and best-loved ancestor, had created before her death in 1920. Maybe I could paint like that someday, I'd daydreamed as a child.

Bettie had managed to scandalize and offend some of Galveston's socialites, they say, with her delightful paintings of nude cherubs. The house was still filled today with period antiques that Bettie had purchased on her trips to Europe.

Bettie was eccentric, a little like me, perhaps. Very unconventional for her time. She'd freely roamed the island, major cities in the United States, even Europe, unchaperoned. Rumor has it that she drove her team of horses and buggy along the beach late at night, smoked, and wore lavish European gowns, always with an elegant silk train and matching lace parasol. She had studied art in Vienna during her twenties, and continued to passionately pursue art throughout her life.

I knew for a fact that her spirit continued to haunt this house that she dearly loved. From time to time she would materialize at the top of the massive carved wooden staircase in one of her elegant flowing gowns, complete with a matching silk train that floated eerily behind her. Semi-transparent, she seemed to glow in another-worldly fashion.

As a child I'd been at first terrified, then thrilled, to wake in the middle of the night to the sounds of somebody playing the piano in the Gold Room. I'd slip out of my pink flowered canopy bed upstairs, trying not to wake Veronica, who slept soundly in her matching bed on the other side of our room. I would creep down the stairs to peer into the room. Nobody was there, but the piano continued to play what I considered to be heavenly music. I would sit on the stairs for hours, utterly entranced, as I was transported into another world that somehow felt like "home" to me.

Once I saw Miss Bettie, a filmy apparition in her glowing white gown. She was sitting on the piano bench playing the most beautiful music I'd ever heard. They say it was her sister, Matilda, who played the piano and violin, while Bettie focused on her painting. But it was definitely Miss Bettie who sat there before my very eyes, playing heavenly music…perhaps something her spirit took up after her demise?

I felt a distinct chill as I swore she turned and smiled at me. I thought I must be special, that Miss Bettie had picked me out to listen to her music.

Why didn't anyone else in my family hear her music or see her?

Veronica told me I was crazy, that there was no such thing as ghosts. But I still remember her running up the stairs one time, her eyes wide with fear. She'd hidden under her covers the rest of the night. She never would admit she'd seen anything like a ghost. Admitting it, after all, would have meant that I was right and maybe not crazy after all.

Veronica and I…we were known as "the sisters," for better or worse. While we'd shared many memorable experiences growing up together, times had drastically changed. People who'd known our family for years whispered behind our backs, "Whatever happened to the sisters? They used to be so close. You never see them together anymore. When you do, they barely speak to each other."

Tonight, memories of Miss Bettie helped me to smile confidently as I bravely entered the room and made my way to the wine and hors d'oeuvres table. It was beautifully decorated with huge bouquets of funeral flowers, and photos of Jimmy and his family.

Fortified with a few gulps of obviously expensive red wine—unlike the box wine I drank—I approached Veronica and her family to exchange the kinds of formal greetings and condolences that were expected on an occasion like this. They all greeted me warmly, especially Maria, who was obviously pleased that I had actually showed up.

"Did you see Mother yet?" Veronica asked me anxiously as she pointed towards an elegant scrolled antique loveseat at the other end of the room.

"Not yet. How is she doing this evening?"

Veronica sighed. "Not as well as I had hoped. We are spelling each other off staying at her side. She is confused and rather testy. Still, I felt she should be here."

"I'll take a turn," I gladly volunteered so I could escape from the stories that family members were sharing about times they'd enjoyed with Jimmy. Times I was not included in. I had my own memories, of course, but it was not possible or appropriate to share them with his *real* family.

"Thank you," Veronica sighed politely. "I hope she doesn't act up and embarrass us all."

"We're family. Don't worry about it."

I would never worry about something as trivial as Olivia having a hissy fit, not at a time like this. But Veronica would. Everything had to be perfect and under control in her prim and proper world. Did she ever let her hair down and just let things flow?

"Hello, Mother." I greeted my thin aging mother with a kiss

on her forehead as I released one of Veronica's grown grandsons from babysitting Grandma. As he hustled off, grinning with gratitude, I sat down beside her and patted her gnarled hand. "Are you enjoying the celebration for Jimmy?"

"Where the hell is Jimmy? Late for his own party?" this prim and proper little old lady blurted out. I'd never heard her swear in her life, not until the past year.

"We are here, Mother, to celebrate his life. Jimmy is dead, remember?"

"Oh no! Dead? Jimmy is dead? So why are we celebrating then?" she frowned, shaking her head, totally confused. "What's wrong with this newfangled world?"

"We're remembering his life, the way he would want us to. Do you want to talk about good times you had with him over the years?"

"Good times?" She sighed. "He was such a darling little boy. He sat on my lap and I read him stories...he died? But he was so little. What a goddamn shame." She pounded her cane on the floor and raised her voice.

This was going downhill fast. She was obviously remembering my Jonathan, piercing my heart once more. "Mother, you are thinking about Jonathan, my little boy, who sat on your lap. He loved your stories...before he died many years ago. Now we are talking about Jimmy," I continued quietly. "Veronica's husband, who just died." Jimmy...Veronica's husband. It was not easy for me to say these words, not when I felt the way I did about the only love of my life.

"Who? I didn't know Veronica had a husband. What's his name?"

"Jimmy," I whispered, as a tear dribbled down my cheek.

"Speak up, young lady. I can't hear your mumbling," she spoke louder yet. I noticed Veronica gesturing nervously to the young woman seated at the piano, urging her to play more loudly.

"It's OK. You are tired. Let's just sit and relax a while, all right?"

Olivia began to pout, fiddling with her cane. At least she was quiet—for a while. Soon her eyes began to dart anxiously around the Gold Room as if she were searching for something. Something very important.

"What is it?" I asked quietly. "What are you looking for?"

"My Christmas village, damn it!" she exploded as she struggled to stand on her own. I grabbed her arm just in time to prevent a nasty fall.

Her Christmas village! She was, of course, remembering the massive Department 56 Snow Village collection that she had acquired over many years, ever since I was a little girl. It had taken up most of the ballroom and had become a family tradition. Galvestonians had flocked to visit Olivia's famous Christmas village every Christmas. What had become of this tradition? I hadn't been here in years. I had no clue.

"The Christmas village?" I asked Veronica as I walked past her, holding Olivia's arm.

"Over there, in the ballroom," Veronica replied icily. I must have intruded on something; or perhaps she didn't want me to be the one to show Mother the village. Who knew?

I led Mother into the ballroom, flipped on the light switches, and was immediately stunned and mesmerized by the Christmas village display that came to life before our eyes. The entire ballroom was filled with tables of Christmas village houses and accessories, lights and Christmas music. It truly was a winter wonderland. Who had done this? Certainly not Mother. Veronica?

Mother's eyes filled with tears of joy as she somehow managed to navigate her way, limping on her cane, around the endless displays. Her memory seemed to return in incredible fashion as she relayed the names of various snow village pieces she had purchased, when, and even the amounts she had paid for them. She was on top of this. She was adamant that her descendants needed to know the value of these pieces.

Shaking my head, I stepped back in awe. My mother seemed to walk between two worlds, remembering things that none of the rest of us remembered...and forgetting the things that she needed to know to exist in this world. Somehow I knew on an instinctive level that I would still love her always. She was my mother, despite the conflicted relationship we'd sometimes had.

"What the fuck?" my mother suddenly exploded, loud and clear. My mother? Her words? Really?

I joined her as she scrutinized the table in the far corner where one of her favorite pieces, Grandma's Cottage, had always been prominently displayed.

"Where is the gazebo? Where are the ice skaters that are supposed to be skating on the mirror in front of my cottage?" she demanded. "And the elves? Where are they?"

"They will be back, Mother," I tried to calm her down. "They will be back, exactly the way you want them to be. For now...." I breathed deeply, hoping I would not upset her further, "Do you remember what Christmas was like here years ago, when you were just a little girl?" I settled her into an overstuffed chair.

I waited with bated breath, not sure if she would strike me with her cane or if this would somehow unleash memories of the past. Time seemed to stand still. She sat stiffly, like a rigid soldier, blank eyes staring into the past, perhaps into a strange world that we were not a part of. The only sound to be heard was the tinkling of Christmas bells ringing out from one of Mother's snow village churches.

Finally she turned to me, a softer, wistful look in her suddenly younger eyes. "Don't you remember what Christmas was like when we were young?" Giggling like a child, she continued. "Oh my! On this special day, our cousins, you, and I were actually allowed into the formal dining room at Ashton Villa. Can't you just see the porcelain bowl in the center of the table, decorated with cupids and flowers? I remember the polished silver salvers with domed lids, full of side dishes, lined up on the sideboards. The beautiful china with gold trim. Fancy little dishes of salted almonds at each place. Sometimes there were forty of us around that gleaming mahogany table. Yes," she sighed, "we always started with oysters on the half shell...and there was creamed cauliflower. But the highlight was a roasted pig with an apple in its mouth. Do you remember?"

I nodded, remembering nothing. Obviously, I hadn't even been born when my mother was a little girl. However, I was not about to spoil her mood by telling her that.

"For dessert, the adults had flaming plum pudding with brandied hard sauce...." She drifted off into another world. "But we children," she confided with a gleam in her eyes, "We had the best dessert of all, didn't we?"

I nodded in agreement.

"Oh yes, we waited anxiously for the maid to bring in the silver platter with a huge nest of spun sugar. In the center of the nest, there was a large ice-cream hen surrounded by yellow baby chicks made of ice cream. We each got our own little chick. That was the best ice cream I ever had. Aunt Bettie, I think, was the one who had the hen and chick molds made on one of her trips to New York. It became a family tradition...."

Olivia's voice trailed off as she came back to the present, a puzzled look spreading across her face. She shook her head as if to ward off cob-webs infiltrating her brain.

"What are you doing here in my home?" she suddenly hissed

24

at me. "I don't recall inviting you, or anyone else for that matter. I think I will go upstairs to bed. Tell everyone to go home, now. I'm sick of this shit!" She struggled to her feet as I grabbed her arm and gestured for Veronica, who came rushing over.

"Party's over. Get these people out of my house." Olivia glared at me as Veronica approached and took her other arm. "And you," she snarled in my direction. "You never could do anything right. Why can't you be more like...more like— what's your name again?" She glanced at Veronica, who looked humiliated.

"It's time to take you home, Mother." Veronica tried to calm her, motioning for her son, Michael, to help Edward escort her back to the nursing home.

We managed to usher poor Mother out to the car while she continued to scold us all. "This is my home. The rest of you just get the hell out! I'm not going anyplace!" Once we got her settled in the back seat of the shiny black limo, her mood suddenly changed. "Oh goody! Are we going for a nice ride?" Olivia grinned. "I want an ice cream cone from the dime store."

"I'm sorry," Veronica apologized to everyone, tears in her eyes, when we returned to the Gold Room. We all assured her that it was all right, nobody's fault. Hopefully Veronica wouldn't blame me later for stirring Mother up, and ruining her carefully orchestrated celebration of Jimmy's life.

"It's time to watch our slide show, I think," Maria chimed in as she led us to the library where the equipment was set up. "Let's get back to remembering and honoring my dad."

I slumped into a comfortable leather chair, thankful that the lights were dim. It was bad enough that Jimmy had died. Almost as bad that my mother had once again pointed out my inability to measure up to my sister.

You never could do anything right. Her harsh words echoed in my mind. Still, I needed to remember that she was not in her right mind. I couldn't help hoping that deep down, somewhere in my mother's heart, there was a part of her that thought well of me, that still loved me. Seemed like I'd spent my life trying to win her approval. That apparently wasn't going to happen.

I soon became lost in Jimmy's life as portrayed in the slide show. Photos of him riding his favorite stallion on his ranch out on the west end of the island. He had loved his ranch, working with his cattle and horses. Everyone knew that he'd had an uncanny ability to train and communicate with animals. We called him "the horse whisperer." Deer and other wild animals seemed to follow him around.

There were photos of him with his real estate awards and investments. He'd built himself an empire, and made himself into a pillar of Galveston society. No, he had not ridden into Galveston society on the coat tails of the wealthy family he'd married into. He had made his own way in the world.

There were photos of Jimmy with his family, of course, in all stages of their lives together. I held my breath when the wedding photo of Jimmy and Veronica flashed upon the screen. No, I would never forget that day, one of the most difficult ones of my life.

I startled when a photo of me from long ago flashed upon the screen. I was posing in shorts on a lonely stretch of the Galveston beach with waves crashing behind me, smiling broadly, lovingly, at the photographer. Jimmy had taken this photo many years ago, on the best and the worst day of my life—shortly before he married my sister.

"Where did that come from?" the words escaped from my mouth.

Maria replied, "I found it in my dad's desk. I'd never seen it before, and have no idea who took it or where it was taken. It looks professional, as if you'd hired a local photographer."

"I...I really don't remember," I stammered. "It was so long ago."

"You were beautiful, Aunt Bella!" one of the younger children chimed in. *Were*, I smiled to myself. *And now I'm a sixty-year-old senior citizen, alone, more alone than ever before.*

I felt Veronica's puzzled eyes staring at me as I stared blindly at the movie screen.

Jimmy had apparently kept that photo to himself all these years, hiding it in his desk. Had he taken it out often, perhaps running his finger over my face, as he remembered our days together?

There was also a photo of Jonathan and me sitting on a swing in the park, beneath a palm tree and surrounded by flowers. I'd always treasured that photo. Yes, we were a part of Jimmy's life, and Maria had made sure that we were included in her slide show.

THREE
BELLA

"I am confident that there truly is such a thing as living again, that the living spring from the dead, and the souls of the dead are in existence."
Socrates

It had been an exhausting, gut-wrenching day. I was happy to say my goodbyes and get back home to my cats on this beautiful starlit evening. The wind had died down and a full moon was dancing across the ocean. Across Galveston Bay, the lights from the mainland glowed.

Both Jimmy and Jonathan consumed my thoughts tonight. I was engulfed in loneliness, lacking energy to work on anything. Even writing in my journal, my faithful friend and source of therapy, would have to wait.

All I wanted to do was sit out by my gazebo with a glass of wine, absorbing the power of the nature that surrounded me — the sound and smell of the ocean lapping across the shore, the magic of the full moon and brilliant stars contrasting with a pitch black sky. Nature had always been my refuge.

I settled down in the old white wicker rocking chair beside my gazebo. It was nestled in a grove of overgrown oleanders, beside

Jonathan's grave. I'd had him cremated long before cremation was popular. I'd been determined to have my little son's urn of ashes buried by our cottage, not in the family plot at the cemetery in town as my family had expected me to do.

Sometimes I sat and talked to Jonathan out there. Sometimes I felt his presence, especially in the early years after he'd died. He'd been able to assure me that he was OK and happy.

Mommy, I come back. I be with you later, his little voice had crept into my consciousness one night in a dream shortly after he died. *I OK. I love, love, love you, and Teddy, too.* (his favorite teddy bear.) Then he had giggled, reaching his chubby little arms out to give me a hug, and suddenly disappeared. The dream had been so real, much more than a dream.

But he seemed to have moved on in recent years, which was the way it was supposed to be, they say. By now, he had perhaps reincarnated into another lifetime. Yes, much to the chagrin of my family, I firmly believed in reincarnation—the theory that souls recycle through a number of lifetimes here on earth. They die and are born again, coming back in another body, another time and place. They face challenges and learn valuable lessons during their lives on Earth, all designed to advance and perfect their souls.

God only knew how much I hoped to be with my little Jonathan again someday—in Heaven or here on Earth, in this lifetime or the next one. Sometimes I carefully watched children I met on the street, looking for any resemblance to my Jonathan, any recognition of his spirit. One more reason for my family to think I was losing my mind.

Tonight, of course, Jimmy was also heavily on my mind. As the moonlight spilled into the ocean like a pot of gold shimmering across the waves, I psyched myself up, trying to absorb its energy, thinking thoughts to Jimmy. *Come to me, please. Hold me in your arms. Let me know you are OK*, I pleaded. There was no response. I could feel nothing except waves of grief seeping through my soul.

Where are you, Jimmy? I searched the stars in the sky, wondering why I couldn't feel his presence tonight. After all, he'd held me in his arms at the cemetery today. I knew that for a fact, strange as it may sound to others. Where had he gone? Was he ever coming back to me? Could he be comforting somebody else tonight...like Veronica? Or maybe his children and grandchildren?

Veronica had her children and grandchildren to comfort her. I had nobody.

Feeling sorry for myself, I became more and more restless. I decided to walk over to the ocean side and hike along the beach. It would be deserted this time of night, which was exactly what I wanted. On nights like this, I was sometimes able to connect with spirits of the past on this lonely stretch of beach — especially my great-grandmother, Isabella, who had perished in the Great Storm of 1900 here in Galveston, along with at least six thousand other people.

First I had to change into the faded black lace Victorian dress that had once belonged to my great-grandmother in the late 1800s. Her wedding dress. The hem of her long flowing dress was wearing thin and ragged at the edges, from my walks along the sandy beach, and sometimes through shallow pools of salt water by the ocean's edge.

After squeezing myself into her dress and buttoning it up, I carefully removed the delicate Victorian cameo broach from its secret hiding place in the locked box beneath my bed and fastened it around my neck. That, too, had belonged to Isabella, my namesake. I was so grateful that the dress and broach had survived the Great Storm.

Although Isabella had been washed out to sea with so many

others on that devastating day in September of 1900, her husband and ten-year old son, Charles, had miraculously survived. So had the trunk containing these family heirlooms.

I wore her dress and necklace every time I walked the beach at night, trying to connect with her. And it worked — sometimes, not always. Her spirit seemed to respond to these items that she'd worn and cherished during her lifetime.

Grabbing a flashlight just in case, although I shouldn't need it on this night of the full moon, I softly closed the door of my cottage, not wanting to attract attention from any neighbors who may still be up this late at night. Lifting the hem of my dress, I quietly made my way towards the ocean that seemed to be calling me tonight.

There had been a time, shortly after Jonathan died, that the howling winds and wild waves had screeched my name so compellingly that I came close to walking into the fog-shrouded sea and ending my life. That was the first time that Great-Grandma Isabella had come to me, a translucent Victorian image in glowing white. She had startled me from behind as I'd approached the sea, forcing me to turn around and look at her. She held out a transparent hand that radiated warmth and love, beckoning me to come back. I did, as if in a trance.

Her unspoken words filled my mind. *It is not your time to leave this world, my dear child. You must live on for Jonathan's sake, in his memory.*

"Who are you?" I'd gasped, shivering from a distinct chill in the air. "How do you know Jonathan?"

I am your Great-Grandmother Isabella, my dear. I am also your spirit guide, watching you from afar and sometimes coming through to help you at times like this. You have been troubled, but you must understand that through your trials, you are learning things you were meant to learn in this lifetime on Earth.

31

"Jonathan?" my voice squeaked. "Is my baby all right?"

Jonathan is fine. He is with loved ones, Bella. He wants you to go on with your life in his honor. Again, she did not speak aloud. Somehow, she implanted these thoughts into my mind. All I could do was stare at her, my mouth hanging open. She was beautiful in a heavenly way, and she looked exactly like the old photos I'd seen of Isabella in a family photo album.

You are special to me, my Bella. I will be here for you. When you need me, walk along this beach that I also love. I will try to come to you.

I nodded my head, greatly relieved. I didn't want her to leave.

And Bella, there is a small trunk in the attic of Ashton Villa that I want you to have. It is hidden beneath the floor boards near the staircase. In it you shall find my wedding dress and a broach that your great-grandfather gave me when we were united in marriage. It shall please me if you wear it anytime you seek me out. And now, I want you to promise me that you will take care of yourself, the glowing image continued.

"I will. Thank you," I mumbled, as she disappeared.

No, I'll never forget that night on the beach. It gave me the strength to live on. Yes, I believed in what had happened, only to find out that my family thought I was crazy. There had been a confrontation at Ashton Villa the next day after I got my nerve up to pay my family a visit. I needed to find that box in the attic.

"There is no such trunk in the attic," my mother snapped in an exasperated tone of voice. "Really, Bella. You've been through a terrible shock losing our little Jonathan. I'm sure that's why you are seeing things like ghosts on the beach. Really! You will be the death of me yet." She fanned herself dramatically. "Veronica, can you talk some sense into your sister?" With that, Olivia left the room, informing us that she needed to lay down for a while.

"Maybe we need to get you some help," Veronica sighed, "to get over Jonathan's death. I know how hard it must be, but the things you are telling us…well, they don't make any sense, Bella. It would not be good for the family if you talk to other people about these fantasies of yours. But we could find you a good therapist who would keep this all private. You will come to your senses soon with a little help."

Someone cleared his throat in the background. I turned around to find Jimmy standing there leaning against the door frame in his jeans and cowboy hat, tanned and relaxed, obviously having just returned from the ranch. He tried to conceal his surprise at seeing me. I rarely ventured home to Ashton Villa anymore. He knew why.

"Hello, Jimmy." My heart caught in my throat.

"Nice to see you here, Bella," he grinned. "What's up?"

After Veronica launched into her version of my story, looking for Jimmy to back up her concerns and recommendations about hiring a therapist, Jimmy was quiet for a moment, knowing he was caught in the middle of a difficult situation.

"Look," he finally began in his Texas drawl. "What harm can it do to let Bella explore the attic? It's still her house too, you know. What if she finds a trunk up there? What if she doesn't? Maybe it was just a dream…but who knows? Stranger things have happened. I say it is up to Bella to decide if and when she needs to talk with a therapist. For God's sake, she just lost her son. Let up, Veronica, will you?"

"Well…," Veronica gasped, glaring at her husband. "You are obviously no help at all. Men, they just don't understand things like this."

"Maybe what she needs is a nice walk on the beach and someone to talk to." He smiled warmly as he dipped his Stetson hat towards me. "I'm at your service, ma'am. Just tell me when and where."

"I'd like that," I replied. Then, catching myself, "Of course, you will come with us, Veronica?"

"Of course not," she snapped. "You know I hate the ocean!"

"Fine, your choice," Jimmy replied. "But first, let's check out that attic. Come on, Bella."

As Veronica stormed out of the room to bend Olivia's ear, Jimmy led me up the grand staircase to the upper staircase and then to the little drop-down stairs leading into the attic. He pulled the folding stairs down, ducking to avoid any dust or debris that had settled over the stairs in recent years.

Nobody went up into the attic anymore—not since "the sisters" had played up there together years ago, digging through trunks of old books and Miss Bettie's treasures from around the world, trying on dusty old gowns and playing make-believe games. We'd had fun together in that drafty old attic, where our imaginations had soared.

Although Veronica and Jimmy had raised their three children in this house, Veronica had never allowed the children to play in the attic. I never understood why. But then, I always felt she was overly protective of her children. But who was I to judge? Me, I'd always been the family rebel, risk-taker, and free spirit.

"It should be behind the eaves, right about here." I pointed to an area behind the staircase. It was bare, nothing but a few old floor boards, nothing that looked like it could contain a hidden compartment. I was feeling discouraged, questioning my sanity. Maybe my mind had been playing tricks on me after all. "I don't know," I sighed.

"Hey, we're just getting started." Jimmy grabbed my arm, sending tingles up and down my spine, as he settled me on an old trunk beside the staircase. Pulling a hammer from his pocket, he got down on his knees and began tapping across the boards, prodding, prying. No signs of any secret compartment here. He was determined to find something, knowing how badly I needed

34

the confirmation. He was the only one who believed in me and didn't think I was crazy.

He expanded his search, still tapping, prying, until he finally yelled, "Bella, there's something here!" He pried several boards loose to uncover a hidden chamber — and a little trunk. Carefully he lifted the trunk out of the hole, his eyes gleaming, as I knelt down beside him, my heart pounding.

"Open it," he whispered, touching my shoulder gently, after loosening the clasp on the trunk.

Holding my breath, I slowly raised the dusty lid and lifted a beautiful long black lace dress from the trunk. Tears filled my eyes. It was true. This was the Victorian era dress that the ghost on the beach wanted me to find. Great-Grandmother Isabella's wedding dress!

And there was more, I realized, as something shiny caught my eye in the bottom of the trunk — an elegant Victorian cameo broach. Lifting it from its grave, I began to cry, tears of happiness and relief.

"Isabella," Jimmy whispered, clasping the necklace around my neck and wrapping his arms around me. We sat together on the dusty attic floor, his arms holding me close, for as long as we dared. Until my tears had dried.

Then we crept back down the ladder. Together, we showed the treasures we'd found to our astounded family. They had nothing more to say — for the time being anyway.

So that was how we discovered Isabella's treasures many years ago. I had cherished them ever since.

Tonight I was relieved to find the beach beside the ocean deserted. I didn't need to be discovered by some late-night-walking insomniac as I danced on the beach in my Victorian clothing, or conversed with spirits. Yes, I danced on the beach sometimes, late at night when the mood struck me and the spirits coerced me into doing so. Isabella loved it for some reason. No, I didn't need any more grief from my family over my escapades. Now and then, well-meaning islanders had reported to my family that Crazy Bella was dancing on the beach, again, in the middle of the night.

Crossing over the sand dunes and down to the edge of the ocean, I kicked off my shoes. Walking slowly, feeling the sand squish between my toes, I tried to clear my mind. Focusing on the rhythm of the waves washing upon the shore and over my feet, on the moonlight shimmering across the waves, I breathed deeply. In and out. In and out. My breath soon aligned itself with the rhythm of the sea, coming in and going out with the tide. I was becoming one with the sea.

Isabella. My mind tried to tap into the universe where she resided somewhere. *Isabella,* I thought as hard as I possibly could, bidding her to come to me. In and out...in and out. Where was she? I really needed her tonight. Didn't she know that Jimmy died and I was devastated by my loss? She truly was the best friend I had on this earth, my spirit guide as well.

Finally I recognized her lovely transparent image gliding in across the waves towards the shore. Brilliant stars overhead seemed to wink at her. Looking closer, I thought she seemed to have a troubled expression upon her glowing face tonight.

"Oh Isabella, I am so glad to see you!" I exclaimed out loud instead of using the telepathy that we usually used to communicate. I'd even learned to use this universal form of communication, sometimes wondering why humans felt the need to "talk" when they could communicate so much better via telepathy.

Dance for me, Bella, she spoke silently into my mind.

What? I don't feel like dancing – Jimmy has died. I thought my words to her, knowing she preferred this kind of communication.

Dance for me, Bella. She repeated her silent message more sternly. *Then we shall talk. Only then.*

She was the boss, the one with the knowledge that I needed, the one who guided me and helped me cope with struggles I'd encountered during this sorry life of mine. Who was I to refuse her request?

So, trying to psych myself up into a more joyful state of mind, I began to twirl around the beach, kicking up my heels, dipping low to scoop up a handful of sand. I danced into the water, splashing and waltzing into the waves, feeling the spray upon my face. Dancing on the night of the full moon and beginning to feel its magic.

Do you feel better? My spirit guide smiled as I slumped back onto the shore. *You need more joy in your life. You need to dance again. You know that you have more to accomplish in this lifetime. It's not an option to live alone with ghosts of the past. You will see us all again someday in the future, but not now. You must move on, and make the most of this lifetime of yours.*

Jimmy? Please, I pleaded silently, *Is he OK? Why can't I contact him?*

He is here, Bella, and doing well. He already contacted you at the cemetery this morning. Did you not feel his arms around you?

She seemed to know everything. *Yes, but I need more. I need him, Isabella. He is my soul mate. Why won't he come to me again?"*

Yes, Jimmy is your soul mate – one of your soul mates, you need to understand. He will come to you when the time is right. Timing is a concept that you people here on Earth do not seem to comprehend. Isabella's spirit sighed with a slight hint of exasperation over my human ignorance.

"So what am I supposed to do now?" I cried out in my frustration.

You are to pursue your mission in this lifetime. You have books to write, books that may help mankind to see the truths of the universe. That includes the book you are supposed to be writing about the 1900 storm. Remember?

Of course. I am working on it, Isabella," I replied with a twinge of guilt, thinking of the copious stacks of notes sitting on my desk waiting to be organized, somehow, into a great book about Galveston's 1900 storm, the devastating event that transformed this island community — and has haunted it ever since.

You are not, Isabella confronted me. *I died in that storm, as you know, and I am waiting to reveal my story to you. Let me know when you are ready.*

I sensed her spirit beginning to retreat into the waves and disappear on me. "Wait!" I called out. "I want to hear your story. I need to hear it. I will get back to this book tomorrow. But first, before you leave, tell me more about Jimmy."

I am truly sorry for your pain, Bella. You need to understand that although he is one of your soul mates, he was not meant to be yours exclusively in this lifetime. He belonged to Veronica this time around. This is all part of the contract you all made before you incarnated into these lives. Someday you will understand.

With that, Isabella's spirit floated up into the sky, escorted by twinkling stars bringing her back "home" again.

I stood on the beach, bewildered. What was she talking about? Contracts? Why did Jimmy belong to Veronica, when he and I had such a powerful bond between us — something I was certain he did not have with Veronica?

As I made my way back home, deep in thought, I almost didn't notice the light glowing from the cottage closest to the beach. It had been dark, like all the others, when I'd arrived.

FOUR
VERONICA

*"Life can only be understood backwards,
but it must be lived forwards."*
Soren Kierkegaard

The old house felt lonely and far too big as I rattled around by myself. Jimmy's funeral was over, and all my family members had gone back home to take care of their own lives. As it should be.

As much as I loved Ashton Villa, the only home I'd ever lived in during my sixty-three years on this earth, it felt strange to me today. Restless, I roamed the big house, touching and admiring all the beautiful treasures accumulated here over the past 150 years. Things. Lots of things. Still, without somebody to share these things with, they seemed to lose some of their value, some of their meaning.

National Public Radio kept me company on days I was home. I loved classical music. In fact, I was a good enough pianist to accompany the church choir, which I did every Sunday morning.

My days were usually filled with volunteer work and serving on various boards of directors. I was active in the Galveston Historical Foundation, and even served as a tour guide for the elegant Bishop's Palace. Maybe I needed to get back into my routine soon. Everybody was giving me space to mourn, but I wasn't sure this was doing me any good.

Jimmy was gone. I slumped into an overstuffed Victorian chair where I sat with a cup of tea, gazing up at the gold-framed portrait of our wedding, some forty years ago. My mind drifted back to that day...I'd thought we'd been happy then.

It had been a beautiful sunny day, with a fresh breeze floating in from the Gulf of Mexico across the lush tropical gardens of the elegant Hotel Galvez, where we were married. Palm trees swayed in the breeze as the fountains sprayed water into the air. Guests of the hotel were seated on benches and colorful Adirondack chairs, enjoying a cool drink, a good book, and the fresh air.

The Hotel Galvez, known as the Queen of the Gulf, was a Spanish Colonial Revival structure boasting an eight-story central section flanked with symmetrical five-story wings on both sides. Four copper octagonal towers loomed into the sky from the Spanish-tiled roof. They were always lit up at night, and quite a sight to see.

The hotel was built in 1911, on the site where many hundreds of bodies, victims of the devastating Storm of 1900, had been burned in funeral pyres. Some claimed their spirits still haunted the hotel. Of course, that would include my sister, Bella.

Drifting back to my wedding day, I find myself dressed in an elegant white satin dress with a long train and veil. It had been imported from Paris. I'm walking down the aisle of the Music Hall on my father's arm. Everybody who is anybody in Galveston society is here, seated in the grand hall with its massive arched window wall overlooking the sea. A harp plays softly in the background, accompanied by a world famous violinist. I can no longer remember their names.

Jimmy is waiting for me beneath the windows, looking a little nervous. He is not used to events like this. He'd never before worn a long-tailed black tuxedo, and would have been far more comfortable in his cowboy hat and well-worn cowboy boots.

Jimmy did not come from a wealthy family like mine. He rarely talked about his past, even to me. He didn't want others to know about the alcoholic father, who had deserted his family and left his mother alone to raise five children the best she could. My folks did not even know his secret, nor did anyone else in this area, which was far from where he'd grown up in poverty. All they knew was that despite an unknown personal history, this young man had done well for himself. He invested in real estate and made himself a small fortune. That was all they needed to know.

Yes, it had been a beautiful wedding, followed by a reception in the elegant Terrace Ballroom down the hall. One of the day's top orchestras had played as Jimmy and I danced together as man and wife for the first time. Of course, the event had been photographed and written up in the local newspaper's society section.

The day had gone off without a glitch, thanks to my wedding planners. The only minor setback had been my sister. For some reason, she had backed out of my wedding party at the last minute, claiming she was very ill. We had scrambled to find a replacement who would fit into her bridesmaid's dress.

Looking back, it seemed to me that this had been the beginning of Bella's self-imposed exile from our family. She even moved out of our family home when she became pregnant, claiming it was better for her to start her own life and let me live mine with my new family. That had hurt. We had been close for years, despite what I considered to be a friendly sense of competition between us.

Jimmy, I sighed, focusing on our family portrait hanging over

41

the fireplace. Yes, we'd raised three wonderful children together. We'd had a good life, although we certainly went our separate ways. He was either gone at his ranch or off on some business dealings. When he was home, which he was most nights, he was buried in his office. I kept myself busy volunteering and fulfilling the social obligations that a family like mine had in this community. Jimmy rarely attended these functions with me. He was too busy.

I sometimes felt we were like two trains passing in the night. At least we usually had dinner and polite conversation together in the formal dining room, sitting at opposite ends of the massive table. There was always a floral arrangement in the center of the mahogany table, flanked by flickering candles. A romantic setting.

The maid would pour water and wine into old Waterford crystal goblets before serving a gourmet dinner on our fine family china. It hadn't been too long, I remembered, before Jimmy started asking for simpler fare, like hamburgers and steaks without all the gourmet sauces. His preferences were soon integrated into the weekly menus that I prepared for the cook.

After dinner, he usually retreated to his office or his bedroom while I drifted through the house looking for a good book or something to keep me company. Or, I'd dress up and attend one of the many social functions that Galveston offered. And as the children grew up and had families of their own, I loved spending time with them all.

Still, we had cared for each other, probably like many old married couples who no longer had much need for intimacy. We weren't very old, however, when he began distancing himself from me, as I saw it. He'd never wanted to bother me with his snoring at night after I'd complained about being unable to sleep. Separate bedrooms seemed to be the best solution for us.

There'd been times when I wondered if this was all there was. Had I expected too much of marriage? To be honest, I'd never felt head over heels in love with anyone, not even my husband. Was that normal? Seemed to me that "love" was an illusion, not based in reality.

There'd been times I wondered why I married at all, aside from the fact that I desperately wanted children and a family of my own. And we'd been blessed with three amazing children, along with seven grandchildren. What more could a woman want from life?

Jimmy had been a good husband in many ways. We rarely fought or had a major disagreement. He tended to withdraw to his ranch when he needed space from what he sometimes called "my nagging."

You see, I liked to have everything organized, down to the last detail. He preferred to fly by the seat of his pants. Sometimes he'd do strange things that made no sense to me—like walking the beaches and hunting for ghosts with my silly sister. I refused to participate in their nonsense. After all, I had a reputation to uphold. So did Bella, but she didn't care. She preferred to be the family rebel, humiliating us at times, especially when she ended up pregnant out-of-wedlock.

No, I did not regret marrying Jimmy. We'd had a good life, I reminded myself. No marriage is perfect. Looking back in time, I realized that timing had been an important factor in our decision to get married. I was of the age that I should be getting married and having children. My father had also been in ill health, and was anxious to marry me off before he passed on.

One evening Papa brought Jimmy home for dinner, a handsome young entrepreneur who invested in real estate and was making it big. He had a ranch down on the west end of the island, and had several business deals going with my father.

43

Papa was convinced that Jimmy was an honorable man who would be a good husband and father. Of course, that implied he would also be a good provider for our family. Jimmy would be able to support me in the lifestyle I'd grown accustomed to.

So Jimmy and I began to date. We enjoyed each other's company and seemed to balance each other. He helped me learn to let loose and have fun instead of always having to be the responsible one. And I taught him to be a little more organized and to plan ahead. Strange how we later drifted back to our original personality traits—after the wedding.

It hadn't been long before we decided to marry, as if this was our destiny. It seemed to be the expectation of others and the right thing to do. We did care about each other, perhaps loved each other. I wasn't sure anymore. What was love? Could we have had more together? Maybe. Maybe not. And now he was gone.

My tears began to fall once more. Were they flowing for Jimmy's passing? For what I'd just lost? Or for what we'd never been able to have together—and never would?

I was startled from my reverie by the ringing of the doorbell. Who would be calling right before dinner hour? I could smell the roast chicken wafting from the kitchen, knowing the maid would soon be bringing my glass of red wine. Listening carefully as the butler answered the door, I recognized the voice of my closest neighbor, Rebecca.

Rising slowly, I made my way to the grand mirror to make sure my hair looked all right. I'd missed my weekly beauty salon appointment, so this would have to do, I decided, as I tucked a few stray strands in place.

"Please come in, Rebecca." I attempted a welcoming smile. I wasn't sure I needed to hear all the island gossip today, which was her specialty. She was also a born-on-the-islander from another prominent family. We'd grown up together, although we'd never been close.

While I had many acquaintances, I'd never been really close to anybody. I had a reputation to uphold, after all. I had family secrets to protect. Over the years, I'd found that it was safer to keep myself at a respectful distance from others. You didn't get hurt if you didn't get too close to others; if you kept your emotions under control instead of becoming vulnerable to the whims of others.

Rebecca entered, her eyes troubled, just as the maid walked in with two glasses of red wine and a plate of hors d'oeuvres on a serving tray. So today's gossip wasn't going to be pleasant, I thought to myself as I returned to my loveseat and motioned for Rebecca to take a seat across from me. We each took a glass of wine, and Rebecca began to munch on the cheese and crackers.

"What a treat!" Rebecca smiled. "I was famished. I also wanted to check to see how you are getting along, Veronica. I remember how it was when my Bill died, after all the kids went back to their homes and their lives. If you ever want company or to talk, you know where I live." She picked up another cracker and began to nibble like a chipmunk.

"I'm doing as well as can be expected, and I appreciate your checking up on me. I'll be going back to my tour guide duties and committee meetings soon. Keeping busy should help."

"That's right. That's what I did after Bill died. I had my sister close by, so…."

I took a long sip of my wine and decided it was a good time to munch on a cracker with smoked salmon and cream cheese.

"So…," Rebecca finally inquired. "I hope Bella is here for you?"

"She was here for the family funeral gathering and at his graveside service."

45

"That was a week ago, Veronica. Surely you've heard from her since then."

"I'm sorry, but I don't care to discuss my relationship with my sister. Please understand."

"Such a shame," she clucked. "What ever happened to the inseparable Brown sisters?"

"Life changes. We change, Rebecca. What more can I say?"

"Well...I'm not sure if I should tell you what I've heard from several reliable sources. It's about Bella. I don't want to upset you, but you may want to know."

I knew it. She had an ulterior motive for her visit. Part of me wanted to ask her to leave and tell her I did not want to hear anything about my sister. But the curious part of me won out. She'd already hooked me. "OK," I sighed. "What is it this time?"

"Well...." She sighed dramatically, a frown creasing her forehead. "I happen to have heard from several very credible sources that Bella was seen dancing on the beach in the middle of the night, wearing some long black Victorian dress. And that's not all. She was talking to someone who wasn't even there."

"How do they know it was Bella?" I asked, knowing in my heart that it had to be. This wasn't the first time I'd heard reports like this. And I would never forget that black Victorian dress, Great-Grandmother Isabella's wedding dress, the one Bella found buried in the attic many years ago. Anger began to sprint through my veins. I had enough to deal with right now. I didn't have the energy to deal with my sister.

"My sources have a cottage on the ocean, near Bella's. It was the night of the full moon, and they had a good view of her. After watching a while, they turned on their porch light just as Bella walked past, close enough for them to see her face. She had a very strange look upon her face. I'm sorry, Veronica, but I thought you'd want to know. Maybe she needs some help, you know."

And so do I, I thought to myself.

Thankfully, Rebecca excused herself as the maid came in to inform me that dinner was served. I picked at the delicious roast chicken with all the trimmings, too upset to eat more than a few bites.

After dinner, I went outside and paced around the gardens, sitting by the fountain for a while, trying to decide how to handle this situation. I no longer had our mother, Olivia, to bounce things off of. Together, we'd tried to handle Bella. Now Olivia was succumbing to Alzheimer's, which was obvious at Jimmy's funeral party. It was up to me now. Maybe I'd drive out to the west end and pay my dear sister a surprise visit tonight.

"No, I won't need you to chauffeur me this evening," I informed Edward, as I retrieved the keys for my classic little Jaguar. He frowned, obviously disappointed, as well as worried about the welfare of his aging employer. "I'm perfectly capable of driving. I just need some fresh air by the ocean. Good night, Edward." I discharged him for the evening.

A vibrating orange sun was slipping silently into the depths of the ocean as I approached Bella's tiny vine-covered cottage. I could hear the eerie strains of Enya's soulful music drifting out from Bella's place. It was the same mystical Celtic music that Jimmy had played endlessly while he worked long hours behind the closed doors of his home office. It had never ceased to release chilling sensations throughout my soul, almost as if the music came from a world beyond ours. Strange.

Ducking through the overgrown flowering oleanders, I made my way along the stone path to the front door. Enya was wailing so loudly that Bella apparently didn't hear my knock. I could see her sitting on a large pillow on the floor, her back supported

47

by the cat-hair-covered sofa, piles of books and papers strewn around her.

"Hello, Bella?" I called out as I opened the unlocked door and walked in. The place was a disaster. Dirty dishes were dumped haphazardly in the sink. The remnants of her dinner and a half-empty wine glass remained on the coffee table within her reach. One of her cats was licking the plate clean.

"Veronica!" She jumped up, surprised to see me. "How are you?"

"I am doing as well as can be expected, but what is going on here?" I shook my head in disbelief at the chaos that surrounded me.

"Sit down." She gestured towards the sofa. "Or, if my sofa isn't good enough for you, grab a kitchen chair. Help yourself to a glass of wine if you want." She pointed to a big box of red wine sitting on the kitchen counter.

"No thank you." I sighed as I settled on one of the rickety old chairs, trying not to be overly critical of the unorganized lifestyle my sister lived. I had more important things on my mind tonight. "What are you working on?"

"I'm finally getting back to my book about the Great Storm, and I'm under deadline. Stories about the people who survived, and those who didn't. My agent is hounding me to get this done, and I'm finally really getting into the story. What a tragedy it was."

"That it was. To think that we even lost our Great-Grandmother Isabella...."

"I plan to include her experiences, what it was like for her," Bella confided, a wistful smile upon her face.

"Well, I guess you will need to make that part up. There are no records of what happened to her, as you know. Just that she must have been swept out to sea."

48

"I will find a way to tap into her memories."

"Not again, Bella! She is gone and there is nothing for you to tap into. You never even knew her. She died long before you were born, of course. You need to stop living in a fantasy world and join the real world!"

Rising slowly and stretching her legs, Bella grabbed her empty wine glass and headed into the kitchen for a refill. Taking a long swig, she returned to plop down on the sofa, shoving several cats off to make room for herself.

"I know Isabella better than any of you could possibly understand," she challenged me in an icy tone of voice.

Here we go again, I sighed to myself. Neither of us spoke for several minutes.

"So to what do I owe this delightful, unexpected visit?" Bella mocked me, using the words I'd used on her in the past on those rare days when she would stop by Ashton Villa to chastise me for one thing or another. Sometimes she'd be looking for Jimmy to go ghost-hunting with her, of all things.

I never understood how he, an intelligent man and prominent citizen, could buy into the local ghost legends. He had a genuine interest in island folklore, and even convinced himself that he had captured psychic "orbs" in some of the photos he took at these "haunted" places. As for me, I would not be caught dead chasing ghosts around Galveston or anyplace else. They simply did not exist.

"I will not beat around the bush with you." I leaned forward in my chair, staring into her dark eyes. My eyes. "You must stop making a fool of yourself and disgracing our family!"

"What the hell are you talking about?"

"Dancing on the beach in the middle of the night in that... that old black dress you found in the attic years ago! Talking to people who aren't there!"

49

A light of recognition seemed to flicker across Bella's face. She knew exactly what I was talking about, whether she was willing to admit it or not.

Defiantly, she rose and strode over to her messy desk, where she rifled through disorganized stacks of papers and pictures. She was obviously looking for something. God only knew what it could possibly have to do with the discussion I was trying to have with her.

Finally she returned with an old photo, which she dropped into my lap. Picking it up, I carefully scanned the black and white image. Very strange. There seemed to be a semi-transparent image of a Victorian lady in a long flowing dress, large hat, and lacey shawl. She gazed out the tall elegant windows of what appeared to be the Terrace Ballroom in the Hotel Galvez.

"What in the world is this?"

"Do you see her?" Bella asked breathlessly, as if trying to reassure herself that she was not crazy. Surely others could see what she saw in this photo.

"Well, it almost looks like an apparition of a Victorian lady from long ago," I had to admit. "Of course, there must be a more rational explanation. People can inject all sorts of images into their photos these days. But I don't see what this could possibly have to do with what we were just talking about."

Bella took in a deep breath before proceeding. "This is the woman I speak with, and dance with, by the ocean, Veronica. Meet our Great-Grandmother Isabella. By the way, she is also my spirit guide. That's how I know her."

A chill suddenly ran through me as Bella looked up towards the ceiling and smiled at something or someone I could not see.

"That is absolutely crazy and you know it! What you are saying makes no sense whatsoever!" I snapped at my sister. "And what does this picture have to do with your dancing on the beach with what you think is a ghost?"

"Do you recognize the place this photo was taken?"

"Of course. The Hotel Galvez."

"That's right." Bella smiled patiently as if I were a slow learner. "I took this picture of Isabella at the Hotel Galvez, the day you and Jimmy were married. She was there to pay her respects to you and Jimmy. That was the first time I saw her. It wasn't long before she, the identical image, began appearing to me on the beach. We began to talk, and I discovered who she was. She has been there for me over the years. Once she saved my life."

None of this made any sense to me. Bella hadn't even been at my wedding! "You weren't even there at my wedding, Bella. You were too sick, remember?"

"That's true. I was very ill." She seemed to hesitate.

"So how could you have taken this photo?"

"As sick as I was, I felt compelled to try to come to the wedding, even if I wasn't well enough to be one of your bridesmaids. I arrived early. As I walked in through the main entrance foyer, something compelled me to meander through the veranda and take a peek into the Terrace Ballroom, which was already set up for your reception. Nobody was in the room. But I felt a presence that was hard to explain, and knew I had to take a photo right then and there. I shot this image. As nausea overcame me, I knew I had to go back home to bed. That is what I did. It wasn't until several days later that I developed this print. Voila, here was this spiritual presence captured on film. I had no idea who this lady was, until I met her on the beach later and she identified herself."

"You should be writing fiction, Bella. Your imagination is out of control."

"There is more to reality, to our existence, than what you see in front of your face, Veronica. So much more. You need to expand your horizons and see the big picture. Quit being so

51

obsessive-compulsive and loosen up."

"Well!" I hissed. Who did she think she was? She was the unbalanced one. How dare she challenge me?

"Has Jimmy ever contacted you — or have you ever tried to contact him?" Bella inquired softly, her eyes downcast.

"Of course not. Jimmy is dead."

"Or living on in another state of existence. I don't expect you to understand that."

"You are losing it, Bella. You need help. I'd be happy to refer you to a good psychiatrist. I'll even help pay the bill. Think about it."

I stood to leave, unable to handle anymore of her nonsense.

"No thank you, dear sister. I'm doing fine — in fact, expanding my awareness more so every day."

As I headed toward the door, shaking my head, bewildered by the photo and the strange things Bella had relayed to me, I turned around once more to face her. "Will you at least quit dancing on the beach and talking to ghosts?"

"Absolutely not. If people don't like it, they don't need to watch!" Bella bristled. "And if *you* need a good spiritual advisor or shrink, let me know!"

"I am perfectly sane, Bella. Don't even try to project your problems onto me!" I flared at her. She had a way of getting to me sometimes. Obviously she enjoyed it.

"Don't let the door hit you in the ass," my twisted sister mumbled to herself.

Shaking my head in disgust, I slammed the door, setting off her orchestra of wind chimes.

FIVE
ISABELLA

"Death is simply a shedding of the physical body like the butterfly shedding its cocoon. It is a transition to another state of consciousness where you continue to perceive, understand, and grow."
Elizabeth Kubler-Ross

Why do these sisters have to continually bicker? I sighed, gazing down upon the latest confrontation between two of my beloved descendants. It hadn't always been this way. Not until Jimmy.

Veronica didn't want to believe I still existed, in spirit form, on the other side of life. However, I do think she was stunned to see the photo of me at her wedding. I was there all right. Oh my, it had been a lovely wedding. One of high society's social events of the season. To me, it seemed like yesterday — or today — although that wedding had actually taken place forty-two years ago in Earth time.

I always enjoyed visiting my old home on Earth. I could come and go as I pleased, effortlessly, without the burden of a dense body slowing me down and keeping me earthbound. I could actually fly, soaring like a pelican over the waves of Galveston as I'd always dreamed of doing as a child.

Invisible to most people, I could observe and learn so much.

Not that I would ever intrude on private moments or interfere in anyone's life. I emerged only as needed. And sometimes, even if needed, I've learned to back off to allow my charge to learn a difficult lesson on her own.

I still had important work to do on this earth in my role as Bella's spirit guide. No, it wasn't easy watching over a free spirit like my namesake, trying to help her understand. Humans had such a limited capacity for understanding things that weren't visible. They were often blinded by emotions — just as I had once been, over a hundred years ago, during my last incarnation on the planet Earth. Someday I'll return, someday after Bella leaves this earth and returns "home."

For now, Bella has a mission to complete, one she signed up for long before she was born. That includes the book she is writing about the 1900 storm — the unprecedented storm that ended my life. Her book needs to be more than a recounting of stories already passed down from survivors. She needs to hear, and write about, my personal story. And I perhaps need the closure of having her do that for me. Then, perhaps, we can both move on.

I'm pleased to see Bella researching and working hard on her book. She is burning the midnight oil, as they say on Earth. I think she is ready to hear my story, ready for me to creep into her dreams tonight.

When I think of the Galveston I knew prior to the 1900 storm, it still brings tears to my eyes. What a glorious existence we shared upon this barrier island, surrounded by the sounds and smells of the sea. The sea, with its many moods, always drew me to a place above and beyond this earthly existence. Perhaps I've always had a deep spiritual bond with this body of water.

54

I believed, as the Karankawa Indians, the island's first inhabitants, had, that Galveston Island was, indeed, a special place, where the veil between this world and the next was very thin. That's why the Indians brought their dead here to the island to bury them. That's why some people truly believed the island was haunted—in a comforting, not a threatening way. We cherished the spirits that chose to bless us with their presence from time to time.

But I digress. Beyond the natural and spiritual beauty of my earthly home, Galveston had developed into a cultural center unheard of in those days. It was the number one cotton port in the nation, also known as The Wall Street of the South. We had one of the first medical colleges in Texas, a glorious Grand Opera House, concert halls, sprawling hotels. Why, we even had electric street cars and electric lights! And many elegant Victorian mansions built by successful business men.

Oh my, what glorious times we had together in those days. I remember oyster roasts on the beach, as well as boat rowing and sailing contests. I loved riding our horses down the beach. One moonlit night we rode our horses bareback into the gentle surf as they swam through the waves, cooling off after the heat of a summer's day.

One of the growing city's biggest attractions was the Victorian bath houses built on piers protruding out over the ocean. Oh yes…there was Murdochs; the Electric Pavilion, an elegant frame building; and the Beach Hotel, the finest resort on the entire Texas coast, which burned down in the late 1800's.

People walked or took the trolley down to the beach to bathe and cool off in the surf. Sometimes the men swam naked beneath a black star-studded sky and the light of a shimmering moon. Of course, that would have been totally improper for a Victorian woman! We wore long wool suits that even covered our arms—

shockingly different from the bikinis I see women wearing on the beaches of Galveston today. Oh my — what has happened to our sense of sensibility these days?

We watched horse races along the beach, and some enjoyed the cock fights. There were freak shows to entertain us, something people today would find totally offensive.

My little boy, Charlie, loved to participate in the greased pig scrambles. The island boys tried to catch a greased pig, pick it up by its tail, and stuff it into a barrel. Charlie had won one of these contests just the day before the big storm, the day that changed so many lives; ending mine, and those of at least six to eight thousand others.

My mind drifts back to that fateful day, September 8, 1900, a day that will live on in history as one of the worst natural disasters ever experienced on Planet Earth.

Strangely enough, the 1900 Farmers' Almanac had predicted a severe storm for that day. Based on crude weather information, all that we had available those days, an ominous red and black storm warning flag had been raised by Isaac Cline, Galveston's weather meteorologist, as he tracked sketchy information about an unusual storm brewing out in the Gulf of Mexico. Many of us BOI's (Born-On-the-Islanders) laughed. It was, in fact, a lovely day. The oppressive heat of the past weeks was finally giving way to a welcome breeze.

Yes, we laughed at Mr. Cline's over-reaction. After all, we had weathered many a storm on this island over the years. We may sustain some damage, but we always rebuilt. Nothing could keep the islanders down or prevent us from enjoying life on this special island. We could certainly handle whatever may be rolling in across the vast ocean surrounding us. Or so we thought….

It's time, now, for me to go back. Time for me to relive that dreadful day as I implant my memories into the dreams of my Bella. Time for her to learn the truth so she can write her book.

I don't want to traumatize the poor child—she will always be a child to me—but she needs to understand what happened. I'll be there with her to lead her through the experience and comfort her along the way.

I float back in time, back 117 years, Earth time, to be precise. I awaken to a gentle breeze flittering through the lace curtains in our bedroom. Peering out the window, I marvel at a delicate pink sky swirling with the pastel colors of the rainbow as the sun begins to peek over the horizon. One of the most beautiful sunrises I'd ever seen. It is going to be a beautiful day.

I smile at my husband, Charles, still sleeping in our bed, as he opens his eyes to greet the day. As always, he will soon be on his way to his office in the Cotton Exchange Building on The Strand. Charles lives and breathes his work, making a respectable fortune in the process and providing nicely for his family—ten-year-old Charlie and me.

I make my way down the massive staircase to the kitchen, where I begin making breakfast, the one meal I prepare every day before the maid arrives. It's going to be a busy day. I will be dropping Charlie off at my cousin, Bettie Brown's, Ashton Villa, while I attend a quilting bee at St. Mary's Cathedral Basilica. We plan to spend the day making quilts for the children in the orphanage.

After eating a hearty breakfast of eggs and sausage, Charles pecks me on the cheek, our goodbye ritual. He frowns a bit as he fingers his handle-bar mustache. Something is apparently bothering him. I watch as he retrieves his hand-carved cane,

57

dons his top hat, and steps out the front door. He hesitates on the doorstep, gazing up at the sky, then comes back in to retrieve his umbrella.

"Isabella." He turns to face me. "Do keep an eye out for the weather, just in case Mr. Cline's predictions about the storm come to pass. You know he's been flying storm warning flags from the roof of the Weather Bureau for several days now. I know we've had beautiful sunny weather for days, but some folks from Washington seem to think there's a big storm brewing out there in the Gulf. Headed for Florida, they say."

I sigh, amused by his concern. He was never one to worry about a little storm. In fact, he, like most islanders, loves taking the trolley to the Gulf to watch storms moving in. "How many storms have we all been through on this island, my darling? And we've all survived, haven't we?"

"Of course, and I'm sure we will be fine. I dare say, however, there is a hint of something strange lurking in the air. Clouds are moving in and the wind is picking up. Please be careful, and come home early if the weather looks at all threatening."

"I shall be fine, my darling," I reply as I clear the dishes, remove my apron, and prepare myself for my meeting.

It is only a few blocks to Ashton Villa, so Charlie and I walk instead of taking the trolley. I hug him goodbye, holding him a little longer than usual.

"I love you, son." I blurt out the words that live in my heart, but were rarely spoken in most households of that day.

He looks surprised as he flashes me a big grin that spreads from ear to ear. "You too, Mama," he calls out as he runs off to play with his cousins and Miss Bettie's white angora cats.

Another six blocks and I arrive at the old stone cathedral. As always, I marvel at the cast iron statue of Mary, Star of the Sea and Mother of Jesus, perched atop the tower and surrounded by twin spires with crosses. Mary was said to be a beacon guiding mariners safely into the port of Galveston over the years. She protects the island, and has weathered many storms.

As I enter the church, crossing myself, I notice the wind beginning to pick up as dainty raindrops splatter against the stained-glass windows. We begin stitching our quilt pieces together, visiting and enjoying each other's company.

"Where is Shirley today?" one woman asks. Shirley is one of the younger members of our group, an avid quilter, not one to miss a quilting bee.

Shirley's neighbor shakes her head, a grin spreading across her face. "You know our Shirley. She can't resist a good storm. Word is out that the tide is up down there on the beach. Huge waves, they say. Shirley told me she and her children were taking the trolley down to the beach to see the waves. She sends her regrets for missing our meeting."

Several of us take a break to peer out the windows. The rain is falling harder now, and large pools of water are forming in the streets, edging up into the neighbors' yards.

Excitement fills the air as children playfully wade into the growing puddles, splashing each other with glee. Some are floating boats. Several of the younger mothers soon join in the merriment, barefoot, drawing their long skirts up above their ankles.

Others are taking the trolley down to the beach to watch the wild waves crashing over the piers. We Galvestonians all love a good storm, especially one that will break the intense heat of the past days.

The church ladies look at each other, searching for an answer, for reassurance that this is just another storm to be taken in stride.

"Issac's folly?" one of the ladies grins hopefully.

We go back to work, a little quieter than before, keeping an ear and eye out for the weather. The sound of rain falling steadily keeps us company. I cannot help but recall my husband's words that morning as he bade me farewell. "Something strange is lurking in the air," he'd advised me.

It is almost time for our luncheon when the church door bursts open and Father Kirwin strides in, water dripping from his clothing and forming puddles on the floor.

"Ladies, you will be safe here until the rain lets up, but you need to know that the storm is moving in. Streets in the low-lying areas near the beach are flooding. The wind from the Gulf is now destroying the Pagoda Bath House and most of Murdoch's Pier."

"What?"

"Oh dear God!"

A chorus of wails breaks out as the good father tries to reassure us.

"We must leave now and get back home," one frightened woman announces bravely.

"I do not advise doing so," he responds sadly. "The rain is getting worse, and our streets, even up here on higher ground, are starting to flood. You're safe here. In fact, people who live down by the beach will probably be joining you here soon. Old Isaac is driving his buggy along the beach, telling everyone to get to higher ground. Some are already heading this way. Others are laughing at him, still enjoying the wild waves."

I am beside myself. I feel I must try to make my way back to Ashton Villa, back to Charlie. It is only six blocks, I tell myself. And Ashton Villa is located on Broadway, the highest part of the island, higher than the church I'm sitting in.

I open my umbrella and step outside into ankle-deep water that is rising rapidly. The wind whips around me ferociously, almost blowing me away, as pelting rain stings my face. Perhaps the father is right, I decide, as I watch a stream of refugees stumbling through the water towards us, trying to get to higher ground.

We usher them inside, find towels for them to dry off, and share our luncheon with them. They relay tales of how bad it is down there on the beach. They are afraid their homes will be destroyed or seriously damaged.

"Not safe, I tell ya." One big black man shakes his head sorrowfully as he shares his plate of food with several strangers who had just arrived.

Father leads the group in prayer as the wind wails outside. More people arrive, looks of horror and fear upon their faces.

"We will be safe here," we reassure each other over and over again.

Will we really? Will Charlie and Charles be safe? What should I do? Where should I go? My mind is reeling with plans and back-up plans. What if the storm gets even worse? What if I decide to leave? Can I make it to Ashton Villa? What would be the best and safest route for me to follow to get there?

The cathedral is a hub of activity as it fills with more and more displaced people, including small children holding tightly to their parents' hands, crying. Some are lugging a few of their prized possessions.

An eerie premature darkness has descended over the island. Nuns are lighting candles around the cathedral, fearing we will lose power anytime. Suddenly, one of the large stained glass windows explodes as thunder shakes the huge building. Colored glass fragments fly into the nave and outside into the driving rain. Rain begins to stream into the building as people scream and run towards the center of the cathedral. We can hear something crashing and battering like a ram against the building, as if trying to knock it down.

Mary, where are you when we need you? But the beloved

statue of Mary on top of the cathedral is also swaying in the vicious storm. Will she survive? Will we?

"We need to get the hell out of here, make our way to one of those mansions on Broadway. That's the highest place on the island," one man screams as the two ton church bell breaks loose from its restraints and crashes through the roof. Thankfully, nobody was injured. But some of the people begin to leave, promising to stick together and help each other along the way.

"Are you coming, ma'am?" the big black man asks me as he holds the door open. "We will take Avenue F up to 23rd Street, then on up to Broadway near Ashton Villa."

Ashton Villa? That was all it took to convince me. I nod and weakly follow the others out into the torrential rain, slogging slowly through swirling water that is now several feet deep. Debris floats by, threatening to knock us down. The large brick buildings on Avenue F provide some shelter from the ferocious wind, thank God. We hold onto each other, helping each other up when one is knocked down into the churning water.

The water rises steadily. It is dark as night. Six blocks seems like six miles or more as we inch our way along. At times we take shelter near one of the buildings before struggling on again. We are finally only one block away from Ashton Villa and my Charlie, when the wind turns so fierce that it rips my umbrella into shreds. The rain pelts my face, stinging like shards of ice. I hunch over into the wind, determined to make my way through water that is now up to my waist and steadily rising. Huge waves of water are suddenly rushing through the streets and into the nearby houses and buildings.

Dear God, I pray, help me! Help us all!

A thunderous crash signals the sound of the trestle bridge, the only remaining link to the mainland, snapping and crashing into the sea in pieces. Galveston Island is on its own.

My God, this can't be happening! We are approaching the massive brick First Baptist Church, just one block from our destination. We pray as we struggle along on our way. One woman says she can't go another step. She wants to seek refuge in the church, which is already overflowing with people. But as we get closer, we hear horrible rumbling, crashing, and terrifying screams. The massive structure leans heavily towards the street and several of its ornate pillars tear loose, crumbling into the street and through the roof.

Bracing ourselves against the fierce winds, we struggle on. I can hardly stand or walk as angry waves knock me from one side to another. Flying timbers and debris seem to be coming at us from all directions.

Charlie! Charlie, my precious little boy, is the only thought in my mind. I must make it back to Charlie and Ashton Villa. We will be safe there in that formidable brick structure built to survive any possible storm, and located on the highest part of the island.

Inching ahead, one step forward, another backwards, I hear crashing and rumbling heading our way, coming from the ocean side. Houses are being torn apart, furniture and debris flying through the air.

Streams of more frantic people are now making their way beside us, fleeing from homes closer to the beach that are being destroyed by this unprecedented storm. Fleeing to higher ground, a river of refugees carrying a few of their prized possessions and holding on to their children for dear life. Some are sobbing. Others are praying.

Will we survive?

The water continues to rise higher and higher. I can barely slug my way through the churning sea that is submerging our island. The Gulf has met the bay. Galveston Island is under water.

Children are screaming in terror, falling into the sea that now surrounds us. Frantic parents grab their young ones from the jaws of death. We have become one with the sea. It is rising, rising still. No longer able to touch ground, we are now swimming, trying to keep our heads above the relentless rising and falling waves.

"Dear God, please help us!" Our cries pierce the sounds of the howling wind and the crashing of the sea. As waves threaten to suck us down into a bottomless sea, we cling to pieces of furniture or rooftops floating by. Bodies float by, some entangled in pieces of furniture or timbers from destroyed homes. Some men are climbing trees that are whipping fiercely in the gale force winds.

I am suddenly thrust, by someone or something, onto the roof of a house that is floating by. Some of my neighbors are already aboard. I hold on for dear life as the wind shifts and whips us around. Our "life raft" suddenly heads out into the ocean.

"Charlie," I scream into the darkness. "Charles!"

We are at the mercy of the sea as it tosses us up and down across the monstrous waves, farther and farther out into the ocean. The remaining lights of the island retreat into the distance.

It seems like hours have passed, like it is night, like death is looming on the horizon. Someone on our floating house begins to sing hymns. Others are praying. One young woman is sobbing and suddenly loses her grip, slipping into the furious waves. The men try to pull her to safety, to no avail. She is gone, as we all shall be soon.

A glimmer of hope suddenly arises, however, as the wind shifts once again and sails us back towards shore. We hold on tight as we ride the waves, faster and faster, sputtering salt water as walls of water crash over our heads.

We can see lights ahead on the high point of the island. Ashton Villa, I breathe deeply. Ashton Villa is still there!

We are almost flying now, with the force of the wind at our backs. As the moon peeks out from behind the clouds, we are stunned to see a massive barrier on the shore, directly ahead of us. A formidable barrier made of debris from what once was houses, pianos, furniture. As we get closer, we see mutilated bodies and animals embedded and buried within the huge mound.

"Oh my God!" a panicked voice screams into the night as an elderly man slips or jumps off the roof we are riding upon and disappears in the sea. The roof plunges sharply to one side, spilling several others into the churning water. I have no idea how many of us are left alive. All I know is that we seem to be driving full force ahead into a solid reef of certain death.

"Charles! Charlie! Help. Oh dear God, help!" I sob hysterically into the screeching winds. Until...until a surreal sense of calm numbs me, numbs everything. I feel nothing. My body is shutting down.

I know that my life is over. Death looms directly ahead of me. I can feel it. I can smell it. It is coming to claim me.

Everything suddenly goes black. Surreal black. Where am I? Am I dead? Or am I alive?

I see a bright light hovering above, beckoning me to follow it. It radiates an ironic sense of peace and comfort. At a time like this? But I cannot go to the light—not yet. I need to be sure Charlie and Charles have survived, to tell them I love them. Dear God, where are they?

I sense other spirits drifting around me, escaping from the shells that once housed their souls. Some are following the light. Others, like me, are trying to figure out if we are dead or alive. If this is all real or just a horrible dream.

Somehow I can now see clearly through the darkness that engulfs me. Looking down, I see my body, crumpled in a heap, broken in pieces atop the pile of rubble. I'm surrounded by the distorted bodies of my friends and neighbors, young children, babies torn from their mothers' arms, horses and cows. Some are still alive, partially buried, sobbing, praying, pleading for help. Others are silent, eyes glazed over in shock as they stare at the horrors surrounding them.

I float silently, grief-stricken but numb, above this sea of terror. Bodies floating. People dying. Railroad trestles from the destroyed bridge battering houses until they crumble, scattering their occupants, furniture, and precious heirlooms into the raging water. But I...I can no longer feel the wind or the rain. I'm floating freely without the confines of my old body. Without the pain and the fear. All I care about now is finding my family.

I look down upon Ashton Villa, relieved to see it still standing as several feet of water pours into the lower level of the house. Peering inside, I see Charlie, Miss Bettie, and other family members—alive, thank God! Terrorized, they huddle together on the second level of the house.

Charlie sits at the top of the grand staircase, hugging his knees, tears running down his cheeks as he watches the water rising below on the first floor. "Where's Mommy?" he whimpers.

I will my spirit to reach out and hug him, to comfort him, to tell him that I love him and will always be with him. He startles, looking bewildered, glancing around him. Can he feel my presence? Does he hear me? He sighs as he begins to calm down.

Miss Bettie puts her arms around him, as I wanted her to, and holds him close. Thanking God for sparing my son, I move on to find my husband. The storm is calming down, the flood waters receding back into the ocean as rapidly as they had crashed in. As the waters recede, the mass devastation is exposed.

Where would Charles have been? I can't find him as I swoop over what was left of The Cotton Exchange. I panic when I see Ritters Café, the place where Charles and his associates always had a late lunch. They dined here on huge platters of oysters and shrimp served by waiters in white jackets and black pants. But Ritters no longer exists. The roof, walls, and supporting beams of the ceiling have collapsed into the building.

Charles, my darling! I scream silently, searching frantically among the crumpled bodies scattered along the water-logged streets. Many are naked, clothes having been torn off by the ferocious winds and waves. I watch dazed survivors searching for loved ones, dodging floating debris. They don't see me. They don't know I'm there beside them.

I do not find Charles, so I float through what's left of the cafe into the remnants of the building. The massive carved mahogany bar is still intact.

Suddenly, I hear a familiar voice screaming for help from beneath the bar. My Charles had apparently taken cover beneath the bar and is still alive! I rush to his side, drifting over the bodies of some of his associates. It's too late for them, but Charles is still alive. I gather him in my arms. He has a deep gash on his forehead, but does not appear to be seriously hurt.

As I hold him close, I gaze into the face I'll always love. He looks in my direction, a perplexed expression upon his face. He begins to calm down, as if he can feel my presence comforting him.

I love you, Charles, and I'll always be with you. Take good care of Charlie for me. I project my thoughts into his mind as forcefully as I can. His eyes widen as he looks around with a bewildered expression upon his face. He sighs deeply. Can he feel my presence, my love? I stay with him until help arrives to clear the debris and help him out of the building, until he makes his way, through the bodies and debris, back to Charlie and Ashton Villa.

I hang around for a while, watching the horrendous clean-up operations. I watch as my body, one of six thousand or more, is loaded onto a horse-drawn cart, then a steamship, and escorted out to sea, where it is weighted down and dumped into the sea. It is the only way to deal with a disaster of this magnitude. No way to bury all the bodies.

But many of these bodies, including mine, end up drifting back to Galveston Island, as if we are determined to go home where we belong, home to our families. Back to life as it once was. Life as it will never be again.

Perhaps some of us don't even realize we are dead yet. It all happened so fast, so tragically. It is more than our minds can comprehend without shutting down. I'm not certain myself if I'm dead or alive. Could this just be some horrible nightmare that I cannot awaken from?

The distraught survivors don't know what to do with the many hundreds of bodies that have washed back onto the beaches of Galveston Island. The only answer seems to be burning the bodies in funeral pyres along the beaches wherever they are found. All able-bodied men are ordered to gather and burn the bodies, as armed guards stand by to make sure they do their sickening duty. Plied with whiskey, these exhausted men pile our bodies in heaps and start the fires.

Day after day they tend the fires, sometimes vomiting as the stench of decaying bodies fills the air. Night after night the sky glows eerily with the flames of funeral fires burning along the coastline. The fickle ocean laps gently against the shore, a funeral choir paying tribute to all the lives it claimed so violently just weeks ago.

I watch my own discarded and decaying body turning slowly into ashes in a massive fire on the grounds of what is now The Hotel Galvez. The towering hotel still stands, overlooking the sea. Perhaps that is why, many years later, I enjoy haunting the old hotel from time to time.

Gazing down at my burning shell of a body, I feel nothing. I am numb. I must really be dead. But, somehow, I feel strangely alive. Perhaps it's not all over. Perhaps it is simply time for me to move on into a new dimension of "life."

It is time for me to go to the light....

SIX
BELLA

"Death is the greatest illusion of all."
Osho Rajneesh

"Oh my God! Help!" I tried to scream out into the night, aware that I was unable to utter a sound. I thrashed around in my bed, drowning, drenched in a sea of sweat. Trying desperately to free myself from the worst nightmare I'd ever experienced.

It's only a dream…only a dream, a tiny part of my subconscious tried to calm me down. Somehow this had always worked in the past, but not tonight. Something was wrong. This was real, more than a dream. And I was caught up in it, reliving something from somewhere that seemed to have happened long ago.

Finally I broke free from the terrors of the night, feeling as if I'd been rescued by an unseen force. Trembling, I felt an invisible hand gently stroking my forehead.

Hush, child. You are all right, Isabella's unspoken words seeped into my mind.

"Isabella?"

Yes, it is I. I'm with you. I'm here for you. She continued to stroke my forehead.

"What? What just happened?"

70

It was time for you to learn more about the Great Storm, from one who did not survive. Time for you to feel it, to understand what happened to those of us who died. Time for you to write about it. Her thoughts continued to infiltrate my mind.

"But you terrorized me, Isabella," I cried out. "I thought I was drowning, dying!"

Precisely, my dear. How else would you know what it was like? She sighed. *You will be able, now, to write your book, one with a unique "slant," as they say, one that nobody else has been able to capture.*

"But...," I stammered. What could I say? Of course, she was right. I had my angle now. Maybe this would be the book that would sky-rocket me to fame. I could almost envision my book launch party, maybe at Ashton Villa — maybe not.

It's not about fame and fortune, she interrupted my thoughts. *Think of how this knowledge will help people dealing with the deaths of their loved ones. How it can help survivors of tragedies like this. That is what this is all about, Bella.*

"So this is part of your unfinished business?" I finally saw the light.

And yours as well, she acknowledged. I sensed her brilliant smile as she swooshed across my bedroom and through the closed window, where the first light of day was beginning to creep in. Then she was gone once again, implanting one final thought in my mind. *Write! Now!*

First, I needed to clear my head with a cool shower and a walk beside the ocean. As I walked, taking in the remnants of a brilliant sunrise, a sky streaked with swirls of pink and gold, my mind reeled with ideas for the book I was about to write. Scenes and characters came to life. Yes, I would embed the truth within fiction. Sometimes that was a very effective way to get important points across to non-believers.

I finally understood the mission that Isabella and I had

71

embarked upon together. Perhaps we could make a difference in this world, a difference for those dealing with the loss of loved ones. Isabella was right. I knew she'd be there to guide me along the way, to push me on when I stumbled or got distracted with life.

"Here's to our book, Isabella!" I cried into the ocean breeze as I splashed barefoot through the gentle waves washing in from the sea.

Something stopped me dead in my tracks, made me glance down at the beach one step ahead of me. There was a perfect sand dollar glittering in the sunshine. I gently picked it up, recognizing this as a sign of good luck. It was rare to find a perfect sand dollar on these beaches. I'd searched often, finding many broken pieces but never a complete one. I would make it into a beautiful necklace, one that I would wear every day as I worked on our book. For good luck.

I was on a roll the next few weeks, consumed with our novel. My first task was to write a detailed accounting of my nightmare about Isabella's life and death. That would be the heart of my story. I didn't want to forget any of this, although I was certain there was no chance of that after what I'd been through.

I buried myself at my little kitchen table, which was overflowing with notes scattered about, books about the storm, my laptop, assorted half-full cups of coffee, and dishes encrusted with the remnants of my last few quick meals.

Sometimes I forgot to eat, almost forgot to go to the bathroom, for hours on end. I would be shocked sometimes to find myself still writing in the dark. This novel was coming together in a way I've never before experienced. Words seemed to flow onto the page, magically, from a source far beyond myself. Isabella?

I shut out the rest of the world while I wrote, ignoring phone calls, making due with whatever groceries I had left in my cupboards. My only excursions beyond my cottage were daily walks on the beach, where I inhaled the ocean air, basking in the sunshine, as more ideas for the book rose from the depths of my sub-conscious. How much information was hidden there, I wondered, inaccessible until we found a way to call it up? Where did it come from?

My only other adventure in life those days, which soon extended into a very productive month, was my nightly glass of red wine out in my gazebo as I watched the sun set over the bay. This was a ritual I'd indulged in since Jonathan died. It was my time to remember him. Now, of course, I also remembered Jimmy.

I talked to them both, sometimes with tears glistening in my eyes. I still longed for a sign from either one of them. They seemed to be silent lately, as if they were giving me space to complete my mission, my book, instead of focusing on them. What I'd experienced with each of them was, in fact, helping me to write this book. Pieces of each of them and memories we'd shared were being woven into the fabric of the book I was destined to write.

One evening as I sat out in the gazebo, I heard my cell phone ring with what seemed to be a sense of urgency. I felt compelled to rush into my cottage and pick up instead of letting it go into voicemail, where many unheard messages were probably already waiting for me.

"Hello?" I grabbed the phone after finding it buried it beneath a pile of notes on the table.

"Thank God you finally answered!" my sister's exasperated voice snapped. "You know your voicemail box is full, and you haven't bothered to return my calls."

"I've been busy working on my book about the storm."

"You're a dreamer, Bella, but that's not why I called. Have you bothered to visit Olivia — your mother, if you recall?"

A twinge of guilt stabbed at me. I'd been too pre-occupied to make my weekly visits to the nursing home. "Why?"

"She is not doing well. You'd better get there as soon as possible if you want to see her again," Veronica scolded. She always had to dramatize situations, to make them sound much worse than they really were.

"What's going on? Something worse than the usual?"

"Congestive heart failure. Old age. She is giving up on life and does not want to go on."

"I'm on my way."

I flipped the phone off, changed into clean clothes, ran a brush through my dirty hair, and headed out the door. Damn Veronica if she was just playing with me. How could Mother have taken such a fast turn for the worst? She'd been all too spunky—and nasty—the last time I saw her. She'd certainly let me know that she didn't approve of me and never had. Still, she was my mother....

Twenty minutes later, I pulled into the parking lot of the Meridian Retirement Home along the seawall overlooking the Gulf of Mexico. Mother's home for the past few years, it was a lovely place, complete with a library, movie theatre, game room, wellness center, and a fireplace lounge with a piano. She took her meals in an elegant dining room with a view of the ocean. We'd placed her in the best possible home once Veronica could no longer handle her. Veronica must have been paying big bucks for her care here, I assumed. I hadn't been asked to contribute.

I made my way to Olivia's room. I could hear Christmas music playing—in late January—from within her room. The room was dark except for lights twinkling from several Snow Village houses that Veronica must have placed there.

"Mother? It's me, Bella," I announced as my eyes adjusted to the darkness. She was sitting in her overstuffed chair by the window, mesmerized by her Christmas village. She didn't look to me like she was dying.

A smile spread across her face as she held her arms out for a hug. I was surprised, in that she never did this. I walked into her fragile arms and held her close, a tear trickling down my cheek. "How are you?" I asked.

She sighed wearily. "It is time for me to go home, Bella. I wanted to tell you goodbye."

"Home? Ashton Villa?"

"Oh no, my dear. Home to God, home to your father. And I know little Jonathan is waiting for me there, too." She seemed so content, as if she were looking forward to dying.

"But Mother, we can do something to make you better. We need to get you to the hospital!"

"Absolutely not," she bristled. "I have the right to decide when to go home, and I'm going now! My Grandmother Isabella is here with me. She's waiting for me."

What? I gasped, searching the room for any signs of her presence. After all, I knew Isabella better than anyone else.

"You can't see her," Mother leaned in to confide in me, "but she was here. And she told me that she is watching over you, Bella. She says you are special, and I should be very proud of you."

I didn't know what to say, so I just held her hand.

"I'm not crazy, you know," Mother continued. "Isabella will be back. Maybe she just went down for a cup of coffee."

"Of course you're not crazy," I assured her. "I'm sure Isabella has been here. How about Daddy, or Grandpa Charlie, your father?" I needed to know more, to fill in some of the missing pieces of my life.

Olivia's eyes glazed over, a faint smile spreading across her face. "Oh yes, your daddy is here, waiting for me." Then her eyes blackened and turned to ice. "As for Grandpa Charlie, he's not here. Never was here for me. No, he never really came back to life after his mother, our dear Isabella, died in that dreadful storm. I never really knew my father."

I thought she was going to cry. I never really knew my Grandpa Charlie either. He was so distant, so removed from life, that I had no idea who he really was. I had no idea what demons lived in the recesses of his mind.

"Tell me more about him, please."

She tensed up, clenching her hands together. "I don't want to talk about him." Her gloomy mood suddenly brightened as she gazed up at the ceiling. "You really believe Isabella is here?" Olivia's voice quivered.

"Of course I believe you. I've also seen her."

"You have? Veronica thinks that is crazy, you know. Veronica doesn't believe."

"Well, I do, Mother," I smiled at her through my tears.

"Before Isabella comes back for me, I have something to tell you," Mother whispered, as if anxious to share an important secret with me.

"Yes?" My heart pounded in my ears as I watched my mother's eyes fill with tears.

"I love you, Bella, and I am proud of you. I should have told you...." Her voice trailed off. "You have wonderful things to look forward to in your future. And someday, I will see you in Heaven. I promise."

I collapsed, trying to suppress my sobs. I couldn't believe I was hearing the words I'd longed to hear all my life. Was my mother delusional, or had the truth finally seeped through a tough veneer that she'd polished throughout her life? Why? To protect herself? From what?

"I love you, Mother." I folded her into my arms, rocking

her tiny body as if she were a baby. I felt her body relax slowly. I thought she was sleeping until her eyes suddenly flew open, gazing towards the ceiling, a look of profound peace and beauty transforming her aged features.

"Isabella, it's time," she whispered, her arms reaching out. I felt her go limp in my arms as the unmistakable feeling of Isabella's presence swished through the room. One last, long, slow breath, and then my mother was still.

My mother, the mother I was never sure I really had — not until now — was gone.

As my tears flowed, I reminded myself that she still lived on in another time and place. I could only imagine the joyful reunion she'd have in Heaven, surrounded by all her loved ones once again. I could almost see her scooping my little Jonathan up in her arms. The two of them had always had a special bond, a bond that had apparently skipped my generation. That was okay. Somehow, my mother and I had re-connected at the very end of her life. For that, I would be forever grateful.

Another funeral, just two months after Jimmy's. Another painful reunion with my sister, a reunion that once again brought us together momentarily. We were sisters, despite our differences. Now, all we had left of our family of origin was each other. That should count for something, I told myself. And somehow, I suspected that the journey I'd embarked upon as I wrote the book may help to heal some of our past wounds. Someday....

SEVEN
BELLA

"It is the secret of the world that all things subsist and do not die,
but retire a little from sight and afterwards return again."
Ralph Waldo Emerson

It was the night of the full moon, the first one since Olivia had passed on. I looked forward to my usual walk on the beach beneath the light of the moon. Hopefully, the power of the Green Rising Moon may help me to connect with the spirits of my deceased loved ones. I longed to feel Jimmy's arms around me again, to feel his presence and hear his thoughts. Why had he not contacted me again since the day of his funeral?

Of course, I also hoped to see my Jonathan…although I suspected he may have already re-incarnated.

And now my mother, Olivia, was among them. Maybe I could connect with her also. Hopefully, Isabella would be there tonight to help me connect with them all. Yes, I planned to wear her black lace wedding dress. That was a given on a full moon night. It was what Isabella wanted and expected of me.

A restlessness washed over me as I paced around my cottage, anxious for the sun to set and the moon to rise. My energy was peaking.

My phone suddenly went off. The ring tone told me it was my sister calling. The last thing I needed was for her to interrupt my full moon outing. Maybe that's why she was calling, trying to prevent me from making a spectacle of myself out on the beach tonight. I didn't answer but, I did check her voice mail message.

"Bella, can you come over? Please?" Veronica's voice shook as if she were terrified. "I'm afraid, and I don't know who else to call. Please…."

My sister scared? Of what? She was always so confident, able to handle any situation. What in the world was she afraid of? I'd never heard her voice shake like that.

"Damn," I muttered to myself. Not tonight of all nights! My first impulse was to ignore her plea for help. She'd never asked me for help before. Never. She'd never needed me before. Why now? Why me? But then, who else did she have except for her society friends who were more like acquaintances?

Reluctantly, I called her back. She sounded like she'd been crying, like a little girl who had lost her mother. Which she had… as I had also.

Was she grieving this much over Olivia's death? Of course, the two of them had always been close. I'd always been the one on the outside of their relationship, the one who never measured up to their expectations.

As a glowing orange ball of fire descended from the sky and slipped into the ocean, I found myself driving along the Seawall on my way to Ashton Villa. How I longed to be out there by the ocean tonight. My heart ached at the possibility that I may not make it back home in time for my walk on the beach.

Veronica was on the porch waiting for me, clutching a bottle of wine and two glasses in her clenched fists. She looked like hell, as if she'd missed her weekly beauty shop appointment and had not bothered to change her clothes in several days. She hadn't even bothered to put her make-up on. I don't think I'd seen her without make-up in many years. Her eyes were puffy and framed with dark circles.

Her eyes darted fearfully towards the house as if she were afraid of something in it. Breathing a sigh of relief when she saw me approach, she gestured for me to follow her instead of inviting me in. We hiked in silence across the lawn and into Sealy Park where the Victorian Pavilion perched, surrounded by a maze of flowers and palm trees. I followed her lead as she settled upon a bench in the gazebo, opened the bottle of wine, and poured us each a glass.

I waited as she gulped down her glass of wine, instead of sipping slowly as she usually did. What the hell? I gulped mine too, still waiting for her to speak.

The magic of the star-lit night and the gardens was not lost on me. Memories flooded through my mind of all the times we had spent together here, long before the pavilion was built. Veronica and I had walked our dolls, in their buggies, around the paths and gardens. We'd had tea parties on the lawn. We jumped rope, played jacks, picked dandelions, and made flower chains. Sometimes we laid on our backs in the grass, gazing up at the clouds as our imaginations turned them into various objects.

Then there had been the summer concerts, a Galveston tradition since 1928. Every Tuesday evening during the summer, the quiet little park came alive with the music of the Galveston Beach Band. Each performance began with the traditional bugle call, followed by the Pledge of Allegiance. As the band played "Stars and Stripes Forever," children marched along the paths, waving their flags. Families came from all over, sitting on the open lawn as they listened to marches, Big Band music, Latin, jazz, rock, and classical music.

Those were the days, I sighed to myself, the good old days

before all the troubles began.... My heart began to soften as these old memories seeped into my consciousness.

Veronica refilled our wine glasses, relaxing a little as she gazed up at the moon. "It's beautiful," she sighed before falling silent again.

"What is going on?" I finally asked her. Surely she had not called me, distraught, to have me look at the moon and drink wine with her.

She wrenched up her courage and blurted it out, "I think I am losing my mind! Oh my God, I am imagining things. Terrible things are happening at Ashton Villa!"

"Tell me," I spoke gently. "I doubt you are losing your mind, Veronica. There must be an explanation. What happened?"

"Well...well, this sounds crazy," she began timidly.

"Somehow I doubt it will sound crazy to me," I grinned. "I'm the crazy one in this family. Remember?" Hmmm...maybe that's why she had called me. Everyone else in her little world was too sane to hear whatever she had to say.

"I don't know where to begin. Strange things are happening. I hear the music boxes in Mother's Christmas village playing in the middle of the night. Nobody is there. Nobody has turned them on! I had the maid pack away the entire village to put an end to this. But the next morning, I walked into the Gold Room and found several of Mother's favorite buildings and accessories on the fireplace mantle. I could have sworn they had all been packed away. I know they weren't there the prior evening. I think I am losing my mind!"

"Did you ask the maid?"

"Yes, and she swore she had packed everything away."

"Was it Grandma's Cottage and the gazebo that magically appeared?"

Veronica gasped and almost dropped her glass of wine.

"How do you know?"

"Just a lucky guess. Those were Mother's favorite pieces. She must not have wanted you to pack them away. Maybe she wanted you to keep them out permanently to remember her by."

"You're saying that Mother…. Mother's dead, for God's sake, Bella!"

"I know that," I sighed, "but her spirit lives on. She is trying to communicate with you. Humor her, will you? Try to think thoughts to her, and she may hear you. She is just trying to get your attention, and you're not listening."

"But I'm scared, Bella." She looked into my eyes. "This sounds crazy, almost as crazy as I feel. There's more…."

"Go on."

"Well, you know that framed photo of her on her eightieth birthday, the one on the mantle above the fireplace?"

I nodded.

"That photo is moving around the house, I swear to God. Either I'm sleepwalking and re-arranging things, or losing my mind, or someone is playing games with me. But who?"

I shrugged my shoulders.

"I'm alone in that big house, Bella. The maid and butler live in the servants' quarters out back, as you know. My doors are locked. Who is moving her picture, from one fireplace mantle to another, one room to another?

"The very worst part," she continued, "was one morning when I woke to find it sitting on my bedside table, staring at me! I screamed and ran downstairs and out the door, in my nightgown!"

The very thought of my prim and proper sister running outside in her nightgown, on Broadway Street, almost made me laugh out loud.

"It is just Mother, Veronica! Why does it scare you to think that Mother's spirit is hanging around? Ashton Villa was her home, too, and maybe she's not ready to leave it yet. Maybe she has some unfinished business. Or maybe she is trying to tell you goodbye."

"That is freaky. I don't believe in ghosts. You know that!"

"Maybe you should reconsider your position. Neither did Mother. Maybe she knows different now that she has crossed over. And maybe she is trying to tell you that."

Veronica was silent but listening intently as she sipped the last of her wine. The bottle was empty.

"Are you afraid of your own mother, just because she has shed her earthly body and is now in spirit form? Has she done anything on her visits to scare you or threaten you?" I persisted, determined to make her see the light. "You should be happy that she cares enough to come and visit you."

"I'm trying to wrap my mind around these bizarre ideas, I really am. If what you say could possibly be true, has she come to visit you, Bella?"

I felt a twinge of pain rip through my heart. No, Olivia had not bothered to come visit me. What else was new? "Not yet," I had to admit, gazing wistfully at the full moon overhead. If only I was out walking the beach tonight, maybe I'd find her there....

"So how can you tell me what I should think if you haven't even seen her? You, with all your strange ideas...." Veronica rose unsteadily from the bench. "We need more wine," she announced as she began walking slowly back to the house. "Are you coming?" She looked back over her shoulder.

"I'll wait here," I replied.

"No, I want you to come and see for yourself what happens in that house!"

We were both getting a little tipsy. Maybe that was all right. Maybe she was actually letting her hair down for once. Maybe it was my chance to prove to her that I wasn't really crazy either. So I followed her back to the house, where she retrieved several bottles of wine from the wine cellar.

First she had to show me the Christmas village pieces that kept reappearing after she had packed them away. But they weren't on the fireplace mantle where she swore they had been this morning. Instead, we found them on the top of the antique rolltop desk. I couldn't help chuckling to think that Olivia was having fun playing games in her old house.

"And what's so funny about someone haunting me and trying to drive me insane?" Veronica demanded as she struggled with the wine opener, trying to open an expensive bottle of Chardonnay. "Which one do you want? Chardonnay or Merlot? One for each of us!"

Suddenly there was a loud crash and the sound of breaking glass in the Gold Room. Veronica's eyes filled with terror as I cautiously made my way into the room. No one was there, but one of the elegantly-framed portraits on the wall had crashed down onto the floor and broken in pieces. It was a picture of Grandpa Charlie, Olivia's father and Isabella's son.

My mind flashed back to something Olivia told me shortly before she died; something about this man never being a real father to her, never being there for her. Did that have anything to do with the fact that his portrait had conveniently crashed onto the floor?

"Who cares? Mother never liked him anyway," Veronica sighed as she picked up the pieces and stuffed them into the trash. "Come on, we have more wine to drink," she giggled as she handed me the bottle of Merlot and led me back to the old gazebo. This time she plunked herself down on a garden bench, patting the seat beside her for me to join her.

"What do you mean she never liked him? Why not?" I was

no longer worrying about my words, what I should or should not say to my sister. I didn't really care tonight, not anymore.

"She never told you?" The puzzled expression upon Veronica's face seemed to turn into one that was taunting me. Taunting me because I had never been in Olivia's confidences like she had been. "He was mean," Veronica continued. "He never got over losing his mother, dear Isabella, in that horrible hurricane. He was never there for anyone. I'm sure he never would have married at all if his father hadn't found him a wife and forced him to marry. Guess he thought that would bring Charlie out of his shell and back to life. But it didn't work. He was an angry man…didn't you know that?"

"Maybe I forgot," I pouted as she started to laugh. "Maybe it's time for me to go home." I rose from the bench.

She sobered up fast, grabbing my arm. "No, stay. Please."

"Only if I can have another glass of wine." I sat down and poured myself a big glass from my own bottle.

"What were we talking about? Oh yeah." She took another swig. "Old Grandpa Charlie! What a bastard he was…never there for anyone but himself. He shut himself off from the whole world. No feelings. Nothing."

"It must have been a horrible thing for a ten-year-old boy to go through, his mother drowning in that awful storm."

"But the thing is…," she stifled a hiccup, "he tuned everyone out, everyone except the ghosts he talked to. They were more real to him than his daughter was, and you know, she was his only child. Go figure!"

A light bulb went off in my head. Did Grandpa Charlie also have a special connection with deceased loved ones? Was I a little like him with all my talk about ghosts? And was that why Olivia was furious when I talked about spirits? Did I remind her of her father? Is that why she never really cared much for me, until the last day of her life when Isabella came to her and she finally saw the light?

Lost in thought, we sat in silence beneath a pitch-black sky. The moon hid beneath a layer of clouds, peeking out now and then. I wondered where Isabella was tonight. I wondered if she wondered why I wasn't out walking the beach in her beloved dress.

Why did my sister know things that nobody had ever bothered to tell me? I began to simmer with resentment. Finally I burst out with, "Well, you know Mother loved me, too. She was even proud of me!"

"Well, goody for you," Veronica hiccupped. "Who ever said she didn't love you?"

"She really didn't like you better than me, you know. You weren't her favorite!" I probably sounded pretty stupid, but I really didn't care. My wounded little girl's voice was coming to the surface after having been repressed for years.

"Nana nana boo boo...." Veronica sang out the silly lyrics we'd sung as children, sticking her tongue out at me. Soon we were laughing together hysterically, like we'd done so many years ago. Of course, that moment soon passed.

"Isabella was there with Mother when she died," I informed Veronica proudly, proud that I was the one with personal knowledge of this fact.

"What the hell you talkin' about?" She slurred her words.

"I said, Isabella was there to escort Mother to the light, to Heaven."

"That makes no sense, you know. Another one of your dumb ideas. Besides...," she hesitated. "How would you know that?"

"Because," I leaned towards her for emphasis, "Mother told me so, right before she died. So there!"

"So there, what?"

"Just sayin. If Isabella can come back, and I swear to God she has many times, then why can't Mother? Why can't you friggin' believe what is right before your eyes?"

"Just shut up, Bella, OK?"

Once again we lapsed into silence, sipping our wine. An ocean breeze began to ruffle the palm trees into a slow dance, swaying softly to the music of the past. I tried to feel the presence of any beloved spirits lurking out there somewhere beneath the fickle light of the moon.

Jimmy weighed heavily on my mind...*my* Jimmy. He would always be my Jimmy, despite the fact he'd been married to my sister. How messed up was that?

Glancing over at Veronica, I was surprised to see tears in her eyes as she stared into the black sky.

"Do you miss him?" The words escaped from my mouth before I could stop them.

She startled. "What did you say?"

"Nothing."

"Are you asking about Jimmy? Of course I miss him. He was my husband, remember?"

I waited, trying to control my reeling emotions, trying not to blurt out how I really felt. Still, I needed to know the truth about some things. Things about their relationship.

Veronica seemed to be lost in her thoughts, still staring out into space, as if I wasn't even there. "It's strange," she began. "He's not here anymore, but then in some ways, he never really was. He was often preoccupied. His mind was someplace else. Still, what we had was good, but it's not like I lost a soul mate or something."

"That's all?" I was astounded, but also reassured that Jimmy had been someplace else for much of their marriage. He'd been in love with me, spending time with me; as friends only, of course, after our initial rendezvous.

"We were just so different. We liked different things." She finally looked at me as if seeing me for the first time. "Jimmy was more like you than me. The two of you loved chasing sunsets and ghosts together. You were both free spirits." Shaking her finger in my face, she continued. "*You* were the free spirit from hell, Bella! Still are in your old age."

"I'm not as ancient as you are," I reminded her.

Ignoring me, she continued. "As for Jimmy, he would have been almost as bad as you if I hadn't reined him in and made him into a respectable citizen in our social circle. All this family needed was two free spirits like you and Jimmy. What a disaster that would have been!"

"Maybe Jimmy would have been happier that way," I glared at her. "At least he wasn't a stuffed shirt like you!"

"A stuffed shirt?" Veronica burst out in laughter. "Now you sound just like Olivia!" Suddenly she stopped and became very serious. "You and Jimmy just might have been happy together...." My heart caught in my throat as she continued. "Of course, that would have been ridiculous. What a silly thought! You and Jimmy?" She began to laugh, stabbing my heart with each peal of her cruel laughter.

I had to get away, back to my cozy cottage by the sea, away from the sister who continued to torment me. First I grabbed my bottle, put it to my lips, and emptied it. I stood up, staggering, telling Veronica good night. But my feet weren't coordinated, and I almost fell on the familiar path.

"Where do you think you're goin?" my sister called out. "You sure as hell aren't gonna drive tonight. Look at you. You can't even walk straight. You will have to stay with me, like it or not."

"Stay with you?" I was horrified at the thought. I hadn't slept in Ashton Villa since I'd escaped many years ago, shortly before

Jonathan was born. The very thought of Veronica and I, alone in the same house, entombed with memories of Jimmy, was too much for me. But I soon realized that driving my car back home was not an option.

The two of us meandered a crooked path back to the house. Veronica locked all the doors. "You can sleep in Jimmy's room," she announced as she climbed the stairs to the upper level, holding tightly to the carved wood railing for support. I wobbled up the stairs behind her. "It's just down the hallway," she pointed towards Mother and Father's old bedroom.

Jimmy's bedroom? They had separate bedrooms?

"We liked our privacy and personal space." She smiled sadly as if hearing my unspoken question.

So I settled into Jimmy's old room, flopping down across the massive four-poster mahogany bed where he'd once slept. Alone? I breathed deeply, trying to absorb his musky scent, trying to feel his familiar touch. Trying to hold back the river of tears building up inside. Oh Jimmy, where are you now?

My eyes scanned the room, taking in a number of framed photos of him on his ranch with his prize horses. Beautiful sunset photos that he'd taken, with me at his side. Photos of him with his family. Where was I?

I wanted to stay awake to take in all that I could of the world where my beloved once lived, but the wine was getting to me. I could no longer keep my eyes open. I drifted off into a deep sleep, still wearing my crumpled clothes, including my favorite white shirt with a fresh red wine stain on the front.

Emerging from my self-induced fog sometime in the middle of the night, I felt the mattress beside me sag with the weight of someone climbing into bed with me. I felt Jimmy's familiar arms holding me close as he intertwined his fingers with mine. I felt his love pouring into my soul in a strange way I'd never before encountered.

"Jimmy," I cried out, turning towards him. But he wasn't there. Nobody was there.

I have to go, my darling. I came back to hold you once more, to give you a proper goodbye. You will be all right. Be strong for me. His unspoken words seeped into my mind. Then, with a squeeze of his hand, I felt him climb out of bed, and his presence disappeared.

Trembling, I flipped on the lamp by his bedside and got out of bed. At first, I tried to dismiss this as a wonderful dream. But I knew in my heart that it was more than a dream. It was real. Jimmy had been here in *his* bed with me. But he was telling me goodbye. I wasn't ready for this. I had hoped for many more visits from him. If Isabella could come back and visit me over the years, why couldn't Jimmy?

Because I am your spirit guide, Bella. Jimmy is not. He has work to do on the other side, Isabella's thoughts drifted into my consciousness. *He's been watching over you all to be sure you are okay. Now it is his time to settle in on the other side of life.*

Sleep was no longer an option, so I opened the Victorian walk through window and stepped out onto the balcony and into the beauty of the night. The clouds had moved out, leaving the full moon casting an eerie glow over the grounds of Ashton Villa. I breathed in the invigorating scent of the fresh ocean air, breathed out my sorrows.

Gazing up at the infinite sky, I was reminded once again that I am just a tiny speck in a gigantic universe. My problems were really insignificant within the context of the big picture of life, and death.

Still, I needed to somehow process my grief over losing Jimmy. Maybe it was time. Up until now, I'd buried myself in writing my novel. Maybe I'd back off for a while, letting it simmer in the recesses of my mind while I focused on letting Jimmy go.

When I finally came back into the bedroom, closing the doors to the balcony, I glanced at the clock on Jimmy's bedside table. It was still ticking, still alive, even without his presence. It was only five in the morning. I tiptoed down the hallway through the shadows of the lingering night, past Veronica's bedroom, and down the familiar staircase into the kitchen to make myself a pot of coffee. My head hurt. I needed coffee.

The maid would not arrive until later, so I had the house to myself. How long had it been? Memories crept in from every corner of this old house, the house I'd always loved and always thought of as my real home. Until Jimmy.

I took my coffee out into the garden to watch the sun rise, sipping slowly, coming back to life. I couldn't believe that my sister and I, after all these years of estrangement, had actually gotten drunk together last night. I suspected that this had been a one-time-only event, and we would revert to our long-entrenched pattern of bickering and disagreeing about anything and everything.

Still, I'd learned a lot last night, things to help me understand myself better. And hopefully, she now realized that she'd been wrong in her belief that ghosts, or spirits, do not exist. Maybe Olivia would quit haunting her and go to the light now that she'd made her point.

It was probably best, I decided, if I left before Veronica woke up. I rinsed out my coffee cup and quietly slipped out the door. Just before locking the door, a twinge of guilt made me decide to leave her a note on the counter beside the coffee pot. "Thanks for a memorable evening. Take care," I scribbled on the sticky note.

I had an important mission to complete — for Jimmy's sake as well as my own. First, I needed to go home to change my clothes and feed my cats.

EIGHT
BELLA

"Though nothing can take back the hour of splendor in the grass, of glory in the flower, we will grieve not but rather find strength in what remains behind."
William Wordsworth

May you find comfort in shared memories of the past...
At least that's what they say. It is common sentiment often expressed in sympathy cards designed to comfort those who have lost a loved one. I was still seeking some semblance of comfort in the wake of Jimmy's death. Today, I would visit some of the places where we'd made and shared memories.

As I pulled off the road in front of the historic Stewart Mansion, I was shocked. The battered old "No Trespassing" signs that I'd expected to greet me were not there. The gnarled and twisted massive live oak trees that once cast an eerie spell upon this haunted estate were also gone.

Instead, I was greeted by an unoccupied entrance station and a fancy sign reading "Bayside at Watermans." The old overgrown estate was being transformed into a luxury housing development, a community of coastal cottages. Freshly paved roads wound through the estate along numbered lot markers.

I was alone, nobody else on the premises, so I decided to take a stroll down the driveway to get a closer look at the property. I was relieved to find that the old white-washed Stewart Mansion was still there, restored to its former glory. A sign beside the mansion informed me that this was now the Stewart Mansion Community Center, a luxury clubhouse and event center. It was surrounded with newly planted large palm trees and flowering shrubs.

I hiked around to the rear of the mansion, holding my breath, hoping to find some semblance of the old Spanish tiled garden. One of the giant live oaks remained in the courtyard near the old, restored stucco arches. But just beyond the arches, there was now a swimming pool and lazy river. The historic flavor of the mansion had been preserved, I had to admit, but it was now a blend of the old with the new.

As I stood there gazing into the courtyard, focusing on the familiar ancient oak tree, my mind flashed back in time to the old days when Jimmy and I had explored the ruins of this formerly abandoned estate. How I wished Jimmy was here with me today. Who knew? Maybe he was…at least I liked to believe in that possibility.

We'd spent many intriguing hours here wandering through the remains of what once was an elegant 8,200 square foot Spanish Colonial Revival hacienda built in 1926, overlooking Lake Como. It had been abandoned for years. Everyone knew it was haunted.

Ignoring the warning signs, we had walked through the old stone arch that framed the rutted out driveway. The massive arched windows of this white-washed stucco structure were boarded up after vandals had thrown rocks through the windows. The red-tiled roof was caving in and the front door had fallen from its' hinges where it laid in a heap covered with weeds and moss. Such a shame, I thought to myself, to let something of this historical significance crumble into the earth.

Jimmy and I had been intrigued with the history of this remote retreat from the world. Located half-way down the island near 13 Mile Road on an elevated ridge made of sea shells, this land had once been the hunting and fishing grounds of the Karankawa Indians. In those days, the island was infested with rattlesnakes down in the marshy bayous and sand dunes. In fact, it was once called Snake Island. The natives camped high on this ridge, away from the rattlesnakes.

They brought their dead out to the island to bury them here, facing the east in fetal positions, since they believed the veil between this world and the next was unusually thin here on the island.

In 1527, Cabeza de Vaca's ship crashed at what is now 11 Mile Road, not far from today's Stewart Mansion. He was a key figure in a Spanish colonizing expedition on his way to Florida when his ship crashed and landed on the island. He lived with the Indians here for several years before moving on.

Later, in the 1800's, the notorious pirate/buccaneer Jean Lafitte set up camp on the island. This was his home base, from which he and his men raided and ransacked Spanish ships sailing the seas. Lafitte contracted with the governments of England and France, who were at war with Spain, to seize and rob Spanish ships passing through the Gulf.

A notorious battle was fought near the present-day Stewart Mansion, near the three twisted live oak trees, between Lafitte's buccaneers and the Indians. Legend has it that the Indians attacked the pirates because they had stolen the daughter of the Indian chief.

When Lafitte was run out of Galveston by the United States

Government in 1821 after some of his men had attacked US ships, he burned his entire village and elegant home before burying some of his treasure on the island. To this day, people try to sneak onto the Stewart property to search for Lafitte's long lost treasure.

Although the Karankawa tribe was extinct by the mid 1860's, legend has it that some of their spirits live on at this sacred place where they buried their dead hundreds of years ago. Now and then, local paranormal researchers picked up on their presence here.

Some years back, Jimmy and I had a surreal experience here. We were leaving the mansion, walking down the driveway towards Jimmy's truck, when I felt compelled to take a photo of one of the sprawling live oak trees in the yard. I felt something strange in the air as I took that photo, but didn't think much of it until later when I looked at the photo.

Zooming in, I was shocked to see a tall dark-skinned, bare-chested man standing beside the tree. Of course, I had not seen him with my naked eye when I took the photo, but my camera managed to pick him up on film. Had I captured the spirit of one of Karankawas, a spirit that had materialized for me? When I showed my photo to some of the local paranormal researchers, they confirmed that I had, and that several others had captured similar photos at this site.

Standing in the courtyard all by myself that morning, my mind drifted back in time once again to a moonlit night years ago. I couldn't remember where Veronica had been that night, out of town someplace on one of her community fundraising events. So Jimmy and I took advantage of her absence to explore some of the haunted sites we loved; at night, when we were more likely to encounter spirits roaming around the island.

Of course, we'd heard warnings about the rattlesnakes and other reptiles that could be lurking in the dark corners or hanging from the exposed rafters of the spooky mansion. Hearts pounding, we creaked the main door open, swinging our flashlights back and forth across the room to make sure it would be safe to enter.

We were greeted by a portrait of a life-size pirate, leering at us from beneath the brim of his three-cornered hat as he flashed a saber sword at us. He seemed to be guarding the entrance, daring us to enter, daring us to disturb the solitude of the ghosts who resided here. I stopped dead in my tracks, feeling a distinct chill in the air.

Jimmy put his arm around me protectively as we gazed in awe at five additional menacing pirate portraits looking down upon us from peeling plaster walls on the second floor balcony. One swung a machete in our direction. Many islanders claim that these portraits sometimes changed places at night.

"Should we leave?" Jimmy whispered, sensing my fear.

"Absolutely not," I replied firmly. "This may be our only chance to explore this place before it crumbles into the earth. Before Veronica comes home...."

So we carefully ventured on, feeling the ghostly eyes of the pirates following us throughout the house. Despite the deteriorating condition of the old mansion, we were awed by the beauty of the Spanish tiles, by the beautifully-carved wooden staircase leading to the second floor, by the massive stone fireplaces.

"If only these walls, these pirates, could talk," Jimmy exhaled deeply, running his hand over the beautifully decorated tiles. He loved history, loved the ghosts of Galveston Island—a passion we shared, one that Veronica and Olivia never understood.

Outside, behind the mansion, we discovered what was left

of a beautiful Spanish fountain. It was the centerpiece of a blue-tiled courtyard, surrounded by gardens that were now filled with weeds, wild berry bushes, and debris from intruders who had partied there. Beer cans, cigarette butts, and old bottles protruded from the rocky soil.

Shaking our heads in disgust at the disrespect of some people, we hiked back down the driveway. Jimmy snapped a few photos along the way, one of which now hung on a wall in his bedroom. It was an eerie night shot of the mansion beneath the light of the full moon, stars glowing in the black sky. Hopefully, he had thought of me and our adventure together when he laid in his bed, alone, gazing at that photo.

Sighing, my heart heavy with memories of the past, I hiked back down the driveway towards my car.

"Hey, lady," a voice broke through my reverie. Swinging around, I found an old man with a bushy gray beard sitting in a rusty truck that had seen better days. "You ain't supposed to be here. It's private property now. Besides, I swear to God that place is haunted! Just because it's all fixed up and fancy again, don't mean the ghosts have moved on. Haunted, I tell you…."

"I know," I smiled at him. "I was just leaving." I hoped the ghosts were still there and had not been driven away by the new developments. I wondered if the pirate portraits had been restored and still hung on the walls of the old mansion. As I got into my car, I glanced back wistfully, one last time, at the Stewart Mansion. Tears filled my eyes. "Thanks for the memories, Jimmy," I murmured to myself.

My trusty old car sputtered a little, then jerked to life. Almost on auto pilot, it headed towards the deserted beaches on the far west end of the island. A place that would remain forever in my heart.

I hiked over the wooden crosswalk that spanned the snake-infested marshes below and crossed over the sand dunes leading to the ocean. I was the only person on the beach this morning, the only soul alone in the universe, it seemed. The welcome scents of an early spring filled the air.

Breathing deeply, drifting back in time, I walked barefoot along the shore, mesmerized by the waves washing over my feet, by the sunlight peeking through the drifting clouds, by the pelicans diving into the surf.

I walked about a mile before I found the secluded stretch of beach I was seeking. The sand dunes had shifted over the years. More cacti and wild yellow flowers had sprouted through the dunes, changing the topography somewhat from the way I remembered it. But it was undoubtedly the place Jimmy and I had made love so many years ago. The place Jonathan had been conceived. The place that had changed my life forever. I sank down into the sand and began to sob. No, I would never forget this place.

Jimmy had been the only man I'd ever loved, despite the fact I could not have him as my husband. Despite the fact that we'd had to settle for a "friends only" relationship after he married my sister. I'd preferred this arrangement to marrying another.

There had been times when Jimmy had encouraged me to find someone else, although I knew in my heart that he would be devastated if I actually did so. He told me I deserved better, that I deserved marriage and more children, things he was unable to give me. Things I was unwilling to accept from him anyway.

Not that I'd spent my life living like a saint. Especially during my thirties, after I'd lost Jonathan, I'd tried dating now and then. Usually it was more like a business arrangement—an escort to accompany me to an art gallery opening or a community event I felt obligated to attend.

Sometimes it was a little more than that. Sometimes I longed so much for another child to love that I tried to find a father for my child—an available and respectable man I could marry and share a life with. But there did not seem to be anyone I could imagine sharing a future with.

The problem was that my heart belonged to Jimmy. I couldn't help that. My friendship with him and the strong emotional and spiritual connection we shared meant more to me than marriage to another. How could I live with and pretend to love another man when my heart cried out for Jimmy?

Memories of our night together, our only night together, huddled together on this stretch of deserted beach, seeped into my soul. Now, I sat alone. All alone. "I'm here, Jimmy," I whispered into the wind. "Do you know now? Do you finally know the truth?"

NINE
JIMMY

"Maybe love at first sight isn't what we think it is.
Maybe it is recognizing a soul we loved in a past life –
and falling in love with them again."
Kamand Kojouri

They all think I'm dead — that I no longer exist!
Nothing could be farther from the truth....

Sure, I've discarded my old, aging body...but my soul lives on. I feel more alive than I've ever been, like I've finally returned to my real home. No, I'm not an angel flapping my wings and floating around in the clouds listening to harp music all day, thank God! How boring that would be.

We actually have bodies here in heaven, although our loved ones back on earth can't see us unless we choose to show ourselves to them by increasing our density levels. We operate here on a different energy frequency.

We create our own looks through projected thought. I haven't changed from the way I looked as Jimmy yet, aside from the fact that I'm now perfectly healthy and much younger. I'm one of the new kids on the block here, and just learning.

I can create my own home and where I live through projected

thought. Who'd have guessed it would be like this? I can visit other departed souls, even an occasional visit to my loved ones back on Earth, just by thinking thoughts to them. Amazing!

This is a real place, shimmering with unconditional love and joy. A place of incredible beauty. There are lush flowering gardens with fountains, lakes, and streams to fish in, wild life and pets we've known and lost in previous lifetimes. There is haunting ancient music everywhere, great concerts, learning centers where you can tap into the knowledge of the universe. There is an endless assortment of things to do and learn here.

One could easily spend an eternity here without getting bored, although it seems that most of us choose to reincarnate from time to time to work on various soul lessons that we identify while we are here at *home.*

Funny thing is, this feels like my true home, like I've been here many times before. I recognized it immediately when I arrived. It felt so good to return to a place that I, as Jimmy Caldwell, had subconsciously missed and longed for during my past lifetime.

My death was a surreal experience, one I sure as hell never expected. I wasn't even sick. I wasn't ready to die. But all of a sudden, there was a crushing pain in my chest. Almost immediately, my spirit soared out of my body.

As I floated towards the ceiling, I looked down at my shell of a body lying motionless on the bed. I actually felt a sense of relief as I gravitated towards a radiant light that projected beams of love and peace. I felt light as air, free from my dense aging body, as I drifted through a spiraling tunnel.

I found myself on the steps of a glowing white marble building with ornate pillars carved in the classic Greco-Roman style. It boasted a huge translucent pale blue dome. Bathed in subtle pastel shades of light, it looked achingly familiar. I now know this is the Hall of Wisdom, the place where we all arrive upon our deaths. The place where we are greeted by our deceased loved ones and spirit guides.

Gazing in awe at the crystal-like buildings shimmering around me, listening to soft heavenly music, I suddenly felt a presence behind me. Spinning around, I was soon surrounded by the love of my deceased mother and father...yes, their love, after all their earthly years of making my life a living hell. I felt their thoughts streaming into my mind as they told me how sorry they were, begging my forgiveness.

Directly behind them, I saw a young boy running towards me, his arms wide open, a joyful smile upon his face. Jonathan! It was Bella's little boy, Jonathan, and he was here to welcome me home!

I scooped him up into my arms and held him close. That little guy had been almost like a son to me for the three short years of his life. I loved him dearly. How many years had it been since his untimely death? Almost forty? He'd apparently decided to appear to me in the little boy form I'd recognize from years ago. I was deeply touched that he was there to welcome me home.

Truth be told, there was a time I actually thought that Jonathan was my son — until Bella set me straight on that. My mind flashed back in time as I sat on the steps of the Hall of Wisdom, basking in the warmth of the sun and the love that surrounded me.

It is 1976. I'd arrived in Galveston the week before my scheduled wedding to Veronica. It was time for me to marry and start a family. I wanted to give my children the kind of childhood I'd never had. Veronica seemed like she'd be a good wife and mother for my children, and her father loved me. I was a real estate broker as well as a rancher, and her father and I had several big deals going together. The future would only bring more big deals my way once I was married to his daughter.

As I said, my children would have a far different life than I had growing up. They would never go to bed hungry or live in poverty. They'd never have to wear ragged hand-me-down clothes to school, clothes the other kids laughed at.

As a kid, I'd been the butt of many cruel jokes. The kids also made fun of my ma and pa. It wasn't funny to me when Pa passed out drunk in a seedy bar someplace after picking a fight with someone. It wasn't funny when he pulled out his pistol and shot the place up, or when he ended up in jail. I died a thousand deaths when the local newspaper reported some of his doings.

"Your pa's in jail! Hahaha." The local bullies would jab me with their elbows. "And your ma?"

"Shut up!" I'd scream at them, tears forming in my eyes. But they'd follow me, making jokes about my ma and the way she dressed—her short skirts, dyed hair, boobs hanging out for the world to see. What they said was true...but she was my ma!

"Look at the baby. He's crying!" one of the boys would taunt me.

Finally I'd spin around furiously and punch one of the boys, knocking him to ground, where I proceeded to pummel him with my fists. Blood flowed, mine and his, while the other boys stood around cheering for my victim. Sometimes one of them jumped in and there would be a free-for-all. I was strong. I'd learned to be tough, and it wasn't often that I lost a fight.

Still, their words tore at my heart. I felt like a total failure. Why was I born into this family? I didn't belong here.

I was a lousy student. I just didn't care. Besides, I was always tired. I worked many hours after school at a local store. We needed the money to buy a few groceries and pay the rent so the landlord didn't evict us from the tiny flat we called home. Somehow my folks always had enough money for booze and cigarettes, but that was about it.

As for my ma…well, the boys were right about her, although I'd never admit it. I'd come home from school or work sometimes to find a strange man in bed with her, with my very own mother. She'd be drunk, laughing, romping around in a flimsy little see-through negligee, her wild red hair flying every which way. I'd be so embarrassed.

Where was Pa? Drunk in the bar, sometimes in jail. He didn't seem to care what his wife did. Neither one gave a damn about me, although I think they appreciated the money I brought home from my job.

When I was sixteen, Pa came home early one night while I was at work. He tried to kill the man in bed with Ma, firing several shots at him. The naked man escaped through the bedroom window with a bullet lodged in his back. I got home from work to find several police cars in my driveway, red lights flashing, as an ambulance tore down the street towards the hospital. Pa was cussing and swinging at the deputies, who were handcuffing him and throwing him into the back of the squad car.

Ma was standing on the sagging doorstep, a blanket wrapped loosely around her in a half-hearted attempt to cover her nakedness. She was sobbing, feeling sorry for herself. Across the street, a woman in a tattered bathrobe with pink rollers in her hair stood beneath the porch light of her home, screaming at my mother, calling her ugly names.

"Whore! Filthy tramp!" Her words echoed through the night as I hid behind a tree, wishing I could disappear. Wishing I was anyplace but here in this crumby little town.

The whole town soon knew that Pa was in jail for attempted murder, possibly murder if the guy didn't survive. And they knew why Pa did what he did. To make matters worse, the man he shot was a neighbor, a married businessman with a family.

His kids went to my school. Ours was a town without pity, as they say. We were ruined.

That was the day I decided to pack my bag and leave. I snuck out of the house late one night while Ma was drunk. She'd retreated to her bed and her booze after the incident, never bothering to talk to me about it or ask how I was getting along. It was all about her, always had been.

I was repulsed and humiliated. I needed to get out. So I hitchhiked a ride to Houston, the big city, where I knew I could get a job. The anger boiling in my veins became my motivating force in life. I would make my own way in the world, despite what they'd done to me. My life would be so much better than theirs could ever be.

Veronica never knew much about the sad story of my early life. I was never comfortable telling her anything more than the fact that I was estranged from my parents. Bella was the only one who knew, and cared enough not to look down on me for my humiliating beginnings.

Maybe all of this no longer mattered here in the spirit world. Maybe if my parents hadn't been such assholes, I wouldn't have been motivated to move on and make something of myself in this world. Besides, they were now begging for forgiveness. Had they learned some kind of lessons in that lifetime?

But I digress. Back to 1976. I was in Galveston waiting for Veronica to return from New York, where she and her mother, Olivia, had gone for her final wedding dress fitting and to bring the dress home. The wedding was only a week away. It would be a lavish affair at the Hotel Galvez.

I was more than a little nervous, pacing around Ashton Villa by myself. Veronica's dad was out of town on business, so it was just me and the servants. Veronica also had one sister whom I'd never met. She was away studying art in New York, but would be home just in time for the wedding.

Wedding jitters, I guessed. I felt the need to go out, to escape from this mansion where I'd soon be living on a permanent basis. It was lovely, but somehow, as spacious as it was, it felt a little confining. I loved being out in the open, near the ocean, out on my ranch on the west end of the island. I was proud of that ranch and the livestock I raised on it. Proud of the real estate firm I was building and investment portfolio I was continually expanding.

Still...something was bothering me. God, I hoped I wasn't making a mistake. I cared about Veronica and knew she'd be a good mother to the children we'd have someday. But what did I know about marriage? I sure as hell never had an example or role model to follow.

It was a balmy starlit night, so I decided to walk down to the Seawall. A quiet walk beside the ocean was perhaps what I needed. I passed the Hotel Galvez, all lit up at night; the place where I'd soon be saying my wedding vows. Music flowed from the ballroom—big band swing era music. Apparently there was an event taking place.

I crossed the street to the seawall, stopping for a moment to gaze out into the ocean at what remained of the historic Balinese Ballroom. It once perched elegantly upon a pier that jutted feet out over the Gulf of Mexico. Storm Carla had severely damaged this icon in 1961 with her hurricane force winds, and the building had been abandoned for years. What was left of this historic structure seemed to be tilting into the sea as waves washed over its crumbling pier supports.

Built in the 1920s, the Balinese Ballroom had endured many

storms and fires over the years. The top entertainers of the day played here in the ballroom with its large dance floor, palm trees and Hawaiian décor. Frank Sinatra. Jimmy Dorsey. Jack Benny. Peggy Lee. Duke Ellington. Guy Lombardo. The list of celebrities went on and on.

Years ago, the back room at the end of the pier had been a den of inequity—gambling and illegal mob activity. The Texas Rangers repeatedly tried to shut the gambling down. The problem was that the casino guard at the seawall entrance would tip off the back room when the rangers arrived. By the time the rangers made it out to the end of the pier, all the illegal gambling equipment and slot machines were hidden in secret closets beneath the floor and in the walls.

I inhaled the fresh ocean air, calming myself as waves lapped against the shoreline and moonlight shimmered over the water. As I hiked along the seawall, I listened to the music drifting out from the Hotel Galvez. I'd always loved swing music, and I found myself almost dancing along to the music.

What the hell? I didn't have anything else to do that night. Maybe I'd crash the party, listen to the band, and have a few drinks. I was convinced when I heard the band playing one of my favorite Frank Sinatra tunes, "My Way." The singer was excellent; almost sounded like Old Blue Eyes himself.

I had no trouble crashing the party, despite the fact that I really didn't know anyone there. This was obviously an out-of-town group celebrating some special occasion, or perhaps here to attend one of the many conferences held at The Galvez.

I found the bar, ordered a stiff martini, and settled into a quiet nook in the back of the room. All I wanted to do was listen to the music and watch the couples dancing. How long had it been since I'd done any swing dancing?

Guess I had more than a few drinks, sitting there alone. The old-time big band music was enchanting, and the crowd was wild.

Out of the corner of my eye, I noticed a young woman sitting alone nursing a glass of wine. She was totally into the music, swaying to the rhythm, almost dancing in her chair. Her long dark hair swung to the beat. I was entranced for some reason, feeling a strange and urgent connection to this stranger. I had to get closer, to see her more clearly. Heart beating wildly in my chest, I approached, my eyes glued to the back of her head.

She spun around as if she felt my presence behind her, and gasped. Our eyes locked together, merging deeper and deeper into the essence of each other. A chill rippled up and down my spine. I felt like I'd known this young woman forever. Like I'd loved her before long ago in another time and another place. Maybe I was drunk. This made no sense whatsoever.

"Do I know you?" she whispered, shaking her head as if to clear the fog. Neither of us were able to break our eye contact. I was speechless. We just stared at each other. Finally, she got down from her stool and walked into my arms. "Let's dance," she purred, as the band began to play a slow love song.

"Strangers in the night, exchanging glances...." The lead singer began to croon one of Frank Sinatra's best loved tunes. "Wondering in the night, what were the chances, we'd be sharing love before the night was through?"

We moved across the dance floor, perfectly in sync, as if we'd always danced together. Moving closer and closer together, our bodies touching in an achingly familiar way. I'd had my share of women, but I'd never felt this way before.

I'd never felt such heat churning through my veins, such comfort. She snuggled her head onto my shoulder as I stroked her back. As the song ended, she looked up into my eyes and before I knew what was happening, we were kissing on the dance floor—deeply, passionately, as if we were the only two people in the world. It just happened.

"Do you want to go someplace?" I finally asked her.

"Let's drive out to the beach on the west end," she whispered huskily. So we did, in her little red Porsche.

Something strange was happening here, and I was unable to control it. We were both obsessed. I had no idea who she was, only that I loved her and needed to be with her. She obviously felt the same way about me.

She pulled off onto the last beach access road on the end of the island. Hand in hand, we crossed over the sand dunes to a secluded place on the beach. We could not keep our hands off each other as we discarded our clothing. I laid my jacket on the beach for a blanket and we fell into each other's arms. Consumed with a surreal passion, we discovered that we already knew every inch of the other's body, what we liked and needed. With a sense of urgency, she drew me in. She felt so familiar. It felt so right. How could it be so wrong?

She lay in my arms afterwards, gazing up at the stars. We made love again; this time, a little more slowly. As the first light of dawn appeared on the horizon, we decided it was time to go home. Home to what? To whom?

"I've been waiting for you a long time," she said on our drive back down the Seawall.

"I feel that way, too, like I've known you forever," I replied.

Damn! What have I done? What was I thinking? And what about Veronica, the woman I was to marry next week? What was I supposed to do now? How could I let this woman go now that I'd finally found her? Nobody else had ever made me feel this way, not even Veronica, my bride-to-be.

"I don't even know your name," I finally continued. "I am James, by the way."

"Isabella," she replied, smiling into my eyes. "When will I see you again?"

"I will be out of town for a week...but please give me your phone number so I can call you," I hedged. What was I supposed to do? She gave me her phone number, and I asked her to drop me off at The Galvez, as if I were staying there. I certainly couldn't risk having her drop me off at Ashton Villa.

What in the hell had I been thinking? What had I done? Still, all I could think of was Isabella. I'd finally found my true love. Was it too late? What in the hell was I going to do now?

I was a wreck, weighing my options. If I broke it off with Veronica, a week before our marriage, after all the money they'd spent on the wedding, after hundreds of people had RSVP'd that they were coming, I would destroy my relationship and business dealings with her father also. I'd be blackballed, my business destroyed. After all my hard work, how could I toss everything away? I was finally making it in the world, and in a big way.

And what about Veronica? She was a lovely woman, and I did care about her. She'd be humiliated and hurt badly if I backed out of our marriage. She didn't deserve to be hurt. Nor did she deserve to marry a man who was in love with another woman.

But what about Isabella, a woman I somehow knew I'd always loved? She was what I'd been searching for my entire life, and she obviously felt the same way about me. What would I tell her if I married Veronica? How could I begin to tell her after what we shared last night?

All I knew about Isabella was that she lived someplace in Galveston. She'd surely see the wedding photos and write-up on the society page of The Daily News.

I hid out in Ashton Villa, tossing and turning at night, unable to sleep. Unable to forget Isabella and how it felt to be with her. Dreaming of her at night before waking up to the crushing reality that I'd soon be married to another. Or would I?

Veronica was so pre-occupied with wedding details when they returned from New York that she didn't seem to notice I was acting strangely and totally preoccupied. Everything had to be absolutely perfect, a trait in her that I later began to resent. I began to resign myself to my fate, dreading each passing day as if I were headed for my execution.

I owed Isabella some kind of an explanation at least, but had no idea how I could accomplish that. She'd be as devastated as I was to realize we had no future together. How could I hurt her like this?

It was the day before the wedding. I was eating breakfast with the family in the formal dining room when the butler came in to announce that Veronica's sister was there. Veronica immediately jumped out of her chair to embrace her sister as she entered the dining room.

"Bella, meet Jimmy, my husband-to-be," she announced proudly.

I almost fell off my chair when I looked up to find my Isabella standing before me, looking as if she were going to faint. Veronica's sister? Oh my God! I plastered a fake smile across my face, recovering nicely, as I mumbled something about being pleased to meet her.

I rose on shaky legs and held my hand out to her. She managed to shake it briefly, her fingers trembling at my touch. She carefully avoided making eye contact with me, trying to hide the pain and betrayal that I alone seemed to see in her eyes.

"Are you all right, Bella?" Olivia asked, stroking her shoulder. "I'm sure it was a long trip. Sit down and I'll get you some breakfast."

I was no longer hungry, so I played with my Eggs Benedict, waiting for an opportunity to escape. Bella also pushed her food around her plate. Nobody seemed to notice. Veronica and Olivia were too busy chattering about wedding punch and the last minute directions for the caterer. Their biggest problem was that the soloist had a cold. What if she didn't sing as well as she usually did?

Before long, Bella stood and excused herself. "I'm not feeling well," she said. "I need to rest a while."

"You've just driven all the way from New York. You should be exhausted," Olivia said. That didn't make any sense to me. I'd been with her earlier this week, made love to her on the beach on the west end of the island.

"No, actually," she replied pointedly for my benefit. "I was in town earlier this week to meet with someone I *thought* was my friend...how wrong I was! After that, I drove up to Houston for a few days to see some of the new art exhibits."

I headed out for a walk as soon as I could break away. Pacing back and forth around the estate, I tried to comprehend what had happened. What a disaster I'd made of things. I was "torn between two lovers" as the old song goes, "feeling like a fool. Loving both of you is breaking all the rules." The song played over and over in my mind.

I couldn't tolerate the memory of the pained look on Bella's face when she saw me and discovered that I was her sister's future husband. How could I ever make this up to her? Maybe I should walk out on Veronica now and keep on walking, never looking back.

I could try to find Bella later, if she'd have me. But what would we live on? I'd be ruined. I'd have to start all over again. Obviously, Bella was used to the finest things in life. What could I give her if I backed out of this wedding, this deal with her father, to be honest?

I waited in the gardens, beneath Bella's bedroom window.

I had to talk with her privately, although I was sure nothing I could say would make any difference. I paced around the garden for hours. Nobody missed me. I was just the groom, typically left out of wedding planning.

Finally the door opened and Bella emerged, her shoulders slouched, walking slowly towards the bench where I sat. "I knew you'd be here," she began in an icy tone, refusing to look me in the eye.

"God, I'm so sorry." My eyes filled with tears. "I didn't know. It was wrong, damn it. I love you, Bella. What the hell am I supposed to do now?"

"I will be out of your life soon, forever." She glared at me through her tears. "Your life is set with my sister. How could you make love to me and marry my sister?" She turned on her heel. "You bastard!" she hissed as I grabbed her arm.

"I need you, Bella, and you need me. We finally find each other…and now this? It can't be too late for us. I refuse to accept that. Will you marry me?"

"Are you crazy? You are marrying my sister, my very own sister, for God's sake, tomorrow!"

"I will back out of it, if you will have me." The words rushed from my mouth before I could stop them.

She was silent, deep in thought, a range of emotions flickering through the eyes I somehow knew so well. Relief. Joy. Love. Anger. Then deep sadness and resignation.

"No," she whispered. "I know all about the Jimmy my sister is marrying, about his business dealings with my father. You would be totally ruined if you walk out of this marriage. My father would destroy you. My answer is no. For your sake and my family's sake."

"What about you, Bella? What do you want?"

She turned her back on me. "I don't need you, Jimmy. Get

over it. It's too late for us. End of story." She started to stomp away as I grabbed her arm.

"You have a right to be angry—"

"I sure as hell do! Do you know what they'd do to me if you married me instead of my sister? My God, they would disown me! They'd make my life a living hell. There is no place for us, Jimmy. No place in this world...." Her already puffy eyes filled with fresh tears.

A tiny part of me breathed a sigh of relief. A larger part felt deep grief and sorrow. "Can we at least be friends? You will be my sister-in-law, you know." I couldn't bear the thought of her leaving like this, of never seeing her again.

"Friends? I don't think so, Jimmy. Please, just leave me alone. I need to find a way to get over this...this stupid one-night stand!"

"One night stand? Is that all it meant to you?" I couldn't believe that for a minute. This had to be her way of striking back at me for the pain she was feeling.

"That's all it will mean to either one of us, if and when we look back on that foolish night. Goodbye, Jimmy." She turned and walked away from me.

The next day, Bella was too ill to attend the wedding, or so she told her family. Veronica was frantic, trying to find another bridesmaid to fit into her dress. All of this wedding crap was driving me crazy. I just wanted to run away—with Bella. That was apparently not an option, so I went through the motions of getting married, my heart aching as I said my vows to the sister of the only woman I've ever really loved.

I didn't see Bella again for six months. She was still in New York studying art. She flew to Paris for some kind of art exhibit, then to Venice. Daddy paid all the bills, of course.

Veronica and Olivia talked about Bella's travel adventures over dinner at night. She needed to find herself a good man, they decided, instead of flitting around the world chasing her dreams. She needed to settle down.

I smiled to myself. Bella would never be content to settle down into a lifestyle like theirs. I knew her, somehow, better than any of them did. Not that this made any sense. It was just the way it was. I knew her heart and soul, and I anxiously awaited her return to Galveston someday.

Maybe she'd at least be my friend, if that was possible after all that had happened. I just needed to see her again. Did she ever think of me? I suspected she did.

So I settled into my life at Ashton Villa as Veronica's devoted husband. I buried myself in my work and spent lots of time at my ranch or my real estate office. My empire grew steadily, as did the value of my investments.

Bella finally came back home to Ashton Villa, six months pregnant!

She was not married, and she refused to tell anyone who the father of her child was. She had no intentions of marrying him, whoever he was. And she flatly refused to get an abortion as Veronica and Olivia demanded of her. Her family was in an uproar, worried about the gossip on the island, about the tarnished reputation of their prominent family.

As for me, I was worried about Bella. Where would she go, and what would she do? Who would be there for her?

Her solution was to move all her things out of Ashton Villa and buy herself a little cottage on the west end of the island. She planned to raise her child there, by herself.

I was deeply hurt and angry over her condition. How could she have hooked up with another guy so soon after our night together? Maybe I didn't have a right to feel that way. Still....

Then the thought struck me. If she was six months along, I could be her baby's father! We had used no protection that night on the beach. This thought kept haunting me. I had to find out the truth.

An opportunity presented itself one day when Olivia asked me to haul some of Bella's things out to her little cottage. She shouldn't be lifting heavy things, Olivia had decided. So I loaded them into my truck and drove out to her place. She was cordial, even invited me in for a glass of iced tea. We made small talk, avoiding each other's eyes at first.

Finally, she looked into my eyes. "Maybe we can be friends. I think I could use a friend right now."

My heart raced as I jumped at the opportunity to be her friend. "But I need to ask you something first, as your friend, and I want an honest answer," I began. "Who is your baby's father?"

She tensed up, her eyes turning to steel, tuning me out. "That's my business only, thank you."

"Am I your baby's father?" I blurted out my suspicion.

"Of course not," she glared at me.

"How do you know for sure? We made love together six months ago, if you recall…."

"And you think you're the only man in the world I've slept with?" she taunted me.

"Damn it, Bella, answer me!"

"Have you considered that I was hurt enough by your actions that I immediately found another guy to go to bed with? Or that I'd slept with someone else before you? You're not the only guy in this world, Jimmy!" She stood and began to angrily pace around her cottage, refusing to look at me.

"How could you, after what we had together?"

"And how could you sleep with—and even marry—my sister, after what *we* had together?"

116

"What did we have together, Bella?" I pulled her down onto the sofa beside me. She sat rigidly, staring at the floor.

We sat in silence for a while. Finally she spoke softly, her eyes downcast, refusing to make contact with mine. "You are not the baby's father. A woman has a way of knowing that. His father is history. I plan to raise my baby alone. I don't want to hear any more about this, all right?"

"Okay," I agreed, hoping to God she was telling me the truth. I didn't think she'd lie to me. Still, my heart was broken to think she'd taken up with another man. It took me a while to accept the fact that I had no right to be hurt.

After little Jonathan was born, Veronica and Olivia encouraged me to spend time with this fatherless little boy. They fell in love with him also, and felt he needed a father figure in his life. It worked for me. I was able to spend time with them both. My ranch was not far from their little cottage.

The three of us had wonderful times together, times I'd always cherish.

It wasn't easy, however, to have to settle for being "just friends," when we both knew deep down that we were—and always would be—deeply in love with each other. How I longed to hold her again, to make love like we did that night on the beach. The only way we could "make love" now was through our eyes. It felt like we were drowning in each other's eyes sometimes, connecting on an intimate soul level.

We did become fast friends, accepting our destiny, sharing secrets and thoughts that we shared with no one else.

After Jonathan died, I was as devastated as she was. I had loved him like a son. I think he thought of me almost like a father. I helped her through her loss and continued spending as much time with her as I could ever since then. Nobody seemed to notice or care. Veronica was a busy socialite, living her own life.

My thoughts of long ago, of my recently completed life on earth, were suddenly interrupted as I felt a presence approach and materialize beside me on the white marble stairs of the Hall of Wisdom. A beautiful dark-skinned Indian woman dressed in a flowing white gown, she glowed with love and light.

"Who are you?" I gasped, stunned to see this vision beside me.

She smiled warmly. *My name is Herneith. I am your spirit guide, Jimmy: I've watched over you throughout your last life, even during the difficult times when I needed to step back and let you learn some difficult lessons on your own. Now I'm here to help orient you to your new home here in Heaven.*

She didn't speak these words out loud. Instead she conveyed her thoughts directly into my mind. I discovered that I could reply to her in the same way. Words were not needed here. She escorted me into the Hall of Wisdom, where we sat side by side on a white marble bench. I began to recall having been there before, perhaps more than once.

In the center of the room there was a large glowing glass ball. It was the life review machine, where I would begin my panoramic life review process. Herneith sensed my fear, my nervousness. I already knew I'd screwed up my last life in many ways. I wasn't sure I wanted to see my entire life play out before my eyes in excruciating detail. Not sure I wanted to find out which of my lessons I hadn't learned this time around.

It's all right, Jimmy, she whispered into my mind. *You are not being judged. You will understand what you learned, what you did well as well as lessons you still need to work on.* She led me by the hand to the glass machine.

As I gazed into the ball, I was drawn into a surreal multi-dimensional virtual reality, complete with all the thoughts and feelings I'd experienced in my recent lifetime. The story of my life as Jimmy Caldwell unfolded all at once. I lived it all over again, this time with astonishing insight into the events of this lifetime. It was up to me to decide what I'd done right and what I'd done wrong.

The next step was watching my life through the eyes of selected people. I could see and feel how my actions had impacted them. I actually became the people I'd loved—and sometimes hurt. I discovered the truth about my relationships with others.

Of course, I decided to merge into Bella's life first. I discovered that I'd given her a great deal of love and happiness, despite the fact that we couldn't be together the way we wanted to be. I'd also hurt her, and that made my heart ache deeply.

As the life review machine whirled around me, I was stunned to discover something I did not know about my beloved Bella, although I had once suspected. I was, in fact, Jonathan's father! There had not been another man for Bella.

This was the one lie Bella told me, and she'd done it to protect me, to her way of thinking. She did not want me to feel guilty and leave Veronica, destroying our family ties and our lives.

Jonathan is my son! Waves of shock, joy, and confusion washed over me.

I needed some fresh air to try to process this revelation. My guide left me at the grounds of the Hall of Justice next door, a serene place where I could reflect and absorb this information.

I wandered along the winding stone paths through luxurious gardens blooming with fragrant red and purple bougainvillea, across foot bridges spanning glittering streams. I drank in the rushing sounds of waterfalls, admired fountains adorned with marble statues of some of the great people throughout history. Philosophers. Artists. Writers and musicians. Doctors of healing. The world's greatest scientists. The statues seemed to live and breathe, still disseminating their wisdom throughout the universe somehow.

Finally I settled in a little gazebo nestled beneath a towering weeping willow. I stared at streams of silver-streaked water flowing from an ornate fountain before me as my eyes filled with tears and my heart began to swell with pride. Jonathan is my son!

Suddenly I felt another presence approach and materialize beside me on the bench.

Looking up, I gazed into Jonathan's eyes. *I am your father! You are my son!* I choked with emotion as I wrapped my arms around him.

I know, he thought back to me. *And I'm proud to be your son.*

God, I'm sorry. I didn't know. Your mother…she never told me. I should have been there for you.

You were there for me, Dad, just in a different way. You loved me, and I loved you. Mommy did the right thing. If you had known, you would have left Aunt Veronica and it would have destroyed many lives. It was meant to be this way. We all learned lessons from the way our life charts played out. We made those charts here on the other side, you know, before we ever incarnated into that past life. We were destined to play the roles we played and learn the lessons we learned.

But you left us so soon, Jonathan. Why did you have to leave? That could not have been a part of anyone's plan, for a little boy like you to just up and die. You weren't even sick. You just died in your sleep. I wiped a tear from my eye.

He smiled patiently before answering. *My mission on Earth was completed once I brought you and Mommy together. The two of you are soul mates, and had almost missed connecting this time around. Once I brought you together, it was my time to come home. I have*

120

*other things, other lessons, to learn here. I know you don't understand.
Someday you will. Trust me.*

How can my son be so wise? I grinned at him.

*I've been here many years longer than you have, Dad. You're just
beginning to remember all that you once knew. That veil of amnesia that
separates our worlds no longer exists for you. You have been here many
times before, you know, in between your past lives. You will discover all
of this when you spend time at the Hall of Records.*

I love you, son. I hugged him goodbye for now.

And I love you, Dad, he replied as his presence slipped away
into the rose-colored glow that permeates this side of life.

TEN
BELLA

*"Just as a body's instinct is to breathe,
a soul's instinct is to evolve."*
A Spirit Guide

I was no longer alone on my secluded beach on the west end of Galveston Island.

The sad sultry song of summer had descended upon the island once again. Hordes of tourists seemed to be everywhere, crowding the beaches as they sought relief from the heat. Driving along the Seawall gawking at the ocean, creating traffic jams.

Tourism, of course, was a major component of our economy. Without the tourists, our businesses and restaurants would not survive. We would not have jobs. Still, it was indeed a "love-hate" relationship for true islanders. Many of us hibernated in the summer, longing for summer's end.

The Winter Texans had headed north once again, some hauling their large RV's behind them. Sometimes I thought about following them. I loved Galveston winters when I was free to roam, when I could walk the beach without seeing another living soul. Just me, the wind, and the sea.

I spent long summer days in my little cottage, working on

my projects and my businesses. My novel about the storm was finished and had been shipped off to my publisher. I felt it was the best book I'd ever written, thanks to a little help from Isabella — actually, a lot of help.

She had whispered in my ear as I slaved away on my laptop late into the night. Exhausted, I'd fall into bed, only to have her come to me in my dreams. She obviously never slept. Instead, she'd stream reams of information into my subconscious. Half-awake, a part of me struggled to grab hold of the flow, but it was going way too fast. At lightning speed. Would I ever be able to access all of this? Finally, when she'd completed her information dump, she'd nudge me awake, insisting I must get up to make a few key notes in my bedside notebook.

"Go away, please," I'd plead. "I won't forget. I'll do it in the morning." I'd turn away from her, pulling the pillow over my head.

Just a few notes, now, to trigger your memory in the morning, she ordered as my pillow flew across the room. She was relentless. Looking back, perhaps that was a good thing.

Now that the book was done, I thanked God for the information she had infiltrated into my mind. Sometimes as I'd sat at my computer staring at the screen, it felt as if she took control of my fingers, walking them across the keyboard. I was astounded, later, to read what I'd written. Where did that come from? I'd ask myself.

Where do you think? she whispered into my mind. *It's good, isn't it?* She smiled proudly.

She not only provided incredible facts about the great event, but she also had a way of spinning off into the world of fantasy. The result was an intriguing blend of fact and fiction.

"We did it, Isabella!" I cried out early one evening after typing "The End" on our manuscript. "Time for a toast," I told her as I poured myself a glass of wine and prepared to head out to the gazebo just before the sun set over Galveston Bay.

How do you toast a ghost? I wondered. She certainly deserved a drink, too, after all her hard work. So I poured a second glass of wine and carried them both out to the gazebo. It was a beautiful evening with a cooling breeze rolling in off the water. The crazy brown pelicans dived into the surf, creating massive splashes as they plopped their heavy bodies into the water.

I turned to make sure Isabella was following me. She was—I could feel her cheerful presence. Sitting in my wicker rocking chair, surrounded by my flowers, I held up my glass, clinking it against the other glass sitting on the little table.

"To us, Isabella, to an incredibly successful adventure with our book. Thank you so much. I never could have done this without you."

You are welcome indeed, my dear, she sighed, then hesitated, as if she had something important to tell me. I instinctively knew what it was.

"You're not going away, are you? Now that our work together is done?" My trembling voice was a mere whisper. I'd grown accustomed to having her around, and I enjoyed her company, except when she deprived me of my sleep at night.

It is time for me to attend to business on the other side, she began slowly. *And time for you to start marketing and attending to your business here. But I shall be back, in a timely fashion of course. And you know I'll always be around when you need me.*

I felt tears well in my eyes, a profound sense of regret searing my soul. Isabella had helped me weather the tragedy of Jimmy's death, as well as Jonathan's so long ago. Now she was leaving. Suddenly I saw the second glass of wine rise from the table and float up into the air. It tilted to one side, as if someone were sipping the wine. Then, it floated back down to the table, half empty.

"Isabella?"

Here's to us, my dear, she spoke gently, as I felt her hug me warmly. Then she was gone.

Once again I was rattling around in my cottage, alone. I busied myself creating a marketing plan for our novel, making jewelry, taking and framing my photographs, and selling my work to the local stores. I made my way through the crowds of summer people, forcing myself to smile. I should smile, I scolded myself. They supported me by buying my work, especially during the summer months.

As the long days of summer passed, I became obsessed with a crazy notion. Jimmy had not paid me a visit in a very long time, despite my requests that he do so. What if…what if it were possible for me to pay him a visit on the other side of life? Perhaps my little Jonathan was also still there — if he hadn't already reincarnated.

I'd heard about astral travel…had once read a fascinating book by the famous psychic, Sylvia Browne. It wouldn't hurt to do a little research, I decided. Nobody had to know — certainly not my sister. She would lock me up if she knew I was contemplating such a crazy idea.

I did some online research and finally decided to pay a visit to The Witchery on Post Office Street, in Galveston's historic downtown district. Strange that despite having lived here all my life, despite my beliefs and experiences with deceased loved ones, I'd never bothered to stop in. I'd pretty much kept my secret world beyond this one to myself, a secret from others — especially my holier-than-thou family. I'd retreated to my remote cottage or walked along the nearby deserted stretch of beach to make contact with my dear Isabella.

First, I stopped at the Mod Coffeehouse just down the block from The Witchery. I sat outside on the brick patio at a little bistro table for two in the shade of the vine-covered overhead trellis. Sipping an Italian soda, I enjoyed the breeze and the music of a fiddler across the street. A perfect place to watch people strolling by. Tourists sporting an array of Galveston T-shirts wandered into the shops and restaurants, stopping to take photos of the historic buildings.

Maybe it wasn't a good day for my excursion to The Witchery...or maybe it was. Maybe I could slip into the crowds so nobody would see me or where I was going. I scanned the crowds carefully for anyone I may know.

Why should I, the free spirit from hell, care if anyone saw me anywhere? Maybe I'd been holed up in my cottage too long, a recluse from the world. After all, why should I hesitate to check out the wonderful selection of books at The Witchery? They also had a gifted psychic reader, and I was very tempted to give that a try. Others had reported receiving some powerful and healing messages from her during their readings.

Many Galvestonians did believe in ghosts. They believed the city truly was haunted, probably due to the traumatic events that took place there over the years. There were the devastating storms that claimed so many lives, the pirate and Indian legends of long ago, and several well-documented murders. Spirits who'd experienced traumatic deaths sometimes hung around long after their deaths. My Isabella was proof of that, although she was also my chosen spirit guide.

The tourists loved Dash Beardsley's "Ghost Tours of Galveston." Dash was, officially, "the ghost man of Galveston," a respected paranormal expert who had done extensive research and investigation here on the island. My mind drifted back to one of his tours that Jimmy and I had taken one spooky evening when Veronica was out of town at some function or another.

Jimmy and I had been waiting on the marble stairs of the old post office building for our tour of the historic Strand district, one of the most haunted places on the island. Suddenly, a sleek black hearse, decorated with images of ghosts, slowly drove up to the curb. Haunting music blared from within the vehicle.

A large man with long blond hair and dark sunglasses emerged from the vehicle. He wore a long black duster that floated around him eerily in the wind. The unusual silver rings he wore on all fingers gleamed beneath the light of the moon. Flamboyant and fascinating, filled with amazing stories, he led us along the historic streets with an old lantern, ghostly music blaring from his boom box.

Jimmy and I had stopped to take photos here and there, whenever we felt the urge to do so. Dash guided us to places where he and previous guests had captured psychic orbs on film, sometimes even an apparition.

"Jimmy, look at this." I'd grabbed his arm, anxious to show him a cluster of glowing orbs of light on a photo I'd just taken. The orbs had floated eerily on the wall and ceiling of the historic café we'd just visited.

Jimmy and I were standing together in a darkened doorway, far enough away from the rest of the group to have a little privacy.

"Wow, you did it, Sa Bella. Amazing!" He'd put his arm around me, holding me close, our hearts beating together as one. Suddenly a strong gust of wind swirled around us as a distinct chill seemed to walk right through us.

"What the hell was that?" Jimmy had called out to Dash. "Did you feel that?"

Dash had grinned, pleased that we'd experienced a visit from one of the spirits on The Strand. "Never fear, my friends, these are friendly spirits. But I will tell you about some that are not so friendly...." His voice grew appropriately somber, deeper, laced with hints of fear. With that he was off down the street, his black coat fluttering behind him, leading us on to more ghostly adventures.

"Bella? What are you doing here?" My sister's voice suddenly brought me back to reality. She stood before me, dressed elegantly as always in a stylish summer dress, a matching wide-brim hat, and high heels. She held several files in her arms.

Only my dear sister would be dressed like this on a hot summer day in Galveston. Even the old-time islanders dressed casually these days. Veronica seemed to live in a prim and proper world that no longer existed, a Victorian world from long ago. Granted, she lived in an historic home surrounded by antiques. Still, she was one of the few who held on to the past so tightly, even in her style of dress.

I startled, not happy to be torn away from this special memory from the past. What was she doing here? "I might ask you the same."

She wiped beads of sweat from her brow, fanned herself with her files, and slipped into the chair across from me. "I had a meeting at the Grand Opera House and decided to walk. It's a little cooler today. At least it was when I left home. But you... you're the last person I expected to find here with all the tourists around. What's going on?"

"Oh, I thought I might get a psychic reading at The Witchery."

She laughed, thinking I was making a joke. That was fine with me. "I haven't seen you in ages. Still working on that book?"

"*That* book is done, finally, and shipped off to my publisher," I announced proudly.

128

"Well, then, congratulations are in order!" She actually sounded happy for me, almost proud.

Why should she care about this book when she'd barely acknowledged my previous books? Maybe it had something to do with the topic—the storm that had claimed our great-grandmother's life.

"I think we need to celebrate, "she announced. "How about one of their delicious pastries and a cool drink? What would you like?"

We settled on Jet Tea Smoothies; peach for me and mango for her. Veronica scurried in to place our order and soon came back out to join me.

I couldn't help grinning to myself as she settled into the chair across from me. Contrasting starkly with her elegant clothing, perfectly coifed hair, and make-up, I wore faded jean capris and shabby sandals, no make-up, hair flying in the breeze. My colorful homemade silver and turquoise earrings dangled from my ears, complimented by a large pendant and matching bracelet. I always wore my jewelry to advertise my business. People frequently commented on these pieces and ended up placing orders with me.

"Cheers! To my prolific sister, and to the success of your storm book!" Veronica toasted me, gently clinking her smoothie glass against mine.

"Thanks, Veronica. It is exciting, my best book ever," I confessed. "It will, of course, be dedicated to our great-grandmother, Isabella."

"I like that! If only she were here to celebrate your accomplishment with you, with us."

Trying to suppress a grin, I replied, "She knows, and she is also very proud. She should be. She provided much of the material, Veronica."

129

"Whatever. Believe what you wish," she sighed, obviously not wishing to argue about anything today. "But," she continued, "Have you planned your book launch party yet?"

"Not yet. Lots still needs to be done. Final edits. Cover design. Internal formatting. Finishing my marketing plan. Social media...."

"Impressive." Veronica sipped her cool drink slowly, a light beginning to gleam in her eyes. "I've got it. You simply must let me host your book launch party at Ashton Villa. That is what Isabella would want, you know. And...and I'd really like to do this...." Her voice trailed off.

"I...I don't know what to say. Why would you want to do this?"

"Because of the storm, because of Isabella and our family, many of whom are no longer with us. I'd like to recognize your accomplishment, believe it or not. And...."

"And?"

"We are the only two left in our family of origin. Maybe we need to start acting more like sisters. Sometimes I feel so alone. I need something more to do, a way to connect with the people I care about."

"You've got your children, Veronica," I mumbled. I didn't. I had nobody.

"And I adore and appreciate them all immensely. But you and I are the only ones with a shared family history, the sisters who grew up together. That should count for something, right?"

I nodded, feeling warmer towards my sister than I had in so many years. "All right. If you're sure you want to do this, I would be pleased to have my book launch party at Ashton Villa."

Isabella will also be thrilled, I thought to myself...if she knows. If she hasn't deserted me completely. On second thought, was it possible that Isabella was playing a role in softening

130

Veronica's heart? Hmmm....

Veronica smiled broadly. "It's set then. Tell me what you'd like and I will make the arrangements." She gathered up her files and stood to leave.

"Oh, you mentioned The Witchery," she continued. "Why don't we go in and take a look? People seem to love that place. I'm always so busy with my volunteer work and board meetings that I've never taken the time to visit."

I almost fell off my chair. What was wrong with my sister? Was she getting Alzheimer's disease? Shaking my head, I followed her to the famous Witchery. Guess this wouldn't be a good day to get a psychic reading after all; not with my sister in tow.

The old brick and mortar storefront of The Witchery was covered with vines and greenery. A sign in the window invited guests to stop in to explore their vast collection of books to help others on their journey to self-discovery, self-empowerment, and spiritual enlightenment.

We slowly opened the old door and stepped into an almost mystical environment that enveloped us in an overwhelming feeling of peace. Haunting native flute music played in the background. Incense filled the air. Candles burned, their lights reflecting upon the old brick walls. A large antique mirrored apothecary unit dominated one wall, filled with incense, herbs, and candles.

Thousands of books filled the shelves, organized by subject; healing and health, angels, dreams, ghosts, herbs and oils, crystals, reincarnation, witchcraft, ancient mysteries, UFOs, and more. I could hardly wait to start exploring these resources. Where had I been all my life?

First we wandered around the room, admiring the crystals, jewelry, statues of Buddha, meditation devices. Things I never knew existed. In the back room, water flowed gently from an

131

ornate fountain beside a large statue of Buddha. Off to the side were two small rooms that were set up for psychic readings. Someday I will come back for one, I promised myself.

"What do you think?" I whispered to Veronica. This didn't seem to be her kind of place. She had always been such a sceptic.

"Interesting," she replied as she seemed to be drawn to the shimmering crystals. She picked one up in her hand and stood there gazing at it as if she were mesmerized. "Maybe I need one of these," she commented when she realized I was standing there beside her. She began to read through brief descriptions of the properties of the various crystals.

I wandered off to begin checking out the books, losing myself in several focusing on meditation and astral projection. While Veronica was exploring the store, I hurriedly purchased several of these books, hoping to complete my purchase before she caught me.

"What are you buying?" She suddenly crept up behind me.

Slipping them into the bag, I casually told her, "Just a few books on meditation. They say it helps to relax and gain insights into your life."

"Interesting. Maybe it would help me relax and slow down a little, do you think?"

"It's worth a try. Maybe it will help you to keep Olivia from haunting the house!"

"Honestly, Bella. That's really not funny. For your information, Olivia is gone. In fact, she left shortly after your visit. After I talked to her and told her to go to the light."

"I'm impressed!"

"You should be." She tilted her chin in her usual dramatic fashion as she handed a lovely dark purple cathedral stone streaked with sparkling white crystals to the clerk. It sparkled in the flickering candlelight.

"You're buying a crystal, an amethyst crystal? For what?" I couldn't believe it.

"It's beautiful, isn't it? The moment I saw it, I simply had to have it. I couldn't take my eyes off of it. In fact, it almost seemed to vibrate when I picked it up. Very strange...."

"Not strange at all," the friendly man behind the counter smiled at us. "Perhaps you were drawn to this particular stone for a reason. Perhaps it will make a difference in your life. It's a healing stone, a stone of spirituality and contentment."

I was intrigued and Veronica nodded her head, encouraging him to continue.

"I don't know your situation in life or what you are seeking, ma'am. But I can tell you what others have experienced with these beautiful pieces."

"Yes, please," I jumped in before my sister could reply.

He leaned closer across the counter as he continued. "The amethyst is one of the best stones to help you meditate so you can reach higher spiritual levels. They help to magnify your personal energy so you are able to connect with universal powers. They help to enhance your creativity, intuition, and imagination. They bring about a sense of peace and calm. And many people swear these stones help heal personal losses and get through the grief process."

"That's perfect," I interrupted. "I'm sorry. Anything else we should know?"

He smiled at my enthusiasm, realizing he had hit on what I was seeking here. Of course, I wasn't the one purchasing this beautiful crystal. My sister was. She stood quietly, mulling over his words.

"It all depends on what you are seeking, ladies. If you are so inclined, once you've learned to properly meditate, this lovely amethyst crystal may help you to make connections between the earth plane and other planes and worlds. In fact, it can open channels to telepathy, past life regression, and communication with departed loved ones."

A slight frown creased Veronica's brow. She was the unbeliever, of course. Me, I was intrigued. This could be the answer to my prayers, if not hers.

"Really?" My eyes widened as I leaned in closer.

"Really." His eyes reflected an ancient wisdom that evoked a deep sense of trust and understanding. "I have used my amethyst stone for years, and yes, it has helped me to communicate with the other side of life."

My sister fiddled with her purse, retrieving her credit card to complete the purchase. "Thank you, sir, for the interesting information. It truly is a beautiful stone, even if all I do is admire it every day."

He grinned. "I have a feeling you selected this stone for a reason that you may not yet be aware of. Perhaps it selected you."

I was bubbling over with excitement as we left the store together with our purchases. "I'm so happy we stopped here, and I am so excited over your crystal, Veronica! Do you know what this means? We may be able to use it to connect with Jimmy!"

She stopped dead in her tracks, glaring at me. "Stop this nonsense right now! Jimmy is dead, for God's sake. He no longer exists—not here, not anywhere. Why are you so obsessed with this nonsense?" she hissed at me in a hushed voice.

"So you're not even going to try? You, his wife, who supposedly loved him...you aren't even going to try? You just don't give a damn, do you? Just forget him, right?" My voice rose a notch or two as my eyes teared up.

"Jimmy was *my* husband, not yours! I will make the decision as to whether or not we try to contact him. And my answer is no! No! Do you hear me, Bella? Let him rest in peace." She turned her back on me and began to hike down the street in the opposite direction. I reeled as though I'd been slapped in the face. How dare she?

"Veronica? Screw you!" I shouted as I flipped her off and ran for my car. Glancing back, I almost laughed as I watched her hustling down the street in her high heels, hiding her head in humiliation, pretending she didn't know me as people turned to stare at the two of us. Good!

I collapsed over my steering wheel, sobbing as her cruel words replayed over and over in my tortured mind. *Jimmy was my husband, not yours!* She'd managed to slice open a wound deep in my soul that was perhaps just starting to heal. Just when I had let my guard down enough to think that the two of us could actually have some semblance of a relationship.

What a fool I'd been! She'd played me good, talking about being sisters again. But why? What was her ulterior motive? She must have wanted something from me to even offer to host my book launch party at Ashton Villa. No way in hell would that happen now, I promised myself.

My emotions were reeling as I pounded the steering wheel in frustration. "Damn you, Veronica!" I spit the words out aloud. "How can you be stupid enough to say Jimmy no longer exists? And if you think for one second that I'm not going to contact him, you are out of your mind! You will never, not ever, control me. Haven't you learned that yet?"

Jimmy...yes, it was always Jimmy in the center of our relationship, always had been. Always the hidden source of conflict between us. Life wasn't fair! I was the one who'd loved him, and he'd loved me. How the hell did Veronica always manage to come between us?

Oh Jimmy, I cried silently. We threw our life together away for this? For her? For someone who doesn't really give a damn about you and how you are doing?

No, my dear Sa Bella, Jimmy's gentle and calming voice penetrated my mind. *We threw our life away because I was greedy and made some bad decisions. I will make it up to you someday. For now, try to cherish all the wonderful times we did have together as much as I do. And try to understand that we each grieve in our own way, even your sister.*

Oh, Jimmy! You're here! I'll always love you, and I'll never stop finding ways to be with you, I promised as the faucet controlling my tears suddenly turned from outbursts of anger to tiny drops of happiness. I'd found him once again! He did seem to come through when I needed him most.

I felt a hand, Jimmy's big hand, gently brush my shoulder. I sensed that big cowboy smile of his, spreading hope and encouragement throughout my heart. Then he was gone. Again.

ELEVEN
BELLA

"The stars that nature hung in heaven, and filled their lamps with everlasting oil, give due light to the misled and lonely traveler."
John Milton

"I'm back," I sang out as I sailed through the doors of The Witchery early the next morning, just moments after the owner unlocked the door. I was revved up after finally calming down from the ugly confrontation with my sister yesterday. After Jimmy's appearance and after spending the night reading my new books about astral projection, I was back and ready to go.

"I knew you would be." Clyde grinned at me, wiping the sleep from his eyes. Long days, I assumed. "How can I help you?"

"I need an amethyst crystal, exactly like the one my sister purchased here yesterday."

"No, you don't," he frowned.

"What?"

"What you need is to take your time to select the crystal that speaks to you. Let it choose you. It will become yours and yours alone, your gateway to wherever you choose to go. Somehow, I suspect you have many incredible journeys in your future — perhaps to worlds beyond this one."

137

My mouth dropped open, recognizing somehow that this was an old soul with incredible insight and wisdom. Was he reading my mind? I scurried to the crystal section to make my selection.

Closing my eyes, I breathed deeply. In and out. In and out. When I opened my eyes, I found one particular crystal sparkling before my eyes, bidding me to pick it up. It was also an amethyst crystal, but different from my sister's. Mine—and I knew it belonged to me the moment I picked it up and felt a strong connection—was streaked with subtle shades of lavender. Mine had spikes of shimmering white crystal reaching up towards the sky.

"Do you think...?" I hesitated as I set my stone on the counter.

"Yes?"

"This probably sounds crazy, a stupid question, but...."

"There is no such thing as a crazy or stupid question," he responded kindly.

Breathing a sigh of relief, I continued. "Do you think this stone could help me leave my physical body and visit the other side?"

"Yes, I do—if you are meant to do so. You will need to learn, and practice, meditation techniques first. Then, when you are ready, start practicing the rope technique that you will read about in that book you purchased yesterday. I highly recommend this technique. But you must practice, over and over again, until you are ready for your journey."

"Thanks so much." I met his eyes, recognizing a fellow soul mate on some level. It felt so good to talk with someone who didn't think I'd lost my mind. Cradling my precious stone in the palm of my hand, I bade him farewell.

"Thank you, and don't hesitate to come back if you have questions or would like to talk."

I began to practice, just as I'd been advised. I didn't want to mess this up. What if I ended up someplace other than the other side of life? What if I couldn't find Jimmy and Jonathan? What if I ended up on another planet, surrounded by aliens? Worse yet, what if I went no place and woke up in my own bed?

Everything I read assured me that once my soul left my body, I would have control of my wandering soul. I could consciously control where it went and when it was time to return to my physical body. It was actually a lot like sleeping, the book said. When you sleep, your soul also leaves your body. Dreaming is nothing more than unconscious astral projection. We have no control over our dreams, but we can control our conscious astral projections.

Days passed. Every day I went a little farther, then pulled myself back to my physical reality. I'd created a ritual that seemed to work well as I learned to go deeper and deeper, and to pull myself back.

Finally, one evening in late summer, I decided I was ready. I chose the night of the full moon, knowing that the full moon had always helped me to connect with Isabella as I walked beside the ocean late at night. Maybe Isabella would even help me out here.

I'd already placed a comfortable day bed in the screened gazebo, to take advantage of the light of the moon and nature itself. I proceeded to the gazebo with my crystal, a photo of Jimmy, and a DVD player loaded with soulful Enya music that Jimmy and I had always enjoyed together.

The golden moon glittered across the rippling waters, creating an effect that looked like a shimmering stairway to heaven. It was breathtaking tonight, one of the most beautiful I'd ever seen. A good sign, perhaps.

Seated on the day bed, music playing softly in the background, I held the crystal closely in my right hand. Breathing slowly, going deeper and deeper, I tensed and relaxed my muscles.

Going deeper, getting drowsy until my mind hovered at the edge of sleep.

Lying down, I focused my energy on the photo of Jimmy, staring at it until I was able to visualize it, every detail of his face, with my eyes closed. I was slipping into a deeper state of relaxation as I gazed into the darkness with my eyes closed.

Light patterns began to dance across my eyes. I ignored them, as I'd previously learned to do. Totally relaxed, I was no longer aware of my physical body, but I began to feel vibrations as my astral body, or soul, prepared to leave.

Focusing hard on the vibrations, I used my willpower to control their frequency, stopping and starting them until I felt I'd mastered them and was in control of this out-of-body experience.

Next, I conjured up an image of a long rope hanging right above me, and began to visualize my hands reaching up towards the rope. Now, I was grabbing hold of the imaginary rope, and instead of turning back this time as I'd done in all my practice sessions, I began to climb that rope, hand over hand. I concentrated totally on climbing that rope as my vibrations began to buzz at a higher frequency and I felt a little dizzy, climbing higher and higher.

Suddenly I felt my astral self, my soul, separating from my body, whooshing upwards towards the imaginary rope. I was free, hovering above my body. Light. Weightless. Focusing hard on my chosen destination. I was on my way!

TWELVE
BELLA

*"They that love beyond the world cannot be separated by it.
For death is nothing more than turning us over to eternity."*
William Penn

Where am I?

I found myself sitting on the steps of a marble staircase winding upwards towards a glowing white marble building with ornate carved pillars. I gazed up at a surreal sky swirling with shades of pastels. Breathing deeply, I inhaled the scent of flowers. Strains of soft, heavenly music surrounded me — harps, violins, flutes, accompanied by a piano. All around me, I saw magnificent gardens, fountains, wooded paths, and stone statues.

I was not alone. Children were playing on the steps above me. Were they dead? Were they spirits? Or were they just visiting, like me?

I was overwhelmed, somehow, with an aching sense of familiarity. I'd been there before! I knew this place, and it felt so comforting to be there. I felt love, peace, and serenity flowing through my veins. Yes, I knew this place...and it felt so good to be back.

I relaxed, taking it all in, not wanting to miss anything. Not wanting to leave ever again.

Sighing deeply, I was suddenly aware of an image materializing beside me on the steps.

"Isabella!" I cried out, reaching out for her.

She embraced me in a warm hug. "And to what do I owe this delightful surprise, my dear?" she smiled.

"I did it, Isabella! I found my way here."

"I can see that, and I dare say I am not at all surprised that you came — on your own, not just in your unconscious dreams as you usually do."

"So you've seen me here before?"

"Of course, many times, my dear," she replied patiently. "Although I'm sure you don't remember."

I was still overwhelmed, gazing around me at the surreal beauty. "It is incredibly beautiful. There are no words...."

"This is our true home, the one we return to in between our earthly incarnations, you know. I'm sure you recognize it."

"Absolutely, but I may need a little help finding my way around."

"And where, precisely, are you wanting to go?"

"I think you know very well why I came, don't you? You are my spirit guide, after all. You don't seem to miss much."

Isabella inhaled deeply before responding. "Somehow I don't think that I am the object of your visit."

"You know I am thrilled to see you, Isabella. I have missed you a great deal since you left. I hope you will return for our book launch party. You simply must be there with me."

Then it hit me that there would probably not be a book launch party at Ashton Villa. Not anymore. Not after my latest disagreement with my high and mighty sister.

"You and Veronica need to mend your fences," Isabella said sternly. "Not just because I dearly want to have that book

142

launch party at Ashton Villa, but because you are sisters. There are reasons for your conflict, reasons that go beyond this lifetime. Someday you will figure that out. It may be the key to healing your relationship."

"I would like to do that—someday. For now...." I tapped my fingers on the smooth surface of the step.

She laughed quietly. "You're in a hurry? Will you turn into a pumpkin if you don't make it back to earth by midnight?"

"Please, Isabella. I need your help to find Jimmy and Jonathan. Don't make me beg."

"I understand. You've come all this way, in a split second, I might add. Let's walk over into the gardens by the Hall of Justice."

I followed her along a wooded path beside a rippling brook that led to a soothing waterfall. Birds chattered and squirrels scampered about our feet. We found a bench nestled amongst fragrant orchids and brilliantly colored roses. We sat together silently, absorbing the beauty of nature as a sense of serenity that flowed through us.

Finally she spoke. "All you need to do is to meditate deeply as you project your thoughts to Jimmy. Tell him you are here to visit so he is expecting you."

"Will he give me directions to his place?"

"You don't need directions. Once you have connected telepathically, you will be there. Just like you thought yourself here. Good luck, my dear. We shall meet again, of course." With that, she disappeared right before my eyes.

So I closed my eyes and began to meditate....

I found myself in a field of wild yellow daisies that were dancing in a light breeze. I was following a trail towards a small red farmhouse, with white shuttered windows and an old-fashioned porch, perched on a hillside amongst majestic oak trees. A large barn stood beside it.

Cows and horses grazed in a lush pasture, which extended down to a little lake surrounded by weeping willow trees. Birds sang. Fish splashed in the lake. A majestic golden eagle flew overhead, making three passes above my head before flying to the farmhouse, where it perched on the roof.

I heard someone playing a guitar — playing beautifully at that. Jimmy always wanted to play guitar. He tried, but wasn't very good at it, I had to admit. Could that be him playing?

My heart beat faster with every step I took. The guitar music stopped. I saw the farmhouse door swing open as a handsome young cowboy, my Jimmy, stepped out. I watched the eagle land on the porch railing beside him. Jimmy talked to him and stroked his head.

Gazing down the path, he saw me coming. A big grin spread across his face and his arms opened wide as he ran towards me. Several tame deer followed him. He always had a way with animals and wildlife. Apparently he still did.

Suddenly we were in each other's arms, merging together, our spirits in sync. I'd never felt anything this intense before, never on Earth.

"Welcome to my heaven, Sa Bella." He swung me around. "Come, let me show you around."

Arm in arm, we walked together towards the house. He carried me across the threshold into his cozy home, which was filled with antiques. A pair of rocking chairs and kerosene lamps framed a stone fireplace. Large French windows provided a glorious view of the lake and woods in the distance.

He led me into a library filled with wall-to-wall shelves, packed with books on every imaginable subject. His ornate carved desk sat in the center of the room. Papers and notebooks were spread across the desk as if he were working on some big research project.

"What do you think, Sa Bella?" he asked as he pointed to a wall on the opposite side of the room.

I was stunned. It was covered with an assortment of framed photos — photos that Jimmy and I had taken together in Galveston. Beautiful sunsets. Ghosts. The two of us together on the beach. One of Jimmy, Jonathan, and me together; my favorite photo, the one I still looked at when I was lonely and missing the two of them.

"I don't understand," I stammered. "How could you have these photos here with you?"

He smiled. "It's my heaven. I can create anything I want. I just think it, and it materializes. Pretty cool, huh? Look here." He pointed at several photos I had never seen before. Photos of the two of us together.

I was more confused than ever. These photos had never been taken, certainly not the one of us on the beach, naked, kissing beneath the light of a full moon as gentle waves lapped over our feet. "But that never happened, not like that!"

"That doesn't mean I can't wish it had happened. By projecting this thought, I was able to bring my image to life. Do you like it?" He pulled me into his arms again. "That is how I create everything here, by projected thought. It's how I built my house and my farm."

"Amazing," I sighed as he ran his fingers through my hair. "God, I've missed you." I fell into his arms, feeling his tight muscles, his heart pounding against my chest.

He led me to his big overstuffed bed. We sank into the pillows, holding each other tight. But then, something strange happened. Instead of making love like we do on Earth, instead of having sex together as I had longed to do for so long, something

145

different happened.

We began to merge into one being. I felt our souls connecting, unconditional love binding us together. We were blending physically, spiritually, and emotionally into a state of utter bliss — sharing each other's passion, joy, wisdom, and experiences momentarily. It felt like the ultimate form of intimacy, so powerful, so passionate. So far beyond a mere sexual experience on Earth, however wonderful that could be.

"What just happened?" I cried out once the moment was over.

"I don't know. It's never happened before. But then, you've never been here with me before. They say there's no sex in heaven. What do you think?" He rolled over, brushing the hair out of my eyes.

"I think this is the most amazing sex, the most amazing love, I have ever experienced."

"Even better than the night we created little Jonathan?" He eyed me cautiously, waiting for my reaction.

I jumped, my mouth hanging open. "What? You know?"

"Of course, I know. I found out shortly after I arrived here at the Hall of Wisdom and did the life review machine thing. I wasn't happy that you lied to me. But Jonathan has helped me to understand why you did what you did."

"Jonathan? You've seen Jonathan?"

"Yes, he was waiting for me when I arrived. And I see him frequently. We are closer than ever. He's my son, always has been and always will be. Although he's one hell of a lot wiser than I am. I'm a newbie here, you know."

"I need to see Jonathan."

"Of course you do. Let's just beam him up."

"What?"

"Project your thoughts to him and he will be here. But first,

146

let's go sit out on the porch swing instead of lying here in bed when he arrives."

"Maybe we should make some dinner to celebrate our reunion," I suggested. "What do you have that we can make for dinner?"

Jimmy smiled that smile, the one that had made me fall in love with him so many years ago. "Anything your little heart desires, ma'am." He dipped his cowboy hat at me. "How about steak? Good old Texas Angus steaks with garlic mashed potatoes, and apple pie for dessert?"

"Sounds wonderful," I responded as we walked out onto the porch and settled in the swing. "What do we have to do to prepare?"

"Nothing. Wait until Jonathan arrives and we are ready to eat. We don't have to eat here in Heaven, you know. But many of us still enjoy the earthly comforts of good old food."

Sitting together closely on the porch, we both began to project our thoughts, reaching out to our son. Within minutes, I saw a young man hiking down the path. He was tall, with a muscular build.

"Are you expecting someone else?" I asked Jimmy.

"Were you expecting to see Jonathan as a three-year-old?" He grinned at me. "He's a young man now, in his thirties."

Focusing more closely on the man approaching, I was shocked to see him suddenly shrink into a little boy, into the image of our son, just as he'd looked before he died so many years ago.

"What?" I cried out as I began running down the path to scoop him up in my arms.

"He shifted back to the little boy you knew, Bella, just for you," Jimmy called after me. "We can do that here to make it easier for humans like you to recognize us."

I barely heard Jimmy's words. All that mattered was being

with my son again. Our son. That sweet smile grinned up at me, his huge eyes full of love. He ran into my arms, allowing me to pick him up and hold him tight. It felt so right. It had been so long.

"Oh my baby," I whispered as tears streamed down my face. "My darling little boy. I've missed you so much."

"I know, Mommy. I miss you so so much!" *Mommy!* My heart sang to hear him call me Mommy once more.

I carried him back to the porch, pulling him into my lap on the porch swing. The three of us together at last...although I was well aware that I didn't really belong there. Not yet.

Jimmy was shaking his head, suppressing his laughter as he watched our thirty-something son sitting on my lap in the form of a toddler. As good as it felt to see my Jonathan again, I was not sure how to relate to him. Was he my baby...or was he a man? I wanted to ask him about his life there, what he did...but how could a baby tell me what I longed to know?

Jonathan seemed to sense my confusion. After giving me a big bear hug, wrapping his chubby arms around my neck, he scooted off my lap and stood beside the chair across from us. A deep man's voice suddenly replaced his soft baby voice as he began to speak. "Mom, do you mind if I revert back to my older self now? It would be so much easier for us to talk."

"No, of course not," I stammered as I watched him grow back into the handsome young man I'd first seen on the path. He sat across from Jimmy and me. I couldn't quit staring at him, taking in every feature, wanting to hold on to this memory forever.

"It is confusing for you, I know. The thing is that, unless we shift our appearance back to another time, or decide to change our appearance via projected thought, most of us here are about thirty years old. We don't get older. We like it this way."

I gazed at Jimmy, a frown upon my face. "Sorry, Jimmy, but

you look a little older than thirty today!"

The men laughed together, their laughter so much alike. Father and son.

"I did it for you, Sa Bella." He took my hand in his. "I didn't think you'd appreciate it if I came across as half your age. Not that you are old, my darling. You still are the most beautiful woman in the world."

After bantering and laughing together for a while, Jonathan started to tell us what his life was like over there.

"I love it here, Mom," he began. "There's so much to do, so much to learn. I spend a lot of time in the Hall of Records, an amazing Greco-Roman building with a glass dome and towering marble columns. It contains copies of every historical record ever written, even those previously destroyed on Earth."

"What do you do there, Jonathan?"

He was animated as he continued. "I research my past lives there, and the lives of my loved ones and soul mates. I have access to scrolls there that contain life charts for every life I've ever lived, and the charts of every other soul as well."

"Life charts?"

"Yes. You see, before we reincarnate on Earth, we each create a life chart to fulfill our unique purpose in that life. It is very detailed, and includes things like what we want or need to learn and accomplish, our specific goals, and obstacles in achieving our goals. We even choose our parents, siblings, and any negative people or situations that will play a part in our lives to help us grow and learn. Of course, we get lots of help from our spirit guides and orientation team."

"That's a lot to digest, son," Jimmy chimed in. He was still learning, of course. "Tell her exactly what you do when you research those life charts."

"Oh yes! It is so exciting! We can merge with these life charts.

By that, I mean that we can assimilate all the emotions, senses, and realities of a particular life. It can be one of my lives, one of my loved ones — or unloved ones — at any time in history. I just merged with Abraham Lincoln recently, and learned so much about the person he was — far beyond anything I've ever read in a book."

"So you do this just to learn and understand yourself and others better?" I was thinking that this could be a fascinating adventure. No wonder he was so excited.

"It can help a person understand conflicts in a past life." He looked at me pointedly. "Reasons, perhaps, why two sisters don't get along."

"I already know why, Jonathan," I whispered, holding Jimmy's hand. Jimmy. We both loved the same man. Jonathan knew that now.

"Of course, but there's more to it than that, Mother," he sighed. "You aren't ready for this yet. I can only tell you that when the time is right you will have access to those charts — yours and Aunt Veronica's. And you will discover some interesting information."

"You've done that? Looked at our charts? Merged with them, as you say?"

"I have," he smiled, "but that is not my story to share. You will know when the time is right."

"Does one have to die before being able to look at those charts?"

"Not necessarily...but this is not your time."

"God, you sound just like Isabella. 'It is not your time....' She is my spirit guide, Jonathan, as well as my Great-grandmother who I am named after."

"I know," Jonathan smiled. "And I understand she's spent time with you recently on Earth, working on a novel you're writing about the Great Storm she died in."

I shook my head. That son of ours seemed to know everything.

"Back to you and Veronica," he continued.

"But you just said the time wasn't right...."

"I did. But the time *is* right for the two of you to make amends. You are sisters, Mother. There is no wrong or right, black or white. No one knows how many days a person has left on Earth to make things right."

I sit in silence for a while, thinking about our last argument, thinking about the fact that she had actually offered to host my book launch party at Ashton Villa.

"Maybe that book launch party at Ashton Villa could provide the common ground you need to re-establish your relationship."

My wise son was obviously prying into my mind. I sighed heavily. "Maybe...but speaking about right and wrong, is it wrong for me to be here, with your father? Does Veronica still have a claim to him?"

"I'm dead, Sa Bella." Jimmy quietly focused on me. "Till death do us part?"

We decided it was time for dinner. As we left the porch and entered Jimmy's kitchen, I saw steaks marinating on the counter. Where they came from, I did not know. An apple pie was cooling on the rack beside the stove, and a big bowl of garlic mashed potatoes was ready.

My guys laughed at my surprise. "Projected thought," they blurted out at the same time.

"That's great, but I'd love to be able to actually put those steaks on a grill and smell them cooking. Can we do that?"

"Of course," Jimmy assured me as he picked up the platter of steaks and took them out to a big grill in his back yard. I was not sure if the grill was there earlier or not. The coals were already hot.

Over dinner, Jonathan told us more about his life there. He had created a beach house that was very similar to our little cottage back on Earth. It reminded him of me, and of Jimmy. It had given him comfort in those early years.

For fun, he attended incredible musical performances that featured music by some of the great deceased musicians—even Bach and Mozart. He fished in his lake and took long hikes in the woods, absorbing the wonders of nature that were beyond anything humans have ever before seen. There were parties, dancing festivals, book clubs. He was never bored, always stimulated, and always had friends to socialize with, as well as time to enjoy the solitude he craved.

Yes, our Jonathan was so much like both Jimmy and me. And I was so proud of him.

It was time for me to say goodbye, to end this incredible visit. Something was calling me back to my earthly home. But I would be back, I promised my loved ones as I hugged them both farewell.

My soul suddenly slammed back into my body where I'd left it lying in my gazebo on Galveston Island, Texas, USA, Planet Earth.

THIRTEEN
VERONICA

"People come into our lives at certain times for various reasons having to do with lessons to be learned. It is not a coincidence."
Brian Weiss

As the morning sun peeked through my lace bedroom curtains, it danced seductively upon my beautiful amethyst crystal. Swirls of purple and white merged, sparkling in the light. I kept the crystal on my bedside table—for good luck or something. All I knew was that it made me feel good, comforted, at peace. I marveled at the way it sparkled and glowed in the shifting rays of light. Not that I believed in all the nonsense that my dear sister did.

As for Bella, I had not heard from her in weeks. To be honest, I was still fuming at times over my encounter with her outside The Witchery. Why couldn't she just accept the fact that Jimmy was gone? Why couldn't she just let him rest in peace? Why must she continually taunt me?

Forget it, I scolded myself as I crawled out of bed and padded down the ornate wood-carved staircase to the kitchen. While the coffee brewed, I wandered around the Gold Room, thinking about the family memories we'd all made there. I ran my fingers over the keyboard of the baby grand piano, admiring the old family portraits hanging on the walls. Miss Bettie's delightful paintings also still graced the walls. What a legend she had become!

While sipping my coffee, I played the messages waiting for me on my answering machine. It was going to be a busy week of board meetings, luncheons with my lady friends, and a visit from my grandchildren. I always looked forward to that. They usually came for Sunday dinner, a family tradition.

For as long as I could remember, our extended family had always enjoyed Sunday dinners together at Ashton Villa in the formal dining room. The food was elegant, served on the family's beautiful gold-rimmed china. The children even drank their milk from fancy heirloom crystal goblets. They were expected to behave like little adults, although it sometimes took a while for them to learn the proper dining etiquette, and to sit still throughout meals consisting of five to seven courses.

In later years, at the request of my husband and children, dinners were not quite as formal. Sometimes we enjoyed a picnic lunch outside, something that greatly pleased the grandchildren.

I decided I'd surprise them all this Sunday with a back yard barbeque—hamburgers on the grill, homemade baked beans, corn on the cob. Would it be too much to make my special Oysters Rockefeller for an appetizer? Maybe a broccoli salad? Key lime pie would be perfect, or maybe not. My grandchildren preferred chocolate chip cookies. I began scribbling out a grocery list. I'd stop at Kroger on my way home from the beauty shop. I always had my hair done on Friday afternoons, always at one o'clock.

Carla, my regular hairdresser, was on vacation this week, so I had a new girl named Mary Ann. She was younger than Carla, by about thirty years. I only hoped she knew what she was doing. I'd worn my hair the same way for forty years now, and that's the way I liked it. I patiently explained to her what I wanted. She also consulted my chart as I tried to relax in the chair, listening to classical music playing in the background.

Mary Ann was quiet as she worked on me. Friendly but quiet. Of course, she didn't know me and apparently had no idea who I was. Or perhaps she did know and was intimidated by me and my position. She'd only moved to the island six months ago, she said.

I enjoyed the silence today, deep in thought, as Mary Ann finished washing and setting my hair and put me under the hair dryer. I browsed through a magazine, drowsing off as the heat swirled around my head.

Suddenly the dryer went off, waking me up. Mary Ann was busy trimming another customer's hair and must not have realized I was done. So I sat waiting, listening to other customers gossiping with their stylists.

"I couldn't believe it," one chubby woman with flaming red hair was telling her stylist. "Here they were, the two sisters, having this fight right in the middle of Post Office Street. Then, get this...." She paused for emphasis. "The younger one—you know, the eccentric one—turns on her heel and gives her sister the finger before storming off down the street. 'Screw you,' she screamed at the top of her voice!"

I froze. Oh my God! She was talking about my sister and me. Someone had seen us. I wanted to shrivel up under the dryer and never come out. What if they recognized me? I looked down at the floor, hiding my eyes. Humiliated.

"So what do you think they were fighting about?" the stylist asked. I didn't recognize her either. She must also be filling in for another beautician on vacation.

"If you ask me," the flaming haired gossip continued in a hushed voice, "it could have something to do with Jimmy. You know, Veronica's husband. I thought I heard them mention his name before all hell broke loose."

"But why Jimmy? What's to fight about? Jimmy is dead, you know."

Carrot top shook her head with exasperation. "So you don't know? You've never heard the rumors?"

"Well, no. I tend not to rely on rumors. People say ugly things sometimes, things that may or may not be true."

"So do you want to know or not?" the gossip sighed in an exasperated tone of voice.

"Well, OK, go on."

"I happen to know that Jimmy spent a lot of time with Bella, walking on the beach together, sometimes playing with Bella's little boy before he died many years ago." She paused, waiting for a reaction.

"Is there something wrong with that? They were related, you know. That little boy probably needed a father image in his life. Maybe it was good that he had Jimmy around."

"But the little boy wasn't *always* with them, if you get my drift. Neither was Veronica. And...." She paused dramatically. "Even after little Jonathan died, many years later, you would still see Bella and Jimmy strolling along the beach together taking photos. Just the two of them."

"Sorry, Shirley, but I don't see a connection here. Not sure where you're going with this. Jimmy was her brother-in-law. Is there a law that they can't be friends and spend time together?" The stylist began snipping Shirley's hair, faster and faster. Probably trying to get rid of this obnoxious woman.

Shirley leaned in for the kill. "Let me ask you this. Who do you think the father of Bella's baby really was? Why did she never tell anyone? Why did she never marry?"

"Jimmy?" The stylist dropped her scissors on the floor. "Are you trying to tell me that Jimmy was the father of his sister-in-law's baby? I can't believe that. Sorry."

Blood churned through my brain. I felt dizzy, like I was going to faint. Shirley's harsh words echoed in my ears, over and over again. Could there possibly be any truth to this? Had I been totally blind to what was happening around me? Had I been betrayed by my own husband?

"Stranger things have happened. Just sayin'," the flaming redhead smirked.

Suddenly Mary Ann was there, lifting the hood of my dryer. "Sorry, I didn't realize the heat went off." She began to unroll and check one curl to see if I was dry yet. "Looks good."

"No, I need a little more heat," I stammered, not sure if I was able to stand, wanting to hide beneath the dryer until the flaming monster left the beauty shop.

"Are you OK?" Mary Ann asked, obviously noticing my pale face, shaking hands, and the look of horror in my eyes. "Do you need a drink of water?"

"I'm fine," I snapped. "Water would be good."

So I hid beneath the dryer until the evil lady waddled out of the shop.

I was in a daze the rest of the day, trying to make sense of what I'd just heard. Trying to put it out of my mind as just another vicious rumor targeted at those who had money and prestige on the island.

Whoever this Shirley person was, she had no class. She was dressed in faded jeans and dirty tennis shoes. There was a tear in her plus-sized plaid blouse, and a missing button.

She was probably just jealous, I told myself. Or was she? Was there any hint of truth in what she'd said?

My mind reeling, I paced around my empty house that evening. Even Olivia had deserted me. The only sound to be heard was the steady ticking of the old grandfather clock. It felt and sounded like a time bomb running through my veins, ready to explode at any moment.

This was foolish, I reminded myself. But why was I so upset? Why did I feel, on a gut level, that there could possibly be some possible element of truth in all of this?

I thought back to Bella's distancing herself from us all over the years. The way she fought with me over anything and everything. The fact that she and Jimmy enjoyed spending time together, doing things I never cared to do. He always had a twinkle in his eyes whenever she was around, and he doted on little Jonathan.

Had I been blind? Dear God, how would I ever find the truth?

I rushed into Jimmy's office and began tearing things apart, looking for any sign of betrayal. Old letters? Photos? Any incriminating evidence? But there was nothing. My oldest daughter, Maria, had cleared out her father's desk months ago. Aside from a few family photos that she'd given me, she never indicated finding anything unusual.

I couldn't sleep that night, tossing and turning as my mind raced in all directions. I felt like a yo-yo, up and down, back and forth, jumping from one conclusion to another. Despite the fact that Jimmy and I had never had the closest of relationships, he had still been my husband. The very thought of being betrayed by my own husband was infuriating. Add my own sister into this alleged convoluted affair and it felt like a double whammy, enough to put me over the edge.

Besides, the very thought of other people knowing, or even suspecting, that he'd been unfaithful to me was the ultimate blow. How could I hold my head high and walk down the street, knowing that people were talking about me? How could I fulfill my social obligations with this scandal looming over my head?

Why should I care? Maybe I shouldn't...but I had a reputation to uphold. One that could be destroyed by my late husband and my sister.

After a sleepless night, I decided I needed to find the truth. I couldn't just fret about this, working myself up into a frenzy if there was no proof of anything. First, I would spend a few days cooling off and plotting my next move. All I knew was that it would involve a secret trip to Bella's cottage. I would need to be sure she wasn't there so I could go through her things looking for any evidence of a relationship between the two of them.

My days and nights began to blur together into a semi-sleepless pattern.

I startled when the doorbell rang sometime around noon one day. I was still in my robe, moping around the house. Peering out through the window from behind closed blinds, I was shocked to find Maria and her family standing there on the doorstep. Several additional vehicles pulled to the curb as my other children and their families spilled out onto the lawn.

It must be Sunday! How could I have forgotten about our Sunday dinner? I hadn't even stopped at the store for groceries for the barbeque I'd planned. I had no food prepared. I wasn't even dressed for the day.

I unlocked the front door before rushing up the stairs to my bedroom. "Come on in," I called out in a forced cheerful voice. "I'll be down shortly."

I hurriedly dressed in an elegant pant suit and matching heels, ran a brush through my hair, and did a fast job of applying make-up. Fastening my brooch and earrings, I turned to find Maria in the doorway.

"Mother, are you OK?"

"Of course, why do you ask?"

"Well, it looks like you're just now getting yourself ready for the day. That's not like you…did you not sleep well?"

"I'm fine. I just overslept. That's all."

159

She frowned as though she didn't quite believe me. "All right, whatever you say," she sighed. "Can I help with dinner? Outdoor barbeque, did you say?"

"Change of plans." I stared into the mirror above my dressing table as I applied my lipstick. "I decided it would be a nice treat to take you all to the Sunday brunch at The Hotel Galvez!"

"Really?" She sounded surprised, but perhaps a bit disappointed that I was proposing breaking a family tradition that had been around for over a hundred years. "Well, sure, that would be lovely. They put out a buffet to die for. I assume you've made reservations? We are a large group, after all."

"Oh dear, I forgot. Would you mind making them, Maria? Just give them my name." Of course, my name carried weight every place we went on this island. At least it always had in the past. Maybe that would change now, if a possible scandal about Jimmy and Bella was exposed to the public.

I was fully aware, as we all walked out to the cars for our drive to the hotel, that my family members were looking at me in an odd way. Several whispered amongst themselves, wondering what was wrong with Grandma. Was she coming down with Alzheimer's just like Great-Grandma?

Still, it was a lovely luncheon. I began to smile again, enjoying the company of my family. I loved them all dearly, and the little ones kept us laughing. It was good to catch up on all the things they were doing in their busy lives, and I was so proud of each and every one of them.

"Do you see Aunt Bella?" my son, Michael, finally asked me during a pause in the conversation.

"Not often," I replied carefully. "We are both so busy, you know."

"That's a shame," he commented. "Is she doing OK out there all by herself?"

160

A devious thought suddenly crept into my mind. This could be the answer to my dilemma over getting Bella out of her cottage so I could explore without interruption.

"As a matter of fact, I think she gets lonely and needs to get out more. She isn't involved in things like I am. If any of you have the time and inclination to do so, perhaps you'd like to invite her out sometime. I know she used to love taking the ferry over to Bolivar Island, and driving out to Stingaree Restaurant and Marina for their delicious oysters."

That should buy me at least four hours of uninterrupted time, I calculated.

"Great idea! We haven't been there in over a year. The kids love taking the ferry over, feeding the sea gulls, looking for the dolphins. What do you say, honey?" He grinned at his wife.

She agreed. "You're coming with us, of course?" my daughter-in-law inquired.

Of course I would not be...but I did need to know exactly when they were going. "I'll see. Just let me know when, once you've spoken with Bella. I'd love to come along, if I can fit it into my schedule. If not, another time. The important thing, I think, is to get Bella out into the land of the living."

A twinge of guilt flittered through my soul. I'd not been exactly honest with my children.

FOURTEEN
BELLA

"A life with difficult relationships, filled with obstacles and losses, presents the most opportunity for the soul's growth."
Brian Weiss

It took me awhile to come back to Earth after my visit to Heaven—back to "life" as we know it. Strangely enough, the "dead" who existed on the other side of life seemed to be so much more alive than those of us living here on this earth. Happier. More content. Much wiser.

My visit had been surreal, like a vivid dream, but so much more than a dream. There were not words to adequately describe that which could only be felt through the heart and soul. Heaven somehow felt like my real home, a place I'd been before, many times.

Sometimes these days as I strolled barefoot along the beach, lost in the waves crashing beside me, I gazed up at the stars and felt an intense longing to go back. To go "home." Still, I'd been told, over and over again, that it was not yet my time to cross over. I had unfinished business here on Earth. But what? The book, of course. What else? Jimmy and Jonathan were waiting for me there. Perhaps Olivia was also....

As I pondered these thoughts and documented every moment of my visit to Heaven in my locked journal, I was interrupted by the ringing of my phone. It was Michael, my nephew. I was surprised to hear from him. He rarely called unless there was a family issue we needed to deal with. Veronica?

"Aunt Bella," Michael's deep voice came across the line. God, he sounded so much like his father, Jimmy. He even looked like him — the way Jimmy had looked years ago when I fell in love with him. "We've been thinking about you. It's been a long time."

"That it has, Michael. How are you and your family?"

"We're fine. I'm calling because we'd like to invite you for dinner at Stingarees, that seafood restaurant on the Bolivar Peninsula. You know, the one with the incredible sunsets over the sea? I'm hoping you could capture some sunset photos for us. I need a nice framed enlargement for my office. And I thought of you. Your photos are exceptional."

"Thanks so much, Michael. I'd love to join you. Just you and your family, or will anyone else be coming?" I didn't want to ask specifically about Veronica, although I was sure she'd decline any invitation that included me after our recent encounter.

He hesitated a moment. "Probably just me and mine... although my mother may decide to join us if she isn't busy with one of her committee meetings."

What could I say? I hesitated.

"Aunt Bella? You still there?"

"Oh, yes. Sure, that's fine."

"Look, I know the two of you have had your differences over the years. But you are still family. I know that she cares about you and wants the best for you. I'm sure you feel the same way. But enough said, right?" He laughed a bit nervously and moved on to setting a date for our visit. It would be subject to change, depending upon the weather. We needed a clear evening to

163

capture the sunset.

As I gathered up my camera, special lenses, and gear on the designated day of our planned dinner date, I was apprehensive. Would Veronica be there or not? If she was, at least we wouldn't be alone. We'd both need to act civilly in front of Michael and his family.

I was out pruning my roses early that afternoon when Michael called. "Aunt Bella, do you mind terribly if we pick you up at five instead of seven this evening? I just got a call from the office, and need to be back for an important meeting tonight that I hadn't planned on. We can eat first, capture the sunset, and then head back on the ferry."

"No problem. I'll be ready. See you soon," I assured him.

At precisely five o'clock, Michael's car pulled into my driveway. I held my breath as I walked out the door of my cottage. Thankfully, I discovered that Veronica was not there.

I'd always enjoyed the ferry ride from Galveston to Port Bolivar. We parked our car on the ferry and got out to watch the sea gulls flying overhead. Michael's two children threw popcorn out from the back of the boat, squealing with delight as hordes of gulls swooped down and surrounded them. I always kept my eyes peeled for signs of dolphins jumping and playing in the surf. It was also interesting to watch the other ships and boats coming and going.

We soon landed on the Bolivar Peninsula, embarked from the ferry, and began our drive to Crystal Beach. Before long, we turned off towards the Intra Coastal Waterway, where the Stingaree Restaurant and Marina were located. Climbing up the stairs to the main dining room overlooking the sea, we decided the weather was nice enough to request a table out on the deck, where we'd have wonderful views of the boats and barges passing by as birds scrambled to retrieve any fish remnants from fishing boats returning to the marina.

The restaurant was a casual, rustic, laid-back kind of place that had been there forever. But it offered stunning views and some of the best seafood around. I was always partial to their Oysters Rockefeller. In fact, my sister had managed to secure their recipe years ago, and made it often for some of the parties she used to host at Ashton Villa. Not that she'd hosted many recently. Not since Jimmy died. Not that I would have been invited anyway.

Michael and Gloria, his beautiful blonde wife, filled me in on all that was happening in their busy lives. They had done well in life, of course, and had the best of everything. Michael had taken over the reins of his father's real estate and investment business, and it was thriving. He had previously served as vice-president, and had been groomed by his father to run the family business someday.

Nobody had expected it to happen this soon, however.

Jimmy would be so proud, I thought to myself. Just looking at Michael, I could see Jimmy. His eyes. The way he smiled and laughed. Like father, like son. My heart ached as my eyes began to water.

I could almost feel Jimmy's presence as I turned away to watch a barge float by.

"Are you all right?" Michael asked.

I smiled wistfully. "It's just that you are so much like your father, Michael. Do you know how proud he would be of you?"

"Thank you, Aunt Bella. That means a great deal to me. I want to do everything I can to carry on his legacy." He dabbed at his own eyes. "I miss him a great deal. We all do."

I could only nod in agreement.

Taking a deep breath, Michael changed the subject. "Now

that we've bored you with all the details of our lives, tell us what is happening with you."

As our seafood platters and Stingaritta drinks arrived, along with hamburgers and fries for the hungry children, I updated them on my art work and my soon-to-be released novel. They were excited about the novel, especially since it revolved around the Great Storm that had claimed Michael's Great-Great-Grandmother Isabella.

"Have you ever thought about throwing a book launch party at Ashton Villa?" Gloria suggested.

"What?" I almost choked on my oyster.

"Brilliant idea, honey." Michael smiled at his wife. "It would be the perfect place, you know. And I have a feeling my mother would be honored to host it. She hasn't thrown one of her big shindigs in a long time. I think it would do her good, especially with the family connection. And Ashton Villa, you know, was one of the few houses that survived that storm. Guess I don't need to tell you that, Aunt Bella." He grinned at me.

"Of course that's a possibility," I hedged, "unless my publisher has other plans. He's in charge of my marketing plan and scheduling events." As if I wasn't in charge of suggesting where and when events should take place. He would, of course, want me to do an event there; it was also my childhood home, after all.

We were just finishing our meal when the sun began to slip into the sea in swirls of soft pastels that began to grow more vivid every moment. I set up my camera and began to shoot. It was an unbelievably beautiful sunset this evening. I knew I'd captured some perfect shots. I couldn't wait to download them onto my computer and begin to edit as needed.

"What a perfect night to shoot the sunset!" I beamed as we piled into the car for the ride back to the ferry. "I'll let you know once they're ready, and you can select the one you like."

It was such a gorgeous evening that I had Michael drop me off on the ocean side near my cottage so I could take more photos of the rising moon. Photography was my therapy. There was something about it that aroused all my senses as I marveled at the beauty of nature that surrounded me. Nature…that's what it was all about. I had to capture the moment.

Feeling happier than I had in quite a while, aside from my recent trip to Heaven, I walked across the road towards my cottage. I stopped dead in my tracks. There was a car in my driveway, and a light on in my house. What the hell? Who could possibly be in my house?

I pulled out my cell phone, ready to call the police as I inched closer, staying in the shadows of the overgrown trees. What the hell? Veronica? Her fancy car with the personalized license plates was parked in my driveway. She wasn't in the car. She must be in the cottage.

My blood began to boil. What was she doing here, invading my home, my privacy? How had she even gotten in? Sure, I didn't usually lock my doors. But she had no right to be here. I'd certainly not invited her to come over. Certainly not while I was gone.

I throttled my initial inclination to burst through the door, swearing at her. I had to remain calm if I wanted to figure out what she was doing here. So I tiptoed around the perimeter of the cottage, hiding in the shadows, peeking in through the windows. Where was she?

As I approached my bedroom window, I heard something inside. Something like a thud, then metal scraping against metal. Peeking in, I saw nobody. Heart pounding, I waited. Something or someone was in my bedroom. It had to be my sister. But where was she?

167

"Dammit!" Veronica's voice suddenly drifted out through the bedroom window, startling me.

Standing on my tiptoes so I could see better, I shifted my gaze down towards the floor. There I found Veronica sitting on the floor at the foot of my bed. The bed skirt was pulled up onto the bed, exposing the box where I kept my journals. Looking closer, I observed my sister holding one of my locked journals in her hand as she tried to pry the lock open with a screwdriver. I couldn't believe it!

That was the last straw. I flew into the house, screeching at the top of my voice. "What the hell do you think you are doing? I'm calling the police!"

Veronica turned white and gasped as she dropped the journal and screwdriver onto the floor. Her mouth hung open and she began to tremble.

"I said, what the hell do you think you are doing? Breaking into my house? Stealing my property?"

"I...I...," she stammered as she struggled to her feet. Her eyes darted back and forth as if she were trying to figure out how she could escape. I stood squarely in the doorway, arms folded, blocking her exit.

We remained that way, in a stand-off, for what seemed like an eternity. Neither of us spoke.

"I can wait all night, if that's what you prefer," I finally glared at her. "But you are not going anywhere until you tell me what you are doing here. And I *will* call the police if I have to. Now, won't that look pretty on the society pages of the newspaper? Socialite Veronica Caldwell busted for breaking and entering, for stealing private property."

She gasped. "You wouldn't...you couldn't.... But, of course, you would. You'd do anything to spite me. That's the way it's always been, hasn't it?"

"Don't even try blaming me for what you've done, Ms. High and Mighty. As I said, I have all night, and I'm waiting for an answer."

Slinking down into the rocking chair by my bed, Veronica wrung her hands, and opened and closed her mouth several times. Nothing came out. She apparently had no idea what to say. I waited, still standing in the doorway. I wasn't going anyplace.

"All right," she finally began. "I'm here because I need to know the truth...the truth about your relationship with *my* husband. I have a right to know...after all these years."

Now *I* was speechless.

"So you have nothing to say for yourself? Is that an admission of guilt? I've already found photos here of the two of you together, and photos of the two of you with your little boy. Whose little boy is he, Bella? Who is the father of your baby?"

"Jimmy was my friend, my brother-in-law, Veronica. Of course I have pictures of him. You're the one who asked him to spend time with my son and me. You apparently felt I was an unfit mother, unable to raise my own child. And you're the one who never had time to walk with us by the ocean or chase ghosts or anything else—"

"Don't even turn this back on me. Quit changing the subject. I'm asking you for the name of Jonathan's father. What kind of a secret have you been keeping all these years?"

"It's nobody's business but mine." I dug in my heels.

"Did you sleep with my husband? Is he the father of your baby?"

"What the hell? No, I *never* slept with *your husband,* for God's sake!"

She stood and began to pace back and forth in my little bedroom, shaking her head as if she didn't know what to believe anymore.

169

"What's going on, Veronica?" I softened my tone. "Are you coming down with Alzheimer's, like Olivia? The way you are acting doesn't make any sense. Breaking into my house when I'm gone? Trying to break the lock on my private journal? Accusing me of having an affair with your husband? That is just plain crazy! I think *you* are the one who needs a good shrink!"

"Well...well, I've heard rumors, and I just needed to know."

"Rumors?" I scoffed. "Join the club. People will talk, they always will. And they love to talk about people like us — especially like you. You're the matron of Ashton Villa, the untouchable Galveston society queen. You're a great target for jealous or bored people. Get over it."

I watched Veronica's eyes fill with tears as she stared at the floor.

"Perhaps I owe you an apology," she whispered. "I don't know what to say. It's just...it's just that it's been very difficult for me since Jimmy died. And then, when you hear things like this — well, I had to find out. I'm sorry, Bella."

She finally looked up at me, her puffy eyes pleading for forgiveness. She looked old and tired, as if she hadn't been sleeping well for days.

What could I do? What could I say? My emotions were reeling back and forth, from anger to guilt to pity. "I accept your apology," I mumbled. "Just don't ever do something like this again, all right?"

"I won't. I'm sorry." She walked up to me and held out her arms for a hug. We hugged each other, in a slightly detached way. Then she left.

Closing the door behind her as she left, I slunk to the floor, crushed. I was nothing but a liar! A pathetic liar.

Still, Jimmy had *not* been her husband when we made love. And he was *not* her husband when we recently merged together

170

in Heaven. Death had terminated their lifetime vows, right? Besides, I continued, trying to justify my behavior — I'd never actually told her that Jimmy *wasn't* my baby's father, had I?

What good would it do to tell the truth now, after all these years? It would only cause more pain for more people. For Veronica. For Maria, Michael, and Melanie, and the grandchildren. At least that's what I needed to tell myself. What I must believe to try to alleviate the guilt that consumed me.

As Olivia might have said, sometimes it's best to *let sleeping dogs lie.*

FIFTEEN
VERONICA

"To err is human, to forgive divine."
Alexander Pope

Was I following in my poor mother's footsteps? Was I losing my mind?

I'd have sworn that Michael told me he planned to pick Bella up precisely at seven o'clock. If so, there was no way they could have returned from their dinner at Stingarees prior to ten, certainly not by eight when Bella arrived and caught me trying to pry her journals open.

Apparently I'd been a fool to think there had been something going on between my husband and my sister. Maybe I wasn't thinking straight. That horrible conversation I'd overheard at the beauty shop had somehow triggered a tiny doubt buried in the recesses of my mind. Why?

I wondered what Maria, my psychiatrist daughter, would say about that. I wasn't about to tell her, however. I was beyond humiliated, mortified by my own behavior and suspicions.

I had no choice but to believe my sister. I had no proof of anything. Did it really even matter anymore? Jimmy was dead. As for my shaky, often turbulent relationship with Bella, I'd

172

actually been trying to pull it together at this stage of our lives. Was that still possible?

A part of me still wished I'd been able to get into those locked journals, however. If nothing else, maybe I'd be able to better understand my eccentric sister.

As I drove back home along the seawall, I opened the windows to let the ocean breeze drift in, trying to clear my head. Trying to erase this ugly episode from my thoughts.

By the next morning, I decided it was up to me to reach out to Bella. I was the one who'd caused this rift with my irrational behavior. For some reason, I had a nagging feeling that it was important for us to resolve our differences now, before it was too late. We weren't exactly "spring chickens" anymore, as Jimmy used to say.

I had several ideas. Of course, I still wanted to host her book launch party, but didn't dare bring that up yet. She'd probably turn me down flat.

I had another idea. There was a performance coming up at the Grand 1894 Opera House this weekend. The Oak Ridge Boys were performing. They always drew a full house with their wonderful old tunes and four-part harmony. Who could forget "Elvira"? It always brought the house down.

As it was, I had standing season tickets to accommodate four in the opera box my family had reserved for generations. Without Jimmy, or my mother, Olivia, who loved to attend performances there, it got lonely sometimes sitting in my ornate box sipping wine by myself. Sometimes my children came with me, but they had very busy schedules.

Bella sounded surprised when I called her that morning, inviting her to the performance. I knew that she adored the Oak Ridge Boys.

She hesitated at first. "I'm not sure if that is a good idea, after last night," she began.

"Just think about it and let me know soon. The show is sold out. If you aren't coming with me, I'll invite somebody else. I'd prefer that you come with me. I know you love their music. And just being there in that magnificent old theater is a treat in itself. The wine is on me."

"I assume I'll need to dress to the nines," Bella sighed.

"Wear whatever you like—tattered jeans, that beat-up old red hat of yours. Your choice!" I tried to lighten the mood.

"I do have a lovely long dress that I've not had a chance to wear yet. Maybe I'll wear that."

"So, is that a yes?"

"It's a yes. Thanks for inviting me, Veronica."

I waited in the elegant lobby of the Grand Opera House, watching for Bella to arrive. Stylishly-dressed people, including many of my acquaintances, streamed through the doors. Where was Bella? I hoped she hadn't changed her mind about coming.

She'd always had a tendency to cancel at the last minute or not show up. I also hoped she didn't wear some ridiculous outfit to embarrass me. *Stop*, I chastised myself. *Aren't you supposed to be turning over a new leaf and trying to have a relationship with your sister?*

I was stunned when I saw her enter. She was beautifully dressed in a long flowing black silk dress set off with a silver scarf and dazzling silver jewelry. She'd even had her hair done up in a glamorous style instead of flying loose the way she always wore it.

"You look stunning." I smiled at her.

"Thanks. As do you." She seemed to be at her ladylike best this evening.

174

Together we walked up the red-carpeted stairway to the mezzanine level. We were greeted at the top by a statue of a Greek goddess holding a torch. Someone was playing a black baby grand piano as people gathered to listen and enjoy a glass of wine from the concession area.

Bella glanced around the historic Romanesque Revival features of this ornate building that had been constructed in 1894. It had survived several storms. After Storm Ike slammed the island in 2008, there had been significant damage on the main level. The necessary restoration was now complete and done beautifully to retain the historic character of the building. Jimmy and I had made a major donation towards the renovation.

We ordered our wine before being seated in our opera box. It was draped in red velvet swags to match the swags framing the stage. We settled into our comfortable chairs, sipping our wine and absorbing the elegance that surrounded us.

There was something to be said for dressing up once in a while, I thought to myself—instead of wearing old tennis shoes and holey jeans like so many people did these days. Dressing up seemed to bring out the best in people. They were nicer, more polite, took the time to converse about subjects other than the daily grind.

It felt good to be sitting there with my sister after all these years. I never dreamed a day like this would come. I glanced at her and she smiled back wistfully, tears in her eyes. My eyes also teared up.

"We've wasted a lot of good years bickering, haven't we?" I broke the ice.

She nodded. "Maybe it's not too late to start over?"

"I'd love that." I reached over and gave her a hug. She hugged me back.

Suddenly the Oak Ridge Boys burst onto the stage and the

175

house lights went out. We were swept into the music along with the rest of the crowd. People were dancing in their seats, clapping their hands. We marveled that an older group like this, with forty years of musical experience behind them, could still perform like twenty-year-olds. They came to life on that stage, bringing the audience along with them. The years may have slipped away since we first heard some of these amazing songs, but they performed better than ever. After a standing ovation, they left the stage and people began to leave.

Bella and I waited in our box while the crowd left. The waiter brought us another glass of wine to enjoy while we waited.

Bella was beaming. We both were. It had been an incredible performance. And somehow, it seemed to help bring us together again. Instead of gauging our words before speaking, instead of suspecting each other of the worst, we seemed to drift back in time to the relationship we once had so many years ago.

"By the way, is your offer still open to host my book launch party?" She asked the question I was wanting to ask her.

"Absolutely! Just let me know when. We can plan it together. I was thinking...how about harp music in the background? And we could have a theme centered on what life was like in 1900 just before the storm."

Bella laughed at my excitement. "You've always been a planner—always threw the best parties in Galveston."

"And this one will be the best I've ever thrown!" I promised her. "Yes! We will have our servers, bar tenders, and the orchestra all wear period clothing. How about that?"

"Wonderful idea, I must say."

"Maybe you should wear a Victorian dress like Miss Bettie wore, or...." I hesitated. "Maybe...maybe that black wedding dress that Great-Grandma Isabella once wore." I couldn't believe I was saying this after all the grief I'd given her over the years for wearing that dress as she walked the beach in the middle of the night.

"What? Really?" She frowned, looking at me as if she were questioning my sanity. Still, she looked thrilled at the idea.

We parted with a hug and a promise to get together soon for coffee or dinner so we could plan the greatest book launch party ever held anywhere.

SIXTEEN
BELLA

*"The past is consumed in the present, and the present is living
only because it brings forth the future."*
James Joyce

Something strange seemed to be happening between
Veronica and me. It was as if all the old hostilities had magically
disappeared. I wasn't sure what to attribute this to. Were we
both getting senile? Or could Isabella somehow be responsible
for this? Was she interfering and planting ideas in our minds?

I grinned all the way back to my cottage. My mind was reeling
with ideas for the book launch party; not that Veronica needed
more ideas. More than anything, I was thrilled at the thought
of wearing Isabella's dress. How fitting, and what a tribute to
my "co-author Isabella." Without her, the book would not have
taken the form that it needed to. How I hoped she would attend
our party.

I trekked out to my gazebo with a notepad and flashlight to
begin making notes for the big event. Stars twinkled overhead in
a pitch-black sky as waves lapped against the shore. I felt more
content than I remembered being for many years. Life was good,
especially now that I was able to visit the other side of life.

Thoughts of Jimmy and Jonathan and of our wonderful visit warmed my heart. "Oh, Jimmy and Jonathan," I whispered into the darkness. "I'll be back soon. First, I have an important book launch party to attend to—at Ashton Villa. With my sister, would you believe it?"

I knew they'd be pleased. I wondered if they'd heard me.

The next few weeks were filled with planning the big book launch party. Veronica and I were on the phone almost daily working out details. Sometimes we met for coffee or dinner. I couldn't remember a time when we'd been closer. Finally the big evening arrived.

Of course, she'd seen to it that the event was well advertised in The Daily News. When I arrived at Ashton Villa, wearing Isabella's freshly laundered black Victorian dress, I was met by one of their reporters and a photographer.

"Tell me about your lovely dress," a reporter stopped me on the doorstep.

"It belonged to my Great-Grandmother, Isabella. It was her wedding dress. She later died in the Great Storm of 1900."

"And your new book about that tragic storm? I hear it is generating rave reviews."

"Why, thank you. Yes, my book offers a unique perspective of the storm, that of one of the many thousands who lost their lives that fateful day. I must acknowledge and thank Isabella for providing the inspiration that made it all possible."

You are indeed welcome, my dear, Isabella's words slipped silently into my mind. *Lovely dress, if I do say so myself!*

I grinned. She was there. I knew she would be. Glancing around, I caught a glimpse of her sitting by the fountain surrounded by people who had no idea she was there.

Veronica hugged me when I walked through the door. Heavenly harp music filled the Gold Room. Candles flickered in the waning light, reflected in the ornate mirrors. Servers, wearing vintage uniforms dating back to the early 1900s, mingled through the crowds, with silver trays filled with glasses of wine and tiny hors d'oeuvres.

Many of the guests were dressed in Victorian-era clothing reminiscent of the early 1900s. Many locals already had vintage clothing that they wore for the annual Dickens on The Strand Festival in early December each year.

The entire scene was a photographer's delight—right out of Dickens.

Veronica introduced me to everyone who was anyone in Galveston society—people I didn't know, but certainly knew of. Some shared their family stories about the great storm. They asked questions about my book and my writing career, treating me like a celebrity. My sister winked at me, looking as though she was actually proud of me. For once!

After the designated social hour, Veronica escorted me to an antique rocking chair by the fireplace. Beside me, there was a table with a white linen tablecloth, a vase of flowers, several flickering candles—and stacks of my new book.

The harpist quit playing and a rousing piano tune flowed from the baby grand piano. Guests began filing into the rows of chairs before me as Veronica rang her little bell to get everyone's attention. Then she introduced me.

"Thank you all for coming to this historic event. It is our great pleasure to see you all here at Ashton Villa, our childhood home, and one of the few homes that survived the Great Storm of 1900. And now I am proud and honored to introduce my dear sister, Bella Brown, the author of a fabulous book about that storm. Please welcome Bella!"

The audience began to applaud, and I felt compelled to rise from my chair and curtsy. *I did what?*

It was a surreal moment, one I'd always remember. Ashton Villa. My sister's generous words. All these people there for me, crazy Bella!

And sure enough, I spotted dear Isabella sitting on the piano bench with a huge smile lighting up her face. Of course, I was the only one who could see her. What more could I ask for?

Once again, I recognized Isabella as the source and inspiration behind my novel. I read a few highly complementary review blurbs before reading several excerpts from the book. As I read the chapter about Isabella drowning in the storm, I watched my audience hanging onto every word, hanging onto their chairs, eyes wide with the horror of that tragic night. They were there with me, with Isabella, reliving the experience.

I then closed my presentation, thanking them for coming and inviting them to pick up a copy of my book. I was humbled at their almost thunderous applause and a standing ovation. Some had tears in their eyes after my last reading.

I signed books for almost an hour afterwards, while a small orchestra played in the background and people mingled throughout the room with their drinks. Veronica had lined someone up to sit at the table with me and handle the book sales. People were buying multiple copies — for friends, family members, and organizations they belonged to. Thankfully, I'd brought along several extra crates of books. I figured I'd sold close to two hundred books by the end of the evening.

"Tonight will go down in my memory as one of the best nights of my life," I confessed to Veronica as we collapsed together side by side on the davenport. The last guest had just left. The staff was busily cleaning up after the party. "I can't thank you enough." My eyes filled with tears.

181

"You are very welcome, Bella." She wiped a tear from her eyes. "This—being together with you again after so many years—means a lot to me."

"And to me." We shared a genuine hug before finishing our glasses of wine. It was time for me to head home to my cottage by the sea. "See you tomorrow for breakfast, my treat, at The Mosquito Cafe?"

"Yes, say ten-ish?"

"Perfect."

I was basking in the glory of the evening as I drove along the Seawall out towards the west end of the island. The entire event had been perfect—more than perfect. Life was good, I decided, better than it had been in many years. My mind replayed moments from this evening.

I was lost in thought, grinning to myself, when a truck suddenly screeched out from a major intersection, shooting through a red light, speeding directly towards me. *Oh my God! Help!* I cried out as I tried to veer out of its path.

Yellow truck. Screeching tires. Black Victorian dress. Feelings of déjà vu washed over me. I knew this scene, this intersection. I knew what was going to happen, because it had all happened before somehow.

Veering wildly towards the sea, trying to escape from this out-of-control truck, I suddenly felt the crushing impact of the truck slamming into my car. Breaking glass. Searing pain shooting through my body as the front end of the car caved in upon me. Then everything went black.

At some point—hours, days, or weeks later…I had no clue—I became aware of waking up in a hospital bed somewhere. Tubes of all kinds were attached to my body as the steady hum and beep of machines surrounded me.

I could hear, but I could not talk. I could not open my eyes. I could not move. I had no idea what had happened to me.

Was I alone? Was I alive?

Your time. It is almost your time, Isabella whispered into my mind, surrounding me with a profound feeling of comfort and peace. *I am here for you, my dear.*

So I was dying? Dying alone on Earth? But I'd be in Heaven soon, wouldn't I?

I heard a door open and the sound of footsteps. Then a male voice approaching my bedside.

"I'm so sorry, Mrs. Caldwell. I'm Dr. Foster, and I'm afraid the news is not good about your sister."

"Is she...is there any way?" Veronica's voice broke down. She was close by, right beside my hospital bed. I could sense her presence.

"As you know, she suffered a severe traumatic brain injury in the accident. The MRI revealed significant bleeding of the brain, as well as a skull fracture. Her brain has swelled significantly, resulting in extremely high intracranial pressure. This has become a life-threatening situation, I'm afraid. Our only hope is to perform a decompressive craniectomy procedure to remove a large section of bone so the brain has more room to swell."

"OK, let's do it. Anything," Veronica pleaded.

The doctor cleared his throat. "Unfortunately, I must recommend against it. Her other injuries are too severe to operate. Her condition does not support the stress and risk involved. We would most likely lose her on the operating table."

Veronica's voice cracked. She was crying as the doctor tried to comfort her. "So...so what do we do now? Just let her die? What if there's a miracle of some kind and she comes out of this?"

"You need to know that if that happened somehow, her

brain function would still be seriously impaired for the rest of her life. She would not be able to lead a normal life, to take care of herself. She would need round-the-clock care, most likely a nursing home. I'm so sorry."

"How much time does she have?" my sister whispered as if she did not have the strength to speak out loud.

"Judging from her deteriorating vital signs, I'd say she will probably pass very soon. It could be only hours, Mrs. Caldwell. You may want to take some time to tell your sister goodbye. She may be able to hear you, or to at least know you are here with her."

The pathetic sound of Veronica's sobbing almost broke my heart. How I longed to speak to her. I needed to tell her something. I sensed that the good doctor was giving her a hug, holding her hand and sitting beside her in her grief. All was silent except for the steady beeping of the machines trying to keep me alive.

"Can I have my nurse call one of your children to come and be with you?" he asked gently. "I know Melanie was just here, and both Michael and Maria have also spent a lot of time here with you over the last week."

"Yes, please. And thank you. I need a little time first by myself. I need to tell her goodbye," she mumbled weakly. Then, the sound of the doctor's footsteps retreated slowly down the hall.

"Oh, Bella." Veronica reached for my hand and held it. I could feel it, but could not respond. "I love you and I'd give anything for you to get through this. But it doesn't look good. I don't know if you can hear me, but...but...." More tears as she choked on her words. "I'm sorry I wasn't the best sister to you for so many years. Why now? Why do you have to die now, when we've finally made peace?"

I wanted so badly to respond. Gathering all the strength I

184

could muster, I opened my mouth to try to speak. She startled. She was listening, waiting. But all I could do was try to project thought images into her mind.

I suddenly found my voice, shocking myself. It was weak. My words were slow, disjointed, but I could speak! "Me...you... love," I whispered hoarsely. "Want...forgive...me?"

"Oh my God, you can speak! Maybe you will get better!! But...forgive? What? You want me to forgive you? For what?"

I was spent and could not formulate any more words. I sensed she was waiting, wanting so much for me to continue.

"Whatever it is, I forgive you, Bella."

I was exhausted. Isabella was there waiting to escort me home. One lingering thought still consumed my mind. Something important that I needed to find a way to communicate to my sister before I left this world.

Help me, Isabella. Help me tell my sister what I need to.

What I wanted to tell her was that the problems we'd had most of this lifetime may be the result of unresolved issues from a previous life we'd shared. I wanted to tell her to keep an open mind. Maybe we could figure this out together somehow, across that bridge that would soon span our worlds.

I was slipping away. It's almost time, I thought to myself.

Suddenly, Veronica broke the silence. "Very strange. A very strange thought just popped into my mind. Something about us having unresolved issues from a previous lifetime we'd shared. And that may be why we had so much conflict. Something about me keeping an open mind so we could both understand what had happened. Is that what you want of me, Bella? If it is, I will do so. Anything, my dear sister."

If I could have smiled, I would have. Thank God for Isabella. I didn't know she had the power to climb into Veronica's mind as well as my own. Or, perhaps, she did this for me and through me.

185

Slipping farther and farther away, I became vaguely aware of the sounds of monitors beeping all around my bedside. Footsteps of nurses rushing into the room. My sister crying as she held my hand, trying to tell the doubting nurses, in between her sobs, that I'd spoken to her. They didn't believe her.

I was flatlining, rising above my broken body. Isabella was with me, leading me towards the most glorious light I'd ever seen. I was swirling through a tunnel of love, peace, and comfort. I was going home.

SEVENTEEN
BELLA

*"I look upon death to be as necessary to the constitution as sleep.
We shall rise refreshed in the morning."*
Benjamin Franklin

Once again I found myself perched on the winding marble steps of the Hall of Wisdom. Free of my body, healthy once more, I sighed with relief.

Something was different this time, far different from my previous visit. This time I wasn't just visiting. I was here for good, until someday when I'd probably choose to reincarnate for another bout with earthly struggles. More lessons to learn.

For now, I was overjoyed at the prospect of being there. Opening my eyes, my gaze fell upon three figures swooping in, their arms open to welcome me home. Jonathan. Jimmy. After sharing warm embraces with them both, I turned my attention to the third figure, advancing more slowly, as if still trying to figure out how things worked here in Heaven.

It was my mother, Olivia. But she looked so good, so much better than her last years on Earth.

"Oh, Mother, it's so good to see you. Are you well?" I hugged her closely.

187

"Better than ever, Bella. My memory is back. I've never been happier, although I must say I miss you and Veronica and all the children. But I have my Jonathan back." She giggled as she reached up to tousle his hair the way she had when he was a little boy. "You simply must come visit my new home," Olivia insisted. "Now, please? You're going to love it!" I hadn't seen her this excited in many years.

I searched for Isabella, not sure if this was appropriate or if there was something else I needed to do first. After all, I'd just arrived.

Isabella suddenly materialized beside me. "Go on, my dear. It means a great deal to your mother. I'll be around to help you later. I'll find you." Then she was gone.

"See you back at my place?" Jimmy's eyes searched mine. "Our place, Sa Bella?"

"Our place," I agreed. I had no desire to create my own home here in Heaven. Jimmy had already created the perfect place for us. A place of our own. Finally.

My mother and I suddenly arrived in a quaint little village tucked into beautiful mountainous terrain. Cozy Victorian-style homes were scattered here and there. The ground was covered with a blanket of pure white snow, and snowflakes fell gently around us. Amazingly, however, it was not cold. There was no need for a coat or hat or snow boots.

Children skated on frozen ponds. Villagers strolled along streets lit with gas lamps as they visited dime stores, restaurants, ice cream shops, and vintage clothing stores. The women wore long Victorian dresses with bonnets, some carrying parasols.

"It's like you've all stepped back in time, Mother, back to the Victorian era," I exclaimed.

"Precisely. Do you like it?"

"I love it. It reminds me of the days Isabella and her parents lived in."

"Except we have snow. I always wanted snow — and mountains," Olivia sighed wistfully. "Come, let's stroll down the main street before we visit my home."

She led me by the arm, greeting her new friends along the way. The entire village seemed to be decorated for Christmas. There were dancing lights, giant candy canes, fresh evergreen boughs trimmed with red velvet ribbons, Christmas trees decorated with strings of popcorn, red berries, and candles flickering in the pastel hues of evening.

Children happily flocked into an assortment of toy stores — stores where there did not seem to be any such thing as computers or technological devices. There were lots of books. Wooden rocking horses. Marbles. Jacks. Sleds and old-fashioned ice skates. Board games, decks of cards. And penny candy of every possible variety, ranging from black licorice to jaw breakers to jelly beans.

We walked towards the edge of the tiny village and turned down a winding lane leading towards Olivia's home. Candles flickered through frosted window panes, reflecting upon the brilliant white snow. The little yellow house was tucked into a cluster of majestic snow-laden evergreens.

As we followed the brick path — which had no snow accumulation whatsoever, despite the snowflakes swirling around us — I heard Christmas music drifting out from the house. Why was I not surprised?

"You've always loved Christmas, haven't you?" I squeezed her arm.

"Always. But wait, you haven't seen anything yet." She proudly opened her front door and led me into a magical snow scene unlike anything I'd ever before seen, or even imagined. The snowy, rolling landscape was filled with Christmas houses, churches, and buildings flickering in the darkened room. Choirs sang. Children skated on ponds.

"What do you think?" she asked. I was too stunned to speak. My mother had recreated the snow village she'd had on Earth. But she'd made it into a true wonder. It seemed to be alive.

Wandering around, I found a replica of Grandma's Cottage, her very favorite piece back on Earth. "Grandma's Cottage!" I exclaimed as tears of joy filled my eyes. "Oh Mother, this is incredible! You really outdid yourself."

Mother looked pleased. "Now you know why I simply had to show it to you. And to think that I was able to do this just through my thoughts."

"I'm proud of you," I smiled as I hugged her close. "And so happy to see you again."

It felt like the differences between us during our recent lives together had suddenly disappeared in this magical place. Unconditional love seemed to flow here.

Mother treated me to Christmas cookies fresh out of the oven. She still liked to bake here, she said, even if she could create her cookies without going through all those steps. And she was happy, she assured me. Someday, she'd take me to see our other deceased relatives who were waiting to greet me. For now, she realized I had to get back to the business of orientation to my new home.

"I assume you're staying at Jimmy's?" Her eyes twinkled.

My mouth dropped open. Did she know? Did she approve? After all, Veronica had been his wife on Earth. And Veronica had always been her favorite daughter...not me.

"It's all right, Bella. I finally understand. He is your soul mate. You and Veronica had some differences to work through. Someday you will figure it all out. The life review machine will give you the answers you need, and will give you both peace."

With that, I was gone. All I had to do was think myself to

Jimmy's and I was there. He was sitting out on the porch playing his guitar when I walked up the path. Hopefully, we'd have a little time together by ourselves before Isabella came to orient me to my new home.

By the time I walked up the steps to the porch, I saw Isabella materialize and perch upon the railing. I sighed, "Already, Isabella? Can't I just rest for a bit?"

"As you wish," she sighed. "I will meet you at the Hall of Wisdom first thing in the morning. You will know when that is. We need to get you into the life review machine, my dear." Then she was gone.

As she'd promised, I awoke the next morning, knowing it was time. I reluctantly pulled myself from Jimmy's arms and prepared for my day of discovery.

"Sa Bella," he whispered sleepily. "You may discover some things that you do not like. Things you will need to ponder to make any sense of. That's the way it is here. We can talk when you get home. Just remember that I love you."

That's strange, I thought to myself. What was he concerned about my discovering?

"Ahhh, I know this place," I sighed wistfully as Isabella and I settled upon a bench in the sacred Hall of Wisdom. "I've been here before, haven't I?"

Many times, every time you come back home. Isabella infused her thoughts into my spirit mind.

Magnificent pillars of iridescent marble surrounded me. Pastel lights representing all the colors of the rainbow streamed into the room through the huge glass dome that dominated the center of the building.

Below that dome, bathed in heavenly light, the life review

machine awaited me. It was a glowing convex dome of soft blue glass.

A sense of apprehension began to creep over me as I vaguely remembered being here before. I recalled walking around that machine, using my all-knowing spirit eyes, as I watched all the events of my past life playing out before my eyes. It was like a three-dimensional movie that I could stop and rewind, playing certain parts over and over again until they made some sense. I could see every moment — good, bad, or ugly. I understood what I did right and what I did wrong. And I also became aware of the impact my actions made on other people in my life.

Of course I already knew what I'd done wrong. I'd fallen in love with the man who was to be my sister's husband. I'd spent one, only one, night in his arms — and had a child by him. I never quit loving Jimmy. Consumed with jealousy, I'd treated my sister horribly — until the very end, when we reconciled. Veronica still didn't know any of this...although she had once suspected.

It was time to face the music, as my mother always used to say. Taking a deep breath, I walked towards the huge machine and peered intently into its depths. Immediately, images began to swirl before my eyes — images of my life. Every moment had been captured in time, every emotion, every reaction of others who had been a part of my past life. I could feel how they felt, could experience what they thought.

But what about things they never knew? What about the secret I'd kept hidden from the world? And why had I done what I'd done? Why had Jimmy?

Isabella suddenly materialized beside me, gently taking my hand and leading me away from the life review machine. "Yes, you do need to know why you did what you did, Bella," she spoke softly. "Why you all played the roles you did in this lifetime. You will understand when we visit the Hall of Records. Come."

She led me through fragrant gardens filled with lush flowers, bubbling fountains, and marble statues to a large building beside the Hall of Wisdom. A breath-taking dome soared above the countryside. The building was of classic Greco-Roman design with towering marble columns.

The Hall of Records, she told me, contained every historical work ever written, including any that had been destroyed on Earth. It also contained every blueprint, or chart, we'd written for all our lives on Earth. The scrolls were all in Aramaic, the universal language which we were all fluent in here.

Here, Isabella informed me, I could study my past life charts, as well as those of others who'd played parts in my past lives. I could essentially merge with those charts, assimilating emotions and senses of past lives. This way, I could begin to figure out conflicted relationships from my past lives.

"Sometimes, karma and unfinished business carry over from one lifetime into another," Isabella whispered, "as I suspect it did between you, Veronica, and Jimmy. But let's start with your most recent life."

Stepping into the hall, I found myself surrounded by endless aisles of shelves filled with scrolls. They filled the walls from floor to ceiling. All I had to do, according to Isabella, was think the name of the chart I wished to review and the approximate date. It would then materialize in my hands.

Settling upon a marble bench, I began my search. First, I reviewed the unbelievably detailed life chart I'd created for myself before I was born into my last life. I also reviewed Jimmy's and Veronica's. Things began to make some sense.

Although it was a lot of information to digest, I felt compelled to reach back to the lifetime I'd lived before this past one. Isabella helped me to access that lifetime since I, of course, had no clue what my name may have been or when I'd lived.

193

This time, however, vivid images began to infiltrate my spirit mind. First, an image of two young ladies wearing long Victorian-style dresses. They were standing on the stairs of an impressive Romanesque-style Brownstone building with a tall clock tower protruding high into a blue sky. The girls were smiling, arms wrapped around each other's waists as though they were the best of friends.

I gasped. "Veronica and I? Friends in another lifetime?" Of course, we didn't look the same, but I instinctively knew. My spirit recognized us. "If we were such good friends, what happened?"

Then, an image of a man and woman together, a wedding photo, taken beside the sea. They wore old-fashioned clothing reminiscent of the 1800s. In fact, the woman's dress looked somewhat like Isabella's black wedding dress.

"Who?" I gasped. "Me...and...and Jimmy? We were married?" I knew beyond a doubt that this was us, together, in a past lifetime, as husband and wife. Again, while our appearances were not the same as in our last life, I could feel the spiritual connection.

"Precisely," Isabella replied. "And I have one more to show you. One you may not care to see...."

I closed my eyes, heart pounding. I wasn't sure I wanted to see the next image. But, of course, it did no good to try to block my spirit eyes from seeing and absorbing this dreadful image. My blood began to boil, or it would have had I still been alive in human form.

There before me was an image of the girl I'd just identified as Veronica—and the young man I'd identified as Jimmy—together. They stood beside a large sea cluttered with steamships and sailboats. Their arms were wrapped around each other and they beamed into each other's eyes, obviously deeply in love. She was dressed rather skimpily for the times, I thought, and her long mane of hair was loose, flying in the wind off the lake. She wasn't even wearing a hat.

"Jimmy and Veronica together? But...but he was *my* husband!" I cried out.

Isabella just looked at me, waiting patiently for me to discover the irony of it all.

"So...." I tried to compose myself. "Which came first? Were Jimmy and I married after he'd been involved with Veronica?"

"I'm afraid not. They became involved after you'd been married for a year or so."

"So he cheated on me, his wife, with my best friend...who now happens to be my sister!"

"We all make mistakes. Sometimes our egos get in the way of staying on track with our charts and soul missions. This can create karma that needs to be dealt with in another lifetime." While I sat frozen on the cold bench, she continued. "You might want to think about anything from this lifetime that carried over into your last one. You. Jimmy. Veronica. Perhaps only the roles have changed, but the theme is the same."

"You're telling me what goes around comes around...."

I know this can be difficult at first. Isabella continued downloading her thoughts into my mind. *This is an important part of your orientation, a review of the most recent lives you've lived. It is how we learn and grow spiritually. While you identify with Bella – and Abigail – right now, and the human emotions they would have felt at a time like this, it won't be long before you align more with your eternal soul.*

I could only shake my head in disbelief. I felt her warmth and a feeling of unconditional love drifting through me. "What happens then?"

You will be operating at a much higher vibrational level, as all souls do, she smiled. *You will understand that all humans have their weaknesses. They make mistakes. It is all water under the bridge, so to speak. You will no longer feel negative human emotions like anger or hatred. Just pure unconditional love – and forgiveness.*

One could only hope, I thought to myself. For now, I felt like basking in my anger.

It's all right to feel angry – for now. It shall soon pass. Isabella sighed, reading my mind. *I think you've learned enough for today, and it is perhaps time to take a break before we meet again first thing tomorrow morning. Send for me if you need me.* She patted my hand gently before disappearing.

I found myself a bench in the garden beside a rippling brook, a serene place where I could sit a while collecting my thoughts; before I went home to confront Jimmy.

How could he? How could she?

EIGHTEEN
JIMMY

*"Spiritual evolution is part of every soul's destiny on Earth,
and each soul grows and evolves at a different rate."*
James Van Praagh

I was sitting out on the porch strumming my guitar, waiting for Bella to show up, worrying about her reaction after discovering the truth about me. I had hurt her with my reckless behavior in the past two lifetimes we'd shared. And that hurt me deeply.

I didn't even see her coming down the path this time. She usually lingered, stopping to smell and admire the wild roses, to marvel at the shimmering blue lake and lush forest surrounding her. This time she burst onto the porch, glaring at me.

"How could you?" she cried out.

"I am so sorry, Sa Bella. Please try to understand...." I rose and walked towards her. She remained rigid, her posture warning me not to get too close.

"What's to understand? You were my husband, and you had an affair with my best friend, my sister! Why? How could you?"

"I have no excuse. You did nothing wrong. You were the one I loved. I always have. I've also been searching for an answer. All I can tell you is that I'd set up a challenge in my chart for that

197

lifetime in Duluth — a challenge to test my ability to be faithful to you, my soul mate."

"Well, you sure failed, didn't you?"

"Yes, I failed. Emma just happened to be there. She was my stenographer in that lifetime. I was a lawyer, and — "

"Emma?"

"That was Veronica's name in 1895 when this happened. Her role was to attempt to seduce me, to test me. So do you want to hear more or not?"

"I can't wrap my head around this. This Emma…Veronica… my sister would never seduce anyone!" She sank into the pillows on the porch swing, swinging back and forth as fast as she could.

"No, Veronica would not. But as Emma, she played a different role. She was rather wild in that lifetime, not at all prim and proper like she is today. You saw the picture, didn't you?"

She nodded, shaking her head in disgust. "So you succumbed to your desires then, is that it? Why didn't you just walk away like any gentleman, any married gentleman, would?"

"Because…well, not to make excuses for myself, but I've learned I'm a relatively young soul, and I was having trouble controlling my ego. I was a hot shot lawyer with all the fine things in life — including my beautiful wife. You." I reached out to touch her hand. She pulled away from me and kept swinging.

"Anyway," I continued. "I always got whatever I wanted. My ego drove me to want more and more. I did have a fine blueprint for that life. But I failed the challenge I'd set for myself. My spirit guide tells me that younger souls sometimes drift away from their purpose. We use our free will, which, combined with too much ego, causes us to screw up. We end up creating more karma for ourselves, karma that has to be worked out in the next lifetime. Does that make any sense to you yet?"

She kept shaking her head, confused, trying to understand.

198

At least she was no longer glaring at me. She was beginning to soften around the edges.

"In time you will understand." I smiled at her. "You haven't been here long yet. You are still in transition. Mind if I join you on the swing?" My heart ached to see how badly I'd hurt my beloved soul mate. I was such a cad.

She moved over to make room for me and stopped the swing long enough for me to settle in. She scooted over to the far end, however, leaving plenty of space between us. We swung together in silence.

Finally she spoke. "What about the karma you created for yourself? How does that fit into our last lifetime?"

I sighed, touching her hand gently, feeling the sparks between us before she abruptly pulled away.

"I paid the piper, as Olivia would say. I wasn't able to have you for my wife last time around. Yes, we connected and had many wonderful times together. We even produced a son together, a wonderful son. But I could never claim you as my wife."

"So you cheated on my sister this time around instead?"

"Not exactly. You and I never slept together after I married Veronica. I honored my commitment—well, in a way. But my heart always belonged to you. And I longed to be with you. That was my punishment. I couldn't have you the way I wanted you. But...." I paused, unsure how to proceed.

"But what?"

"But I wound up hurting you, Sa Bella. You paid for my karmic debt. You wanted to be with me as much as I wanted you. You and me and our little boy. We belonged together as a family. Instead, you carried the burden of giving birth out of wedlock. No father in the picture. How the islanders must have gossiped about that. God, I'm sorry."

199

"I was the one who refused to marry you, remember? You asked me to marry you the day before you married my sister. And I was the one who refused to tell you that you were Jonathan's father. So maybe we both screwed up, as you say."

I sighed. Hopefully, she would forgive me after all.

"What does this karma thing mean for our future, Jimmy?"

"I'm not sure yet. Not completely. I have another sixty—maybe a hundred or more years in Earth time—to figure that out. As do you. All I know is that I still owe you, my darling. Next time around, we will get it right. Please forgive me?"

I put my arm around her and drew her close, basking in the scent of roses that she always wore.

"I forgive you," she finally sighed, and fell into my arms. We held each other for a long time, swinging slowly, silently.

Later in the evening, we decided to go for a walk by the lake with our fishing poles. We'd catch some nice walleye for dinner. Yes, she still loved to cook "real food," as she put it, instead of producing our meals through projected thought.

Over dinner, she grew quiet and began to frown. "Veronica." She shook her head sadly. "What am I going to do about this Emma person who betrayed me? She, Veronica in this lifetime, sure doesn't seem to be working off any karma to make up for what she did to me as Emma. She's got the perfect life!"

"Are you sure about that? Sure, she's got a wonderful family—children and grandchildren. But do you really think she was happy with our marriage? I don't. We pretty much lived separate lives, you know. She never really had me as her husband."

"That may be true. I'm struggling with my desire to get even with her for what she did."

"Perfectly normal human reaction." I shook my head. "But Bella, she doesn't know what she did. I'm willing to bet she has no clue about the life she lived as Emma."

"That's it, Jimmy. Maybe she needs to know. Maybe she needs to take responsibility for what she did. She needs to feel the pain, to know how she hurt me. If only I can find a way to show her what she did."

"Will that help her in this lifetime? God, I sound like my spirit guide." I almost laughed.

"Well, maybe it will. Maybe she can start working off bad karma from her Emma lifetime. Besides, she promised me on my death bed that she would be open to the possibility that our conflict stemmed from a past life. I need to find a way to get her to one of those past life regression therapists."

"Why do you care? Does she really need to know?"

She sighed. "Despite what she's done, she's still my sister this time around. I want her to understand why we didn't get along for so long. I owe her that," she said softly.

I couldn't help but grin. After all the feuding these sisters had done most of their lives—and granted, I was probably much of the reason—now, all of a sudden, they seemed to love each other again.

"What's so funny?"

"I'm just surprised that you and Veronica made up before you died. Maybe the two of you worked off some of that bad karma by doing so. After all that has happened between you, you still care about her, don't you?"

She had to admit that she did. "I'm beginning to think that the three of us have been together in many lifetimes."

"She is most likely one of the closest spirits in our soul group. I suspect we will be together, the three of us, in another lifetime."

"Interesting idea. For now, I need to come up with a plan to project some images into Veronica's mind—the ones I saw today in the Hall of Records. And I need to convince her to see one of those therapists. I'd love to know what she discovers."

"Hmmm...I don't know how to do that. I'm still a newbie here, remember? Not as new as you, obviously. How long have I been here?"

"Time really doesn't matter much here, does it? You died last Christmas, Jimmy, about eleven months ago, Earth time." Her voice was soft, wistful.

"I'm so glad you're here, Sa Bella. Isn't being dead a wonderful thing?"

"It's so strange. I feel like we are more alive than we've ever been. Once I get through this orientation, I'm going to love it. It's just the secrets from the past that throw me for a loop, you know?"

"Believe me, I know. But we soon make peace with it all. We see our mistakes and problems as learning experiences. And we move on."

"As for Veronica, I have a feeling my dear spirit guide Isabella will be able to help me get through to her."

As she spoke, I glanced over my shoulder to watch Isabella materialize. She was smiling at Bella, who grinned back at her.

"Thanks, Isabella," she whispered. "That's perfect!"

"What's perfect? What did she say or project into your mind?"

"She's happy that we made up. And yes, she will help me get through to Veronica. We start tomorrow morning, when we meet in the gardens of the Hall of Justice."

NINETEEN
VERONICA

"I believe that the soul of man is immortal and will be treated with justice in another life, respecting the conduct in this life."
Benjamin Franklin

I still couldn't believe Bella was gone. One minute we were hosting her book launch party — one of the best and most memorable days of her life, she told me. We'd hugged each other goodbye, planning to meet for breakfast the next morning.

I'd been relaxing in my favorite chair by the fireplace with a good book later that night after she left, wrapped in a cozy afghan, when someone knocked on my door. Who could possibly be calling at this hour? I wasn't expecting company. Peering out through the peep hole, I was puzzled to see two police officers standing there with solemn looks upon their faces. Something was wrong, very wrong.

"Please come in," I opened the door, my heart pounding. "What's wrong? Has something happened?"

"Let's sit down, Mrs. Caldwell." One of the officers gently steered me back to my chair. "I'm so sorry to have to tell you this," he began, "but your sister, Bella, has just been seriously injured in an automobile accident. She's been rushed to the hospital."

That's all I remember about that dreadful night. They say my face turned white as a ghost and I passed out. When I came to, I found my children fluttering around me, tears in their eyes. We immediately left for the hospital, and I stayed at her bedside most of those hellish days—until she took her last breath.

Everything was pretty much of a blur after that. I couldn't focus on the details of what had happened. I was no help at all planning Bella's funeral. Thank God my children had their wits about them, and took care of everything for me.

How could she be dead? Bella, who had been so full of life, so full of energy. How could I have lost my only sister when I'd just found her again after so many years?

Why, God? I cried out over and over again as I tossed and turned in bed at night, or sat out by the fountain in my garden trying to absorb the healing power of the nature that surrounded me. Why was life so unfair?

The birds still chattered. The sun still cast a blanket of warmth upon me, trying to thaw the chill that consumed my soul. My flowers still bloomed beautifully, as if life somehow went on. Without Bella. Without Jimmy. Without my mother.

I spent the next few weeks rattling around my big lonely house. I declined a number of invitations for dinner, from my family and some of my acquaintances. I didn't even attend my usual committee meetings.

What was life all about, anyway? Loved ones died and went away. It had been a year from hell. I'd lost my husband, my mother, and my sister, in less than a year. Thank God, I still had my wonderful children and grandchildren. Still, a part of me seemed to be missing these days.

I thanked God that I'd had the opportunity to reconcile with Bella before she died. Something had tugged at my heart, urging me to do so. Had I known on a sub-conscious level that she was

204

going to die? She'd been in good health. Whoever would have thought she'd die in such a tragic way?

I wasn't sleeping well at night. My mind was spinning with "what if" scenarios. What if she'd spent the night here instead of driving home? What if she'd taken another route? What if the drunk who hit her had not been released from jail recently? What if…?

I'd eventually fall into something like a twilight sleep and begin to dream. But these were not normal dreams. They were so vivid, so real. I seemed to be living and breathing these surreal dreams. I was there.

It was the same dream, the same old-fashioned images, night after night.

It always began with a faded sepia-toned image of two young women standing on the steps of an ornate stone building with a huge clock tower looming up into the sky. The ladies wore long dresses, hats, and gloves reminiscent of the Victorian era of the late 1800s. Snowflakes swirled around the two. They smiled at each other, arms locked around each other's waists. Good friends, I assumed.

The disturbing part was that I identified strongly with the young woman on the left. She wasn't as well dressed as the girl on the right, not as proper. She didn't look a great deal like me, but I almost felt that we were one and the same. When I focused on those eyes, I could almost feel her inviting me into her world. Our world. It was eerie.

I'd struggle to escape from the haunting image, sometimes waking up shivering as an unnatural chill seeped through my body. But soon, the dream would reclaim me.

I didn't relate as strongly to the next image. It was a picture of a Victorian era bride and groom, standing amongst rock formations beside a sea. Steamships and sail boats dotted the landscape behind them. The bride looked almost like the girl in the first image, the one on the right. The groom…I had trouble focusing on him. I kept turning away in my dreams, unable to make myself look at him. I did not want to see his face.

I transitioned easily into the final image. It was a photo of a young couple, arms around each other, beaming at each other. Very much in love. I could almost feel their emotions. It was the girl on the left again, the one I identified with so strongly. But this time her hair flew freely in the wind. She wore no hat, and had traded her proper long dress in for a short one that revealed her legs. And she was barefoot. Shocking, I thought to myself.

The man in the picture? I felt a strong sense of familiarity with him also, as if I should know him. I couldn't figure out why. Something kept me from knowing, a part of me that did not want to know, perhaps.

As the three images faded away into the recesses of my mind, I'd feel angry waves washing over me, battering me against large boulders in a frigid sea. *Help me*, I'd scream into the darkness as I struggled to the surface, over and over again, only to be pulled back down into the depths of the sea. Finally, I went under for the last time. The fight was over.

I'd awaken in a sweat, thrashing around in my bed. Trying to come back to reality.

One day I called Maria and told her what I'd been experiencing. She was concerned, and tried to assure me that it was probably a delayed reaction to Bella's death, on top of Jimmy's and Olivia's. But she did want me to see one of her psychotherapist friends. Of course, as a reputable psychiatrist, Maria had many contacts, and was able to get me in to see a Dr. Vandershoot the next day.

As I waited in his comfortable reception room, sleep deprived and nervous, I glanced up at a wall displaying the good doctor's credentials. He was also a past life regression therapist, I noticed.

That triggered a memory of my last conversation with Bella, just before she died. Something about our current conflicts being the result of unfinished business from a previous lifetime? I'd assured her I would be open to that possibility.

What did that mean? And why had I ended up here, with a therapist who delved into past lives? Was this my destiny, or just a coincidence? As I pondered my dilemma, I was called into the doctor's office.

His kind smile immediately put me at ease. He wasn't judging me, just listening, nodding, encouraging me to continue telling my story.

"I know this sounds really crazy," I began to apologize, wringing my hands.

"Nothing is crazy. Everything happens for a reason. If you can share what is happening, we can work together to figure this out. I've been there, Mrs. Caldwell. I know how you feel. I want you to proceed at your own pace, whatever you are comfortable with. There is no rush. No pressure. Let's take a few deep breaths. Relax."

He closed his own eyes and breathed deeply, in and out. I found myself following his lead. His voice was soft and soothing as he guided me into a relaxed state.

"Now, are you feeling a little better?" He opened his eyes.

I soon found myself spilling my guts, somehow trusting this professional with secrets I'd never dream of sharing with one of my friends. I told him about my dreams, about losing Bella, Jimmy, and my mother in less than a year.

He assured me that most people would be struggling after all I'd gone through. Then he just waited. Waited for me to speak again. I listened to the methodical ticking of the grandfather clock.

Something compelled me to ask the question lurking in my mind. "Do you think these dreams, and the conflicts I had with my sister for most of our lives, could have anything to do with a past life?"

He smiled, nodding his head. "It is entirely possible. If you would like to pursue a past life regression, we may discover the answer to that. I've done this for many people, and it has made a difference in many lives. It is entirely up to you, Mrs. Caldwell."

He assured me that I'd be safe as I explored another lifetime, that I could come back any time I wanted to, or I could go into an observer position instead of experiencing the emotions I was dealing with. I'd still be aware of what was going on basically, one foot in each lifetime. He would guide me and pull me out himself if he thought it was best for me.

I couldn't believe I was actually going to do this...but I'd promised Bella, hadn't I? And I certainly did not want to continue dreaming those disturbing dreams.

I settled into a comfortable leather recliner in Dr. Vandershoot's office. Soft classical music played in the background. The shades were drawn to create a relaxing atmosphere. After listening to the music in silence for a few minutes, his soothing voice began urging me to close my eyes, to relax.

"Breathe in. Breathe out. Slowly...." He paused. "You can feel your body becoming more and more relaxed. A warm, positive feeling is starting to flow over and through your body, from the top of your head, going down, slowly, slowly, down towards your toes."

I felt myself relaxing as he waited.

"We will soon begin counting backwards from five to zero,

slowly. Very slowly. As we count down, you will feel yourself going deeper and deeper. You will be descending down a golden spiral staircase into the recesses of your unconscious mind. At the bottom of these heavenly stairs, you will find yourself stepping into a past lifetime. One that will help you to understand your current lifetime."

My eyes were getting heavy. My hands fell limply onto my lap. I was still here, in my doctor's office, but I felt a part of me beginning to drift away.

"Five. You are comfortable. Secure. Sinking deeper and deeper into a state of total relaxation. You can feel the warmth, the love, flowing through your body.

"Four. You may feel yourself drifting back in time, further and further back in time.

"Three. You are relaxed and comfortable and safe. You are looking forward to this past life experience.

"Two. You may have the sensation of floating out of your body as you go back in time. It is a good feeling. You will soon be able to experience this past life with all your senses.

"One. You are almost there. You will be able to step into a past life at count zero. You are still in control, and can move away from any image that is uncomfortable for you.

"Zero. You are there. Your unconscious mind is ready and open to receive memories from your soul. Take some time to adjust to your surroundings. Breathe it in. Feel it. Smell it. Hear it."

I could still hear his soothing voice penetrating my consciousness as I slipped into another world, the world I'd recently seen in my dreams.

"I'm here," I heard my voice exclaim.

"It's all right. Let's go slowly. Can you describe where you are?"

"Why, yes, I'm back in my dreams! I'm.... I'm...." I had to pause to focus on the information streaming into my subconscious mind. "I'm in Duluth, Minnesota, my hometown. I'm standing beneath the clock tower on the grounds of our new high school, Central High School. It is a magnificent brownstone structure overlooking Lake Superior."

"What are you wearing?"

"A long dress and shawl. Hat and gloves. Button shoes. What we wear to school every day."

"Do you have any idea what year it is?"

I had to think hard. Suddenly, the answers came flooding into my mind. "It's 1893, and I will graduate from high school this year. Then I shall go to stenographer school, so I can help to support my mother and siblings. Daddy died, and we need the money."

"Can you see a name on your diploma? What is your name?"

"My name is Emma. Emma McDougall."

"Emma, you are doing very well. Do you see anybody that you know?"

I searched the crowd milling around the beautifully landscaped courtyard as a gentle breeze from the lake lifted my skirt. "There she is, my best friend. Yes, the same girl in that photo with me! Abigail, I'm over here."

"Abigail, your best friend...."

"Oh yes, she is my blood sister. We swore we will do anything for each other. Someday we will have a double wedding. She is of a higher social class than I am, so her wedding dress will probably be nicer than mine...." My voice trailed off.

"That's all right. I'm sure you will still be a beautiful bride someday."

Something made me freeze. Perhaps the mention of me being a bride? That disturbed me.

Apparently the doctor picked up on this. "Everything is fine. Remember, you can step back and observe anytime you choose. Perhaps we should move on to another moment in this lifetime, one that it is important for you to understand. Let me know when you're there. Take your time."

I smiled somewhat flirtatiously, unlike my usual persona as Veronica. "I'm at work in my office."

"Where is that?"

"I work on the lower level of a narrow three-story stone building here in Duluth. It has a turret and carved arches over the tall windows. There's a beautiful carved stone arch that I walk through every morning when I come to work. The date 1886 is inscribed over the entrance. That's when it was built."

"What do you do there, Emma?"

"Since I graduated—with honors, mind you—from the Graham School of Shorthand here, I came to work for the best and the brightest attorney in the entire state of Minnesota." I sighed deeply. "He is so utterly handsome, irresistible. And he pays me extremely well. He even takes me out for dinner and on secret little trips." I began to giggle like a young school girl, then stopped abruptly, shaking my head. "I'm telling you this in confidence. Others cannot know, do you understand?"

"Of course I understand. Anything you tell me will be held in strict confidence. Your secret is safe with me. Does he have a name?"

"Karl Faust."

"Can you tell me more about Karl? What is he like, Emma?"

"Sweet. Understanding. Gentle. Married!" The words shoot out of my mouth, surprising me.

"I see. Is he there now?"

Suddenly he, the man in my recent dreams, walked through the doorway of Karl Faust's law office, Jimmy's grin spreading

211

across his face when he saw me there at my desk.

Jimmy? Oh my God! I gazed deeply into this man's eyes, searching for an answer as I begin to visibly shake. There was no doubt in my mind whatsoever. This Karl from my past life was, in fact, my Jimmy!

"It can't be! No! It can't be true!"

Once again the doctor reassured me, offering to bring me back, suggesting I step back into the observer position. "Emma, you are all right. You are safe. You are learning lessons to help you in your journey through your current life. But you can come back anytime."

"No, I need to stay," I finally responded, my mind reeling. *I had an affair with a married man in this past lifetime? And ended up with him again this time around, but in a different role?*

"I need to know what happened to us, to Karl and Emma, in that lifetime," I finally announced.

"You may go there if you wish, or you may go elsewhere and come back here. It is up to you."

My unconscious mind moved me ahead, but back to the last image in my dreams. It was Karl (Jimmy) and I (Emma) on the shores of Lake Superior. So much in love. I did not fit my current prim and proper Veronica persona, however. I seemed to be defying all conventions of the Victorian era for ladylike behavior.

My mind drifted out towards the big lake. Suddenly I was slipping on an ice-covered rock and plunging into the depths of the lake on a blistery cold winter night. Waves were crashing around me. I was alone, with no one to save me. I hadn't meant to fall in. I was just out walking by the lake, trying to get some fresh air. Upset with Karl for some reason....

"What's happening, Emma?" The doctor's voice pierced my memories. "Are you all right?"

"Help! I'm drowning! God help me!" I began to sob, shivering with the cold, gulping for air, as I gripped the arms of my chair.

"Observe. Step back. You are watching now. You are not drowning." The doctor's firm voice penetrated my flashback.

I took some quick breaths, stepping back, watching the horror of my old self drowning in Lake Superior. But I could no longer feel Emma's physical reactions or emotions.

"Are you ready to leave that lifetime, Emma?" He finally broke the silence. "Can you tell me what your final observations and thoughts are?"

"Wait! I can't leave yet!" I suddenly cried out as I found myself hovering over Emma's casket at her funeral so many years ago. My funeral....

"I'm...I'm watching my funeral. There he is! Karl is here." My eyes filled with tears. "He came to bid me farewell. He looks devastated, although he is trying so hard not to show any emotion."

"Is he alone?"

I searched the little group gathered around my casket until I saw a familiar face—my old friend, Abigail, dressed in funeral black, with tears streaming down her face. She walked to Karl's side and he put his arm around my dear friend's shoulders, offering her a small degree of comfort.

"Karl, is your wife all right?" another gentleman asks, nodding at Abigail. "Perhaps she needs to sit a while."

His wife? Karl? Married to my old best friend?

"No, no, that's not possible," I blurted out, shaking my head, refusing to believe the images streaming through my subconscious mind.

"You're sure this is your old best friend?" he asked.

I could only nod, too stunned to speak. Once again we retreated into silence as my breathing slowed and I regained control of myself.

213

"Now, try to look closely through the eye of your soul. Is it possible that you know this soul, this Abigail person, in your current lifetime? Take your time. Relax."

I'll never know why he asked me that question, what prompted it. But I did what he asked. Searching Abigail's eyes, I was shocked to recognize my sister, Bella. There was no doubt in my mind. Abigail and Bella were one and the same—same soul, different lifetimes....

My head was reeling when I suddenly found myself back in the recliner in the doctor's office. I was humiliated and disgusted with my behavior as Emma. How could I have stooped so low as to have an affair with a married man? How could I have betrayed my best friend, Abigail? And how could Karl have cheated on her?

It was mind-boggling to think my friend Abigail had come back as my sister, Bella, and that my married lover Karl had come back as my husband Jimmy. Was that why Bella and I had had so much conflict this time around? Because Jimmy had been in the middle of our relationship once upon a time?

It was just too much to process. This couldn't be true. Perhaps I was only imagining it all, making it up. Perhaps I wasn't thinking clearly. I had to ask the doctor about that.

"There are several things that make me sense you did not make this up, Mrs. Caldwell," he began. "First of all, you tapped into genuine emotions. You were there. Second of all, you came up with some incredible details. Names. Dates. Places. You may want to think about a little trip to Minnesota to see if you can find any evidence to back up your past life experiences."

"Well, maybe I could do that on the Internet? Through Ancestry.com?"

"Certainly. However, it can be important sometimes to return physically to the site where you may have lived in the past. It can trigger memories. You may feel like you've been there before. Of course, you must decide what is right for you."

TWENTY
VERONICA

"Life is a succession of lessons that must be lived to be understood."
Ralph Waldo Emerson

The more I thought about it, the more obsessed I became with discovering the truth. I could not simply accept the crazy flashbacks I'd experienced in my past life regression session as being real.

I had to know if I'd actually been Jimmy's mistress in a past life. If I'd really betrayed my best friend, my own sister. I could not imagine doing that. I could not picture myself dressing like Emma did, or behaving like she did.

Maybe I did need to take a little trip to Minnesota, a place I'd never been before. At least not in this lifetime.

I sincerely hoped to discover that my recollections of a life as Emma McDougall were not true, that I'd just had some strange trip into someone else's mind. If they were true, what did that say about me?

If they were real, I owed Bella an apology...but she was dead. It seemed strange that she was the one who had asked *me* to forgive *her*, on her death bed. Something I never understood. Now, I may be the one needing her forgiveness. But it was too

216

late.

As for Jimmy, I didn't even want to think about what he had done — if he had actually done it.

Fretting about this situation wasn't doing me any good. The only solution was to book a flight to Duluth, Minnesota.

"Why in the world are you going to Duluth, Minnesota?" my children asked in unison when they came for Sunday dinner.

I didn't want to tell them what I was doing, didn't want to explain why I was going. It sounded entirely too crazy. However, I knew I had to at least let them know I was taking a little trip. They would worry if they tried to call and I wasn't home for days. Anytime I traveled, they always wanted a copy of my itinerary.

These days, they seemed to be treating me more like one of their children instead of their mother. Did they think I was taking after my mother, in the early stages of Alzheimer's disease?

"I've heard about it from some of my friends and wanted to see it, that's all. Lake Superior is supposed to be beautiful this time of year." I grimaced, recalling Emma's alleged drowning.

"There's snow there this time of year — and ice, Mother. You could fall. You don't even have any warm winter clothing." Melanie frowned.

I shivered as I recalled Emma slipping on the rocky shoreline and drowning in that lake.

"Mother? Are you listening?" Melanie's worried voice broke through my reverie. I nodded.

"Why not wait until next summer?" Maria suggested.

"Maybe we could all take a little trip up there together, when the weather is nicer," Michael suggested.

"Yes! Let's all take a trip, a trip, a trip...," my grandchildren chimed in, bouncing in their chairs.

"I want to throw snowballs!" Little Mickey pretended to toss an invisible snowball across the room.

217

"It doesn't snow in the summer, stupid." His older sister scowled at him. "Not even in Minnesota."

"That's enough, children," Michael quieted them. "Mother?"

"I'm sorry, but I need to go now. You see...." I tried to come up with a logical reason based on the research I'd already done on line. "There's an excellent performance of The Nutcracker Ballet at the Duluth Playhouse. And the historic Congdon Mansion is decorated elegantly for Christmas. I want to see it now." I dug in my heels.

"Maybe you just need a change of scenery before Christmas? And some alone time?" Maria suggested quietly. "I know the holidays will be difficult this year—the first Christmas without Daddy, or Grandma, or Aunt Bella. It's been a tough year for you, for all of us."

"Precisely." I sighed. "Of course, I'll be back in time to plan a nice Christmas for us all."

"All right," Michael sighed. "I don't like it, but if it's that important to you, I understand. Just keep us updated on where you are and what you're doing. Keep your cell phone with you at all times."

"I'm perfectly capable—" I began.

"Of course you are. Just stay in touch, all right?" Melanie also gave in. "As for Christmas, we can plan something a little different this year to make it easier for you when you return. Maybe a little side trip?"

"Or maybe our usual traditional Christmas in honor of those we've lost this year," I whispered as a tear dribbled down my cheek. "We shall see."

So I had permission, even approval, from my children. I got online that evening after they left and booked my flights and hotel. No direct flights, so I had to transfer in Minneapolis/St. Paul.

My next priority was buying a few warm clothes. Current temperatures in Duluth were averaging about twenty degrees above zero. I'd never experienced that kind of cold. With the wind chill factor and lake winds, they said it felt more like zero degrees. Unfortunately, I had a horrible time finding winter boots and warm clothing in Galveston. So I had to order several items online and have them shipped by priority express mail.

My departure day soon arrived. I was to fly out of Houston Hobby, the closest commercial airport. One of my grandchildren dropped me off at the airport on his way to a meeting in that area.

I'd been too busy preparing for my trip to spend much time mulling over my past life experiences and regretting what I may, or may not, have done in a previous lifetime as Emma McDougall. Once I was on the airplane, however, taxing down the runway, I began to worry about what I may—or may not—discover in Duluth, Minnesota. There was no turning back now.

So this was Duluth, Minnesota. The place where Emma McDougall may, or may not, have lived back in the late 1800s.

I gazed out the airplane window at a world shrouded in a fluffy blanket of white snow. The city seemed to be perched on rolling wooded hillsides overlooking an endless lake. A large ship slipped beneath the aerial lift bridge just beyond the lighthouse. Others were docked beside massive grain elevators.

"Weather's moving in, ya know," my flight companion observed. "Shipping season's about shot. Yup, they're breakin' ice to keep the lake open for the last ships comin' in. But she's gonna freeze over soon."

I'd tried hard to avoid any conversation with this gentleman sitting beside me, sometimes pretending to be asleep. My mind was too busy to converse with anyone, too busy reeling with conflicting thoughts. Was I crazy to embark upon this journey into a past that could reveal secrets I'd prefer not to know?

He looked pleasant enough, sporting a beard and wearing a red-checked flannel shirt, old jeans, and a pair of heavy insulated rubber boots. Minnesota nice….

"Have a nice visit," I dismissed him as I slipped away down the airplane aisle.

"You betcha…but I live here. Comin' home from a visit to my folks in The Cities. Have a good one yerself," he grinned at me.

Soon I was packed into my rental car, gripping the steering wheel as I drove cautiously along roads covered with a light dusting of fresh snow. There could be ice under that snow. First time for everything, I told myself. I could do this. Other drivers swerved around me, shaking their heads. The snow didn't seem to slow them down.

Following my GPS's instructions to my hotel, Comfort Suites in Canal Park, I drove along Central Entrance Street towards Lake Superior. I passed the sprawling Miller Hill Mall, numerous stores, and restaurants of all kinds. Nothing looked familiar to me. Nothing triggered any recollections of having lived here in the 1890s. None of these buildings would have even been here in Emma's day.

Maybe this whole trip was ridiculous, a waste of my time. At least I'd be able to leave here with a clear conscience, knowing that I hadn't really lived a scandalous life as Emma McDougall.

After several miles, the road began to wind down along the cliffs towards the lake. I was mesmerized by the stark beauty of massive waves crashing against the rocky shoreline, sending splays of water high into a flawless blue sky. Burgs of ice floated on the big lake sparkling in the sunlight. Several giant ships were slowly making their way into the harbor, dodging the growing pack of ice, trying to get in and out again before the lake froze over for the winter.

The closer I got to the lake below, the more my muscles tensed up. Could I have actually drowned out there as I had seen in my past life regression? I gripped the steering wheel tightly. I had to find out.

After negotiating several dead-end streets, I finally arrived on Superior Street, heading towards Canal Park. I gasped when I saw, standing directly before me, on the shores of Lake Superior, the old Brownstone Fitgers' Brewery, with its smokestack looming high into the brilliant sky.

Fitger & Company Brewers, my subconscious shouted into my mind. *Oh my God, that's where Papa worked — until the day he died!*

I began to shake as tears filled my eyes. I pulled over to the side of the road as flashbacks washed over me.

"Emma, my little pumpkin." Papa bounced me on his lap. I reached up to tug on his beard. I felt so loved by this strong but gentle man. He worked hard at the brewery to make a good living for us.

One night he didn't come home from work. Mama cried. She tried to tell us that Papa was gone someplace in Heaven and wouldn't be coming home again. We were sad, and we were hungry.

As I grew older, I wanted so much more from life. I wanted to be like my friends, especially my best friend Abigail. She was beautiful and had the most fashionable clothes of anyone in our school. But we didn't have money for things like that, no matter how hard Mama worked mending and sewing clothing for others.

The flashback suddenly disappeared and I returned to the

221

reality surrounding me. Pulling myself together, I decided I couldn't just sit here parked illegally. I needed to get to my hotel and rest a bit. I needed to block this experience from my mind for now. That's the way I'd always handled troubling situations in my life—locking my emotions away someplace deep down so I wouldn't have to deal with them.

As I slowly made my way down the street, I noticed that Fitgers' was now a shopping mall of some kind with a hotel, shops, and restaurants. The sprawling stone building was covered with dense climbing vines. I tried hard to concentrate on the road before me, afraid to look around at the buildings. Afraid I'd have more flashbacks if I did.

Finally, I turned left into Canal Park, which was right on the waterfront. My hotel room looked out over Lake Superior. I wasn't sure if that was a good idea or not. I flopped onto my bed, weary, in need of a nap. But I couldn't help gazing out the window, watching the boats and bundled-up people strolling along a boardwalk, listening to the ships blowing their horns as they approached the harbor. Eventually, I drifted off into a troubled sleep.

The sun was setting in a dazzling display over the hillside when I finally woke. The wind had calmed considerably. I decided I needed some fresh air, so I bundled up in a warm coat, hat, and gloves and walked out towards the lake. I began to stroll down the boardwalk, admiring the beauty of the sun setting over the lake. Seagulls swirled through the air above me, squawking loudly. The old lift bridge now glowed with lights dancing over the harbor as a steady green light rotated from the top of the old lighthouse.

The boardwalk and streets of Canal Park were lined with modern hotels, shops, and restaurants. There were also some very old stone buildings that called to me, tried to speak to me.

I ignored them. All I wanted to do was absorb the peace and beauty of the lake. I'd deal with my flashbacks later.

I was suddenly startled by the familiar sound of chimes resonating through the air. A chill ran through me as I gazed up towards the hillside, following the sound. A huge stone clock tower jutted into the sky above Central High School. I knew that place. I'd been there. That's where I, Emma McDougall, had graduated from high school in 1893!

My heart beat wildly as I sank down onto a bench beside the lake. I couldn't keep my eyes off that old school. I was rushing back in time, back to my life as Emma.

Mama had been so proud that day when I graduated from high school. All she ever wanted was for me to have a better life than she'd been able to give me as a single mother struggling to make ends meet. Somehow she'd saved enough money from her seamstress wages to pay for me to start stenographer school soon.

But today, my graduation day, I stood in my very best long dress on the lawn in front of our fancy new school. It was made of Minnesota Brownstone shipped to Duluth on barges from nearby rock quarries. The focal point of the large Romanesque style building was a 230 foot clock tower. It had been designed to look like London's famous Big Ben, and the chimes were programmed to sound like those at Westminster Abby.

Duluth was a prominent shipping port in those days, growing rapidly. I was one of four hundred students attending this school.

Yes, there I was, standing beside Abigail on the steps in front of the school, just like I had in my dreams. We were blood sisters, Abigail and me. We swore that nothing would ever part us, not even a man. We'd often giggled together about that.

223

As I sat there on the bench by the lake, I felt drawn to that old school. It was getting dark, but I simply had to go there. I had to find out if all of this was real, or just an illusion. I drove my car instead of walking in the dark. I'd get there faster that way.

The closer I got, the more intense the flashbacks were. Oh yes, I knew this place. I'd once loved my school and all my friends. I parked the car and got out, breathing deeply. How many times had I walked up the massive staircase to the grand entrance? Today, it was roped off to prevent intruders like me from trespassing. It looked like most of the old school had been abandoned. How sad.

Standing there by the ropes, I was mesmerized by the majestic elegance of my old school. Details began to creep into my consciousness. How I'd loved the smiling angelic cherubs carved into the stones above the entrance to the tower. And how I'd feared the grotesque animal figures beside them. Gargoyles... that's what they were called.

I had to find out if they were still there. I had to know if I'd really been here before or was simply making all of this up. I cautiously ducked beneath the rope and climbed the old stairs to the entrance. There was just enough light from the old-fashioned street lights for me to make my way up to the entrance and get a good look. Sure enough, the cherubs and gargoyles were still there lurking in the shadows, just as I remembered them.

Shivers ran through me. Had I really lived before as Emma McDougall? If not, how would I know some of these things? Why did I feel such a strong sense of having been here before?

The lights of the city danced around me as I started driving back towards my hotel in a daze. First, I decided to drive through the old part of town, down Superior and Michigan Streets. My need to discover the truth was overpowering my desire to hide from it. I was on a mission. This was no time to fall apart. I had to be strong.

As I drove along the brick-lined streets, my mind drifted back in time. I was suddenly surrounded by rutted dirt streets, horses and buggies, and a few street cars pulled by mules. Women wearing long dresses and bonnets swept past me. They were escorted by men sporting top hats, beards, and handle-bar mustaches.

On the next block, music blared from seedy old taverns. Several ladies of the night walked the streets beneath flickering gas lamps. Scantily dressed, they flirted with the sailors who'd arrived on the steamboats and were out for a night of drinking on the town.

Trying to clear my head from these haunting images of the past, I found myself slamming on the brakes at the all-too-familiar sight of the old Duluth Union Train Depot. It was an elaborate French-Norman style building with dramatic towers and steep roofs. I always thought it looked like a fairy tale castle.

Back in Emma's day, fifty trains arrived and departed daily. It was such fun to hear the train whistles signaling their arrival. We would run down to the station to watch the steam engines chugging in. Ah, those were the golden days of the railroad....

My eyes began to tear up as I remembered standing there on the platform bidding dear Abigail farewell shortly after our high school graduation. Her parents were sending her away to the University of Minnesota in Minneapolis, where she would major in liberal arts. They had big dreams for their daughter in a day and age when few girls went to college. Traditional choices for women were to get married, become a teacher or a stenographer.

I felt like I'd lost a part of myself the day Abigail went away.

225

We both cried, promising to keep in touch. We wrote each other every day for a while. She gushed on and on in her letters, telling me she'd found her soul mate and was deeply in love. This was supposed to be our secret. Her parents would disown her if they knew she had found a man already. They'd be devastated if she didn't finish college and secure an important job.

Before long, however, my dear Abigail seemed to drift away from me. Looking back, that was when I began to change, and not in a way that Mama was proud of. She didn't like the modern way I dressed. She didn't like my friends, or my frequenting various establishments without a proper escort. I had been determined to break out of my shell, to experience all that life had to offer.

"Ma'am?" A male voice broke through my reverie. Startled, I looked up to see a police officer standing beside my car window.

Yes?" I stammered, coming back to today's world.

"I didn't mean to scare you. Are you all right?"

"Yes, thank you. I'm fine."

"You can't park here, I'm afraid. There is a public lot just down the street." He smiled politely.

"Oh. I'm sorry, sir. I will move along." *What was I doing sitting in this car directly in front of a "No Parking" sign?*

"No problem. Sure you're okay?"

"Absolutely."

I waited for him to move on, then proceeded slowly down Michigan Street before turning back up onto Superior and heading towards my hotel. My stomach began to growl. I was starving, and needed to find a place to have dinner. I hadn't eaten since breakfast, and it was now almost nine in the evening.

My dinner plans screeched to a halt, however, as I was again compelled to slam on my brakes at the sight of a narrow, quaint three story stone building, with a windowed turret and carved stone arches framing tall windows that dominated the second story. The date 1886 was carved prominently onto a stone arch over the entrance.

The lower level of the building had old-fashioned windows protruding from both sides of a beveled glass door. Letters painted on the window read Lizards Art Gallery.

As I focused on the building, the words seemed to vanish. In their place, elegant gold letters in a calligraphic style sprawled across the window. The words Karl Faust, Lawyer danced before my eyes.

My head began to swim. I could barely breathe. "Oh my God! Karl!" I cried out. "Our place, you and me."

My tears began to fall as I slipped back into the year 1895. I'd graduated from my stenographer school and got my first job right here in this building. The offices were on the lower level of the building. That's where I worked for Karl's law firm. He was a brilliant young lawyer, and utterly charming.

He awakened something in me that I'd never known before. Strange, uncontrollable feelings surged through me every time he was close, every time his hand accidentally brushed mine while we were going over the briefs I'd typed for him. I found myself wanting to look especially nice for him. I wanted to make sure he noticed me in a special way. He did.

It wasn't long before we became a couple. I no longer cared about being a nice girl, one who waited until I was married to enjoy the benefits of married life. I wanted to love and be loved now, not later. After all, one never knew how long they would live. I remembered my father, who had died so young. He never saw me grow up. He left my mother alone, a widow for the rest of her life.

Perhaps one had to seize the moment when love came

knocking on the door.

I felt so loved, so cherished, by my darling Karl. I knew he loved me. He just wasn't ready for commitment, he told me. He had other obligations of which he would not speak.

When our day's work on the lower level was done, we sometimes climbed the narrow wood stairs to the upstairs suite he kept for out-of-town guests and clients. That's where we made love in the ornate canopy bed and held each other close. That's where my world felt so right, regardless of how wrong others may have found it to be.

Sometimes I'd linger on, after he'd leave for another meeting or dinner with a client. I'd stand out on the tiny circular wrought iron balcony gazing down at Lake Superior below. Listening to the sound of the waves crashing against the rocks. Relishing the feel of the wind whipping my long hair around my face.

I wore my hair long and loose those days, unwilling to roll it up into a proper bun like most of the ladies did. Karl liked it that way. He'd run his fingers through my hair, telling me how beautiful I was. He made me feel special.

I was a free spirit. I almost felt like I could fly as I spread my arms and inhaled the scent of the endless lake far below me. Sometimes I'd watch the goings-on in the red light district down by the lake. Fancy ladies of the night. Drunken sailors staggering back to their ships. So naughty. Naughty, but somehow intriguing....

I was happier than I'd ever been. Karl brought me flowers, brilliant red roses. He bought me beautiful dresses and jewelry that glittered in the dark. Sometimes he took me along on business trips to exciting destinations. I could hardly wait to become his wife someday; someday when the time was right, of course.

Then one day, my world came crashing down around me.

I was in the office alone. Karl was away at a business luncheon with a client. The bell over the door rang and a well-dressed woman sauntered in.

May I help you?" I asked her.

"Is Mr. Faust available?" She peered down at me in a superior manner, as though I was obviously not of her class.

"I'm sorry, but he is not here. May I take a message?"

"I've just arrived on the train to tend to family business," she began. "I'm only here a short while, so there is some urgency to my request. I'd dearly love to meet up with him and his lovely wife. She and I attended college together."

His wife? I thought I would faint, but I tried to pull myself together.

"Perhaps you could give me his home address so I can call on his wife?"

My face flushed. I'd never thought to ask him for his address. I'd never thought to ask him what his other obligations were, or if he was married! *Oh my God, what have I done? Karl is married?*

"I'm sorry. I don't have that information available," I mumbled, staring down at my desk, trying to hide the tears that were threatening to spill from my eyes.

She rolled her eyes at me and sighed. "Good day, then." She pivoted sharply, her long skirts swirling around her. Walking out the door, she left me in a state of utter shock.

Waves of fury began to wash over me. How could he possibly be married? To whom? I was the love of his life—at least that's what he'd told me. How could he?

Tonight, as I sat there in my rental car, gripping the steering wheel, a voice from within shouted at me to come back. Come back now!

Young Emma suddenly vanished, transforming herself into

Veronica. Sixty-five year old Veronica, sitting in a modern car gawking at a building that once again sported a window sign advertising Lizards Art Gallery. I glanced around nervously, hoping the friendly police officer wasn't tailing me. Hoping I wasn't parked illegally once again.

I took several deep breaths to clear my head as I tried to shove these dreadful memories out of my mind. I would not deal with them, not now. Still, I decided I must write down Karl's full name and the name of his law firm. I would need to check this out tomorrow when I did some research at the public library's genealogy center.

Thank God I had the ability to repress feelings and memories. I felt almost normal as I started the car once again and turned down into Canal Park. People were still out and about, dining at quaint old-fashioned restaurants or shopping. I decided I must get some dinner.

Just across the street from my hotel, I found an intriguing old brick restaurant called Grandma's Saloon & Grill. It was located at the far end of the peninsula, right beside the aerial lift bridge which was already lit up for the night.

The moment I entered the building, I knew I was in the right place, the perfect place to distract myself from things I could no longer bear to think about. Everywhere I looked, there were fascinating objects from the past. Old advertising signs and memorabilia covered the aging brick walls. Antiques hung from the ceiling, including a vintage wicker baby stroller and an elaborate metal crib. A huge elk head was mounted on one wall beside a moose head. Below, a stuffed black bear bared its teeth.

I was escorted to a table in the corner, overlooking the massive antique bar. The floors were made of old wood planking, the ceiling covered with scrolled tin tiles. Beautiful carved wood support beams were covered with black and white photos of Duluth long ago. The lights from the aerial bridge outside shimmered through stained glass window hangings.

It was hard to concentrate on the menu when there was so much to see. Directly beside me was a large wood statue of an Indian chief, complete with a feather headdress. But what caught my eye more than anything else was a framed oval photo of an elderly lady from long ago. Grandma herself, perhaps?

As I gazed at the photo hanging beside my little table, my waitress returned.

"Is that the legendary Grandma?" I inquired.

"That it is," she smiled. "There's an article about her on the back of the menu, if you're interested. Can I start you off with anything from the bar?"

"Do you have a specialty drink you'd recommend?"

"If you like Bloody Marys, you'll never find one that can compare with our Minnesota Prairie Mary," she boasted. "It's garnished with a venison stick, pepper jack cheese, pickled baby corn, and pickled herring."

"I'll try it," I decided. Oh yes, I could use a drink after the day I'd had. As I sipped on my drink, I absorbed Grandma's photo. She wore a black velvet bonnet that tied beneath the sagging folds of her chin. Elegant white lace flowers sprouted from the top of her hat. Her dress was black, with a white lace stand-up collar and matching Victorian jabot.

Grandma had short gray hair, parted in the middle, with tight curls on both sides. But I was most intrigued with her piercing blue eyes that seemed to look right through me. A slight frown wrinkled her forehead. Half a smile played upon her thin lips, as if she were up to something. She was undoubtedly a woman of great determination.

Breaking away from Grandma's spell, I decided I'd better order my dinner. As always when I traveled, I enjoyed trying local cuisine. So I ordered the fresh Lake Superior walleye with a cup of Grandma's famous chicken wild rice soup. The wild rice was harvested locally on Minnesota lakes, as the Native American tribes had done here for centuries.

I then turned my attention to the article about Grandma. Her name was Rosa Brochi. She was a feisty Italian immigrant who opened a boarding house and brothel in the original building on this site in 1869. She became known as "Grandma" because she took such good care of her girls, and catered to the lonely sailors coming in off the ships traveling through the Great Lakes. She allegedly created some of the recipes that were still used here today. Legend also has it that Rosa returned to her home country to assist in World War I efforts. She was never heard from again.

"She must have been a fascinating person," I said to the waitress when she brought my food.

"That's what they say," the young woman sighed. "Whether it is all true or not, however, is a matter of speculation. Still, it's a delightful story, eh?"

I pondered her words as I ravished my excellent dinner. What was true, and what was not? And who had the right to determine that?

Exhausted by the time I returned to my hotel room, I barely had the energy for a quick shower before I slipped beneath the comforter and drifted into a sound sleep. But it wasn't long before distorted images of the past and the present began to infiltrate my dreams once again.

Side-by-side images of me today and the Emma persona I'd seen in my previous dreams merged together, then split apart. Then, another side-by-side of Jimmy blending with an image of Karl. And finally, images of Bella swirling around and dancing with Abigail.

The images played over and over again in my subconscious

mind until I heard a loud whisper from someplace. "That's enough! She's got it!"

I stumbled out of bed to get a drink of water. It was only midnight. Maybe I'd take a sleeping pill. I needed sleep. I needed to break away from the dreams that were haunting me.

I groaned and pulled the covers over my head when my alarm clock went off early the next morning. I was trying to shut out the day—to shut out the facts I feared I'd learn, or confirm, during my research at the library.

Did I really want to know the truth? Or was it better to hide in ignorance? Yet, as much as I'd already discovered, I was afraid that I was doomed to recognizing a past reality I did not like. Not at all. One that threatened the very essence of my current day persona.

Get up, Veronica, I prodded myself. I gazed out the window towards Lake Superior. It was perfectly calm today. Hardly a wave on the lake.

This was an unpredictable lake, I'd learned. The weather could change in the beat of a heart; from a day like today to storm-force winds and blizzards that had overcome many a ship over the years. The bottom of this huge lake (31,700 square miles) was dotted with shipwrecks. While a part of me admired the beauty and strength of the lake, finding peace and solitude beside it, another part of me feared it greatly.

I went down to the lobby for breakfast, then put on my warm jacket and walked out onto the deck overlooking Lake Superior. There I lingered a while with a cup of hot coffee. Despite the thirty degree temperature, the sun warmed me. I didn't want to leave.

Give me strength to face this day, I whispered to the powerful body of water stretching endlessly before my eyes. Then I found

233

my car and made my way to the public library, well aware that my fate may lie in old genealogical records hidden away in the archives.

Just the facts, I prayed silently, *all I need is the facts. No emotions please.* I would take my psychiatrist's advice and go into observer mode, I decided, instead of experiencing anything that may upset me.

Soon I was settled in a comfortable chair in the genealogical research center. The kind librarian had connected me with an Ancestry.com database, where I'd begin my search for Emma McDougall. As I bravely began to search, she scurried off to find more resources.

I found a number of Emma McDougalls. None, however, had lived in Duluth, Minnesota. Wait—there were more! I cautiously scrolled down until I stopped suddenly, gripping the arms of my chair for support.

Emma Jean McDougall, Duluth, Minnesota. Born 1875. Died 1897. Could it be? She died when she was only twenty-two years old?

There were some little green leafs to follow, taking me back to Emma's parents: Henry McDougall, born 1845, died 1880. Emma would have been only five years old. I shivered, remembering my flashbacks of losing my father at a young age. Further research of old Duluth newspapers confirmed his death as the result of an accident at Fitgers' Brewery.

Delving deeper into Emma's past, I discovered a brief news clipping. Emma McDougall had drowned in Lake Superior, an apparent suicide, in 1897.

No, I screamed silently into the empty room. *It was an accident, not suicide! I was simply upset after learning that my lover had a wife, upset enough that I threw caution to the winds and went walking beside the lake on that stormy night. I slipped on the rocks and slid into the angry sea. I didn't want to die!*

"Ma'am, is everything okay?" The voice of the kind librarian brought me back.

"I'm fine," I whispered, "just finding some rather shocking information. Do you have any information about the old Central High School and its graduating class of 1893?"

She scurried off, and soon returned proudly with an old yearbook. 1893. I began to carefully page through the old book. The interior of the school was just as I remembered it, including the alcove above the stairs where Abigail and I had sometimes sat, peering out the window as we plotted our future paths in life.

Memories came flowing back as I recognized some of my former classmates and teachers. Where was Abigail? Halfway through the book I found a photo of the two of us on the lawn by the entrance to the school. It was almost identical to the image haunting my dreams.

Abigail Adams and Emma McDougall, Class of 1893, the caption read. Yes, Adams, that was her last name.

With that information, I began an online search for my dear friend, Abigail. The one I had unknowingly betrayed in our past lifetime together. There she was, her vital records on the computer screen before me. Born 1875, just like I was. Died in 1925 at age fifty in Duluth, Minnesota.

Holding my breath, I clicked on her marriage link. She had married none other than Karl Faust in 1894. I began frantically clicking on links to find more vital statistics and archived newspaper clippings. The full story, the one I swore I never knew during my lifetime as Emma, began to unfold before my eyes.

Abigail and Karl met while both were attending the University of Minnesota in Minneapolis, Minnesota. She majored in liberal arts. Karl, born in 1865, was completing his law degree when they married. Abigail never had the big wedding her mother had always planned for her, back home in Duluth. Instead, she and

Karl were married in a quiet ceremony at Augustana Lutheran Church in Minneapolis. There was no mention of the Adams family attending the wedding.

I remembered the letters Abigail had sent me from college. She'd been in love. It was a secret. Her parents had already selected a future husband for her from among their associates. The plan was for Abigail to obtain her degree, and then come home to marry a man she did not even care for. She feared they would disown her if she followed her heart and married the man she loved.

So, according to the records I found, she had married in 1894. There were no records of her obtaining a college degree.

Karl obtained his law degree in late 1894, and soon set up his law office in Duluth. That, of course, was where I met him—the husband of my best friend.

Oh my God! How could I have betrayed my dear Abigail? And how could he have betrayed his wife? I began to fume. *Damn you, Karl — or Jimmy, or whoever the hell you are!*

The librarian quietly placed several old books on my table, disrupting my internal tantrum. Perfect timing, I thought, as I distracted myself by paging through the first book. It was a collection of photos of some of Duluth's old historical buildings.

I soon found a faded photo of Karl's law office, just as I remembered it. The words "Karl Faust, Lawyer" were prominently displayed on the front window, just as I'd recalled them last night when I'd driven past that old building. I lingered, staring hard at the photo, as I was once again swept back in time.

"I've never seen your upstairs suite." I'd smiled seductively into Karl's eyes as my hand brushed his. We were just closing the office for the night, and we were alone.

"Perhaps we should call it a night, Miss McDougall."

He cleared his throat. But I could feel the electricity sizzling between us. I'd known for a long time that he was attracted to me. And I hated it when he called me Miss McDougall.

"Emma. Please call me Emma," I purred, tracing my fingers along his arm. "Please? What can it hurt to take a look? I've always wanted to stand out on that balcony, to enjoy the view of Lake Superior from way up there."

He shuffled his feet as if he were struggling, as if he was torn between running out the door and climbing the stairs leading to who knew what.

I bent low to retrieve a file from my desk, exposing my cleavage. This was the most daring dress I'd ever worn to the office. I'd hidden it beneath a sweater when I left the house that morning, knowing that Mama would not be pleased. Then I proceeded to walk towards the narrow staircase leading up to the third level of the building.

"Emma," he sighed. "This may not be a good idea."

I did not reply. I merely glanced at him over my shoulder as I hiked up the hem of my long dress and began climbing the stairs. He followed.

He opened the door to an elegantly furnished suite dominated by an ornate canopy bed. I circled the bed, admiring it, before opening the French glass doors onto the balcony and stepping out. I let down my hair and spread my arms into the wind.

He stood in the shadows watching me. The look in his eyes told me everything I needed to know. He wanted me, almost as much as I wanted him. I twirled around on the balcony, dipping low, waltzing by myself.

"Emma." He stepped out onto the balcony, grabbing me around the waist. "Please stop. You could fall. Come in." He was breathing heavily as he held me.

"Why?" I moved closer into his arms, sighing as he led me back into the suite and locked the door to the balcony. "Dance with me, Karl." I began to lead us around the room, humming a tune.

We began to dance slowly, moving closer and closer, hearts beating wildly—until he suddenly broke away, shaking his head in disbelief. "What the hell are we doing? This is not right. We must leave. Now."

"But it is right, my darling." I found his eager lips and slid my hand beneath his shirt. I began to massage him gently. "Do you know how long I've waited for you? How can it be wrong when it is meant to be? You know that you want me as much as I want you."

He grabbed me and kissed me passionately. Our bodies were on fire. We could not stop. Not now. It wasn't long before he'd undressed me and eased me out of my corset. I'd never before seen a man naked. Never before made love. All I knew was that I needed this man, and he needed me.

We made love gently, then more passionately. Our fate was sealed that evening. It was the first of many passionate trysts we shared up there in the hidden suite. Until that fateful day in 1897, when I learned he was married and ended up at the bottom of Lake Superior.

Coming back to today's reality, to the desk at Duluth Public Library, I shuddered. So, if this flashback was true, I was equally at fault—perhaps more so than Karl! How could I have behaved like such a cheap little tart? *Tart*...where did that word come from? From Emma's days, of course.

Still, I hadn't known he was married, not then.... And I certainly didn't know he was married to my former best friend,

238

my true blood sister.

My head was spinning with all I'd learned. My last task of the day was a visit to the cemetery—a visit to Emma's gravesite. According to the burial records I'd found, she was buried in Forest Hill Cemetery on Woodlawn Avenue. I plugged the address into my rental car's GPS and began my journey.

I wound my way up the wooded hillsides overlooking Lake Superior to the old cemetery. It sprawled along rolling hills overlooking a frozen pond where children skated. Massive trees sheltered an assortment of beautiful tombstones and mausoleums from long ago.

I stopped short before a rust-colored brick mausoleum inscribed with the year 1890. I'd been here before, I suddenly realized. I knew this place. Mama and I had been here to pay our respects when this prominent citizen had passed on into the afterlife. The two of us had huddled together in the background. We weren't of his class. I think Mama had served as a seamstress for his wife in those days.

Looking around, I became aware that this was a pretty fancy cemetery, with many dignitaries and important people buried here. Mama could never have afforded to bury me here. Perhaps I was in the wrong cemetery. Perhaps Emma was buried someplace else.

I pulled out the lot and plot numbers I'd found at the library to direct me to Emma's grave. I soon found it, nestled beneath a massive tree overlooking the pond. An eagle soared overhead as I walked up to a very impressive tombstone, now aging with the years.

It was inscribed *Emma Jean McDougall, 1875-1897, Beloved daughter and special friend.*

Tears filled my eyes as I brushed the light snow off my old tombstone and rubbed my gloved hand over the inscription.

239

Special friend? What did that mean? Special friend of whom?

Stepping back, I looked around the site and focused on a large double tombstone adjacent to mine. The style was almost identical to mine.

Something compelled me to brush the snow off the stone so I could read the inscription. Stunned at what I found, I slumped down onto the snow-covered ground.

The inscription on the side closest to my grave read, *Karl James Faust, 1865-1920*. The other side was inscribed *Abigail Adams Faust, 1875-1925*.

The three of us, despite our conflicted relationships in that lifetime, had come together in death. And now we'd apparently returned — together again — for another go-round. Was this our destiny? Why?

I could no longer deny what was happening. The facts were all there, facts that confirmed the crazy dreams and flashbacks that had been haunting me.

Shivering, I rose from the frozen ground. Shoving my numb fingers into my pockets, I walked down to the pond to watch the children skating. How simple life had once been, I sighed to myself. Why did it have to get so complicated?

As I stood silently beneath the falling snowflakes, I cursed at myself. How could I have been so stupid? How could I have betrayed my own blood sister? Had she come back this time, as my biological sister, to teach me a thing or two?

But she'd done nothing to get me back...nothing aside from shunning me for years and always disagreeing with me. Until the end, when we finally made peace. Thank God for that.

I deserved to be punished for what I'd done to her, I decided, for having a disgusting affair with her husband. It was so humiliating. I really wasn't that kind of person. I wasn't the wild one — at least not in my present lifetime. Many considered me to be almost too prim and proper. How could I possibly have done the things Emma did in my past life?

A scene from Emma's lifetime suddenly took over my mind....

Mama was scolding me as I stood beside the wood stove in our over-sized shabby kitchen. "You will be the death of me yet, Emma. I tried so hard...." She slunk down into the wooden rocking chair beside the stove and picked up her bag of knitting. Needles flying, she stared down at the peeling floor tiles.

"I'm sorry." I pivoted away from her, gazing out the window at the falling snow. "I'm a grown woman, Mama, and I just want to have a little fun. Is that so bad?"

"But look how you dress! That dress...the bodice is cut way too low. What will the young men think? You know this is a shipping port. There are sailors all over. You need to dress decently so they will show you some respect."

"Mama, I do not stroll through the red light district! Please! Give me some credit!" I turned to see her brilliant blue eyes flashing with anger.

"I swear she takes after Rosa instead of me or her daddy," she mumbled to herself.

What was she talking about? "Who? Who is Rosa?"

She startled, apparently realizing the words that had slipped out of her mouth in a fit of anger.

"Who is Rosa?" I repeated my question. "And why would I take after her?"

Her lips tightened as she continued to knit furiously, avoiding my gaze.

"Is this some kind of family secret I should know about?"

"Best you not know, child." She tilted her chin defiantly.

241

Mama was Italian and had a temper to go with it. I usually knew enough to back off, but this time I was determined to find out what she was talking about. If I took after somebody named Rosa, I needed to know who she was. It might help to explain my recent feelings and behavior. I had to admit I baffled myself at times. I was sometimes overwhelmed with feelings that I could not seem to control.

"But I need to know," I pleaded. "It could help me to understand myself. Am I adopted, Mama? Is that what you are hiding from me?"

"Heavens no, child!"

"You need to tell me if there is somebody named Rosa that I take after. I have a right to know the truth. Who is Rosa?"

Mama exploded in her native Italian language as she threw her knitting bag onto the floor and scurried out of the kitchen. I followed her, unwilling to let this go. I needed an answer.

Once she'd calmed down, she relented. "I will tell you something. Then I do not want to ever discuss this again. Do you understand?"

I leaned in closer, holding my breath, not sure what could be so terrible that Mama had hidden this information from me for my entire life.

"You once had an ancestor named Rosa. She spent her days—and nights—in the red light district, in a brothel, if you must know. She was the madam, exploiting young girls for the benefit of despicable sailors coming into port on their ships."

I was stunned. "So how am I related to this Rosa?"

"I've told you all that I'm going to tell you, young lady. Nothing else is of any importance. Your daddy and I never spoke of her in this house, and I do not intend to speak of her again. Do you hear me?"

I could only nod in agreement.

242

She softened a bit. "I'm sorry for comparing you to someone like her. I did not mean it. I was just upset, that's all. You're my only daughter, all that I have left in this world. I just want to be sure you don't turn out like she did. Truth be told, you do bear a physical resemblance to Rosa." Her mind seemed to drift off into the past.

Finally she stood and scooped me into her big arms, her eyes full of tears. All was forgotten. All was forgiven. She was once again my doting Italian mama.

As I emerged from my trance into Emma's life, it suddenly hit me. Rosa...the woman in the portrait at Grandma's Saloon...the photo I couldn't take my eyes off of. Rosa had been the madam of a brothel at this site. Her eyes in that photo...those brilliant blue eyes...were identical to those of Emma's mother. They were both Italian, and there was a distinct resemblance. The eyes. The prominent Italian nose.

Were they related? How?

I scurried from the cemetery and headed back to my hotel room, where I settled down with my laptop and began a search on Ancestry.com. I found my past mother easily, and traced her back to her parents in Italy.

Mama had never spoken of her Italian ancestors. I always thought it was too painful for her to remember those she had left behind in her homeland. She had been an only child...or so I thought... until a sibling named Rosa Brochi popped up on my computer screen. Rosa, the famous madam, had been seven years older than Mama.

I'd discovered the notorious aunt that Emma never knew she had, the one who'd been disowned by the family. Could that connection somehow account for the wild streak that had ultimately cost Emma her life?

I shuddered, pulling myself back to today's reality. My head hurt. I couldn't think any more. I couldn't bear to replay the shocking events of the day and all the discoveries I'd made. I needed sleep. First, I consumed several breakfast bars before falling onto the bed in my clothes. I flipped the television on to block out any noise.

Soon I was sound asleep. But sometime around midnight I awoke, to discover Irving Berlin's classic 1954 movie, *White Christmas*, playing on the TV.

"'Sisters, sisters…,'" the Haynes sisters sang as they danced across the stage before getting on the train for the Vermont ski lodge, where most of the movie took place. "'Lord, help the mister who comes between me and my sister, and Lord, help the sister who comes between me and my man,'" they sang as the audience applauded.

I snapped the television off with the remote, tossing it across the room, and hid beneath my pillow.

TWENTY-ONE
VERONICA

*"If this world could only grasp the power of forgiveness.
Being able to forgive someone breaks the cycle of bitterness and
vengeance."*
James Augustine St. John

By the time the airport shuttle dropped me off at Ashton Villa the next evening, I had a plan. It was time for me to go through Bella's cottage and decide what to do with all her things. I was, by default, the executor of her estate.

Aside from my duties, I felt I needed to spend some time there. This would be the place I'd beg for her forgiveness, hoping she could hear me. Hoping she was still looking down upon her beloved cottage. After all, she was the one who'd always believed in communicating with the dead.

Me, I'd been the unbeliever. Now I wasn't sure what I believed anymore, aside from the unavoidable fact that we'd lived together in a previous lifetime.

It felt good to escape from the snow of the Northland, although it had been a beautiful place to visit. After paying my driver, I walked up to the door, where I found three beautiful Christmas wreaths waiting for me. A note was attached, in

Melanie's distinctive scrawl. "Mom, these are for the cemetery. I thought you'd want to be the one to place them on the graves."

How thoughtful. Maybe I'd make the cemetery my first stop tomorrow morning, before I drove down the island to Bella's place.

I pulled into the cemetery early the next morning, just as the sun was rising over the Gulf of Mexico. It was hard to believe that it had been almost a year since I'd lost Jimmy. Then Olivia. And now Bella. They were all buried in our family plot.

As I walked to the site carrying the fragrant evergreen wreaths, it hit me. I'd buried Bella in a single grave beside the double headstone I'd someday share with Jimmy. Jimmy rested between us—just like Karl laid in peace between Emma and Abigail in the Duluth cemetery.

The only difference was that I (as Emma) had been buried alone in a single plot last time around. This time, Bella (Abigail) was buried alone.

The three of us—together again.

But Bella didn't deserve to be alone in this lifetime, did she? She'd done nothing wrong. Aside, perhaps, from having a baby out of wedlock.

As for Jimmy…I felt totally conflicted as I stood beside his grave, trying to make sense of what he had done during his lifetime as Karl Faust. How he had betrayed his wife. How he'd also betrayed me in a sense. And how I'd been at least partly responsible for what happened.

I carefully laid the wreaths upon the tombstones of Jimmy, Olivia, and Bella, wishing them all a Merry Christmas in Heaven as tears filled my eyes. Were they together up there somewhere?

Bella's orchestra of wind chimes greeted me as I pulled into her overgrown yard. The cats were all gone. My children had taken them to the animal shelter shortly after she died, aside from one they had saved for the grandkids. Midnight, Bella's favorite old cat, deserved a place in the family, they decided. That would make their eccentric Aunt Bella happy.

It felt strange to creak the door open and walk into her abandoned cottage. It felt like she should be there, somewhere, working on one of her many projects. Her working table was still strewn haphazardly with her photos, artist sketches, letters from her publisher, polished stones, and fixings for her jewelry.

Boxes of her books, the one she had just released about the storm, filled a corner of the room. They were unopened.

Where to begin? First, I decided to make myself a cup of her instant coffee and take it out to the gazebo, where I could look out across the bay. That had been her tradition for many years. I wanted to share it with her now.

As I sipped the muddy concoction, I focused hard, thinking thoughts to her. *I am so sorry, Bella, for what I did in our previous lifetime; for having an affair with your husband. I swear I didn't know he was married. Certainly not to you, my blood sister and best friend. I'm sure you know the truth now. Please forgive me. Let me know if you hear me, if you can forgive me.*

I tried to tune in to any vibes, any surges of energy, anything unusual. Something to make me believe she was there and had heard my message. There was nothing. Maybe this wasn't the time or place. Maybe later.

I dumped the rest of my coffee in the flower garden and returned to the house to begin sorting through her things. As I sat at her table, sorting through her art work, I found a breathtaking sketch of Jimmy, my Jimmy. She'd captured his eyes beautifully. They sparkled with love, a look I'd rarely seen in his eyes. Nevertheless, it was a wonderful sketch. I would keep it.

Something suddenly compelled me to go into Bella's bedroom and retrieve that old box of journals from under her bed — the box I'd tried to break into that day when she arrived home earlier than expected. That had not been one of my finer moments in life, to say the least.

This time, I successfully broke the lock and carefully retrieved almost a dozen journals. A part of me felt it was not appropriate to be prying into her life like this. But she was dead. Maybe there was important information that we needed to know. Maybe even the identity of Jonathan's father.

I never did buy her story that it had been a one night stand, that she didn't even know his full name. Eccentric as she had been in many ways, she'd still been what Olivia would call "a good girl."

I curled up on Bella's well-worn davenport, throwing her afghan over me, and began reading the story of her life. I hoped she was there with me in some way, guiding me through this process. It would take many hours, days in fact, to get through all of this. Where should I begin?

Suddenly, one of the journals lifted off the table and seemed to drift into my hands. How odd! Was Bella there, playing tricks on me, guiding me on my journey?

The pages flipped on their own to an entry in the back of one of the journals. I began to read.

Dear Veronica,

Just in case something happens to me, there are some things you should know. I am telling you this to come clean, as they say. I have not been honest with any of you. I regret that, but I still think that telling the truth would have hurt you all deeply. Things are different now that Jimmy has died. He, himself, did not know the truth, Veronica, until he passed on to the other side of life.

You see, Jimmy is Jonathan's father — conceived before you ever

248

married him.

What the hell? I dropped the journal onto the floor. The two of them, together? How could they? When? Where? Rage flashed through me.

What a fool I'd been! But wasn't that what I had suspected earlier? She'd lied to me. And he'd lived a lie, pretending to be my husband. How could he?

"How could you?" I glared at the picture of her hanging on the wall. I wasn't sure I wanted to read any more. But something finally compelled me to pick the book up and continue. I had to face the truth, painful as this was going to be.

There, she described in detail the entire affair. She swore they'd never been physically intimate once he'd married me. But she was clear that she'd always loved him and that he loved her. They were soul mates, she emphasized, destined to be together. But something had gone wrong this time around.

I'm so sorry, Veronica. We both love you and beg your forgiveness. Hopefully, we will all understand more once we're together again in Heaven.

I needed some fresh air. I escaped down to the beach, where I began to hike through the sand dunes, marching to the steady rhythm of the breakers crashing along the shoreline. Pelicans swooped overhead, diving into the sea in search of food.

What had gone wrong, and why hadn't I noticed what should have been obvious? All their photo shoots together, the way he treated Jonathan like his own son. He'd always been anxious to run off to his ranch on the west end of the island, stopping to visit Bella. And I, fool that I was, had encouraged him to do so. I thought the little boy needed a male role model in his life.

Even after Jonathan died, I'd felt responsible for Bella and encouraged him to stop and check up on her. Oh, I'd been totally blind...perhaps too busy with my social commitments and volunteer work to pay attention to what was happening.

Suddenly, I found myself laughing out loud, almost hysterically, as tears ran down my face. This was so ironic! I'd come here to beg for her forgiveness for having an affair with her husband in the previous lifetime we'd shared. Instead, I discover that she's the one who needs my forgiveness for her relationship with my husband in this lifetime.

What goes around, comes around, Olivia's words echoed through my mind. Perhaps Bella and I were even now. Perhaps we'd worked off our bad karma. And we had actually made peace in the end. That should count for something.

As devastating as this news was, I decided that I could at least quit beating myself up over what I'd done in my past life as Emma. My guilt was erased. I could move on with my life.

Still, what about Jimmy? He'd been the one who had come between us for at least two lifetimes now. He'd deceived us both. This was his fault, I decided — at least, mostly his fault.

He would have to pay, someday, for all the heartache he'd caused both of us. Someday…some way. But he was dead….

TWENTY-TWO
JIMMY

*"True forgiveness is understanding that each creation has their
own method of learning and producing; and they're
entitled to mistakes, as I am."*
Michael Newton

You appear to be distraught this fine morning, my spirit guide
announced as she materialized beside me in the Hall of Records.
Herneith was an exquisite dark-skinned beauty, and had once
been an Egyptian princess. She always seemed to know when I
needed her, and she had a calming effect upon me.

I'd been busily researching my past lives, trying to figure out
why I'd failed, why I'd made such a mess of my lives. Why I'd
hurt the two women who meant the most to me.

I could only shake my head, frustrated with myself over the
total lack of control I'd exhibited in my past lives. I was afraid to
go back any farther than my life in Duluth as Karl Faust during
the 1800s. I'd betrayed my wife, Abigail, my true soul mate. I'd
also been responsible for the death, the suicide, of my mistress,
Emma.

Ah, but Emma's unfortunate drowning was not a suicide. Herneith
conveyed the message into my mind.

251

"But, it says so in this article," I began.

Not true. It was an accident. You will find the truth in the archives of her life. She slipped and fell into the lake. She did not want to die.

I heaved a sigh of relief. One less burden for me to cope with. I couldn't wait to get through all of this orientation, through this past life review process, so I could get on with my life in Heaven. I'd do good things here. I'd make up for my mistakes.

Let's walk, Herneith said, guiding me out into the tranquil gardens. We walked silently. I began to relax. I could feel her comforting spirit surrounding me. Yes, unconditional love abounded on this side of life. Someday, I'd be ready to embrace this concept. Someday, I'd even be ready to give and receive this kind of love.

Finally we sat on my favorite bench, beneath a majestic oak tree beside a rippling brook. She waited for me to speak, to ask her the questions that she knew were brewing in my mind.

"So how can I make up for what I've done to Bella and to Veronica? I'm at a loss. I was wrong. I know that."

You will figure that out when the time is right. Perhaps the three of you will return to another lifetime on Earth together....

"Oh no!" I interrupted. "I don't think I want to go back and make more mistakes. Can't I just stay here?"

She sighed patiently. *Yes, of course you can stay here. You don't need to go back. Some souls remain here where they study, research, and perhaps discover things that will help others back on Earth. They do good work here to help all of mankind.*

"That sounds good to me!"

However, many souls, after consulting with their spirit guides and the Council, decide to return for various reasons. Sometimes they return to try again, to make up for previous mistakes. To do something to help others. Or to play a role in someone else's life. That is entirely your choice.

I was greatly relieved to hear that. Still, I was troubled. My Bella was also struggling with the things she'd learned. With the knowledge that I, her husband in our Duluth lifetime, had cheated on her with her best friend.

These days, Bella and I sometimes tiptoed around each other at home, lost in our own worlds. Sometimes we disappeared on our own journeys. I think she spent a considerable amount of time in Olivia's little village and visiting with Jonathan. Perhaps making up for lost time on Earth. At least she hadn't left me. Not yet.

I probably didn't deserve to be forgiven by either one of them, Bella or Veronica. Still, I longed to see my Bella smile again, really smile. And I wanted Veronica to find the happiness she deserved.

Timing is everything, my spirit guide informed me once again. *Before long, you – and Bella – will feel the unconditional love of the universe surrounding you. You shall be a part of it.* With that, she bid me good day and disappeared.

I walked back home, preferring the exercise, the opportunity to lose myself in the nature surrounding me. My pet eagle landed on my shoulder, welcoming me home.

The house was empty. No Bella. She was totally preoccupied these days with monitoring Veronica's past life experiences. At least they'd made peace, each one forgiving the other. Good for them. But what about me?

Feeling lonely, I grabbed my guitar and took it out onto the porch, where I settled on the swing and began to strum lonesome songs from long ago. As I played, I lost myself in the music.

"Beautiful," she sighed, as she materialized on the swing beside me, cuddling up to me. She smiled that smile, her eyes once again brimming over with love.

"Sa Bella, you're back. I mean, the old you is back."

"I am, Jimmy. I just needed some time. I've had so much to digest, so much to think about."

"And?" I set my guitar down and wrapped my arms around her.

"And, I forgive you. We all make mistakes. We're human. We hurt each other. Some day we will understand the reasons we each did what we did. For now, all I know is that God forgives us and wants us to forgive each other."

Tears filled my eyes as I held her. "Thank you, my darling."

"I've also made mistakes, as did Veronica. But we learn from our mistakes. I think it's time to put all of that behind us, don't you think?"

"Is Veronica doing all right?" I was genuinely concerned.

"She is now. We have forgiven each other. She's now free to move on. Of course, she's still wondering what your fate will be...."

I shook my head. "How do you know so much?"

"I've had lots of help." She grinned as Isabella materialized on the porch beside us.

"My pleasure," she replied with a smile. "Now, I hope you can both move on and settle in to the wonders of life here."

"Thank you, my dear Isabella," Bella said as she hugged her spirit guide.

"As for me, I'm ready for a little break," Isabella laughed. "You've kept me quite busy as your spirit guide, I must say. I'll still be around, of course, if you need any more help transitioning here. But I also need to begin planning my next life."

Then she was gone. A profound sense of unconditional love and peace remained, surrounding the two of us as we swung together on the old porch swing.

TWENTY-THREE
BELLA

*"There is a land of the living and a land of the dead,
and the bridge is love — the only survival, the only meaning."*
Thornton Wilder

Jonathan eagerly guided us through our first Christmas in Heaven. We attended surreal musical concerts performed by some of the greatest musicians who'd ever lived on Earth. The music seemed to seep into our souls, surrounding us with a profound sense of peace and joy. We attended church services, where we prayed for our loved ones on Earth.

Olivia went all out for Christmas, of course, as she always had. While she still liked to bake her own Christmas cookies, she did use her newly developed gift of projected thought to expand her Christmas village into and around her large wooded lot. She even added snow, giggling as she managed to create a beautiful snowfall for us as we arrived on Christmas Eve.

Yes, we had a winter wonderland in Heaven. We ate the feast Olivia had prepared for us, exchanged gifts, and sang old Christmas carols as she played her antique pump organ.

Life in Heaven was good, we all agreed, so much better than anything that anyone on Earth could possibly comprehend.

255

"I wonder how Veronica and the children are celebrating Christmas this year," Jimmy commented wistfully.

"It seems strange, doesn't it, for us to be celebrating here without any of them?" Olivia sighed.

"And it must be a little sad down there," I chimed in. "After all, three of us are no longer with them. Three of us gone home in less than a year."

Jonathan, who was settled into an overstuffed chair in the midst of the twinkling Christmas village houses, suddenly startled. "Wow, I just had a flashback. I'm about three years old, and I'm running through a village just like this in a beautiful brick mansion...."

"Ashton Villa? You remember Ashton Villa?" Olivia beamed, asking him for more details about the house. He went on to describe it perfectly.

"I'm having such fun running around the village, giggling, trying to touch all the houses. Then, suddenly, a pair of strong arms scoops me up from behind and holds me close." Jonathan's eyes filled with tears.

"Yes, my son, that was me holding you on your last Christmas on Earth," Jimmy whispered, wiping a tear from his eye.

"You always insisted on taking him there for Christmas Eve." I gazed deeply into Jimmy's eyes. "I finally agreed to tag along during those years."

"And he loved it! Didn't you, son?"

"I must have! Actually, I'd love to see it again, to see what they're all doing tonight at Ashton Villa," Jonathan replied.

"So would I," Jimmy whispered. "I'm so proud of them all. Sometimes I look down and can't believe how fast our grandkids are growing up—without us, I'm afraid."

I hugged him close. "I have an idea...let's do something to let them know we are thinking about them and loving them all."

"Like what?" Olivia asked.

"I may need Jonathan's help here," I began, as he came to my side and put his arm around me.

"Mom, you are doing remarkably well with your newfound powers. Believe in yourself. Believe you can do this. I'll back you up if you need any help. I know what your plan is, and I think it's a great one."

Olivia and Jimmy just shook their heads.

Closing my eyes, I took several deep breaths, psyching myself up—almost like I used to do back on Earth when I'd try to call Isabella to my side or communicate with deceased loved ones. But this time I found myself going deeper, deeper yet, transporting us back to our beloved Ashton Villa.

Suddenly, the star on the top of the Christmas tree in the Gold Room began to blink as several bells on the tree rang.

"Look, Mommy." A little boy, about three years of age, pointed in amazement at the bells. "Look, Daddy!"

"Does that mean an angel is getting its wings?" an older child asked her Grandma Veronica. "Just like in that old movie we watch every year?"

"*It's a Wonderful Life*," Veronica sighed, putting her arm around her granddaughter. "It *is* a wonderful life. We need to remember that. Even though there are times—"

"But what about the angels?" another grandchild interrupted her. "Maybe Grandpa got his wings and he is ringing that bell."

"Or maybe it's Grandpa, and Great-Grandma Livia, and Aunt Bella. All of them," another chimed in, jumping up and down with excitement.

"Yes! Maybe they are thinking about us tonight." Veronica wiped a tear from her eye. "And we are missing them, aren't we?"

They all nodded solemnly, even the little ones.

257

"It's OK to miss them, to feel a little sad sometimes," Maria whispered. "But I think they want us to be happy again, don't you?"

All heads nodded quietly once again.

The bells quit ringing and the room was engulfed in total silence—until four little gift packages magically floated to the base of the tree. Wrapped in gold foil, they glittered beneath the lights.

"This is really strange." Michael shook his head as he picked up one of the packages and began to carefully unwrap it. The family gathered around him, trying to get a peek.

He retrieved a beautiful gold ornament with an inscription on the front, which he read aloud to his family.

"'Merry Christmas from Heaven! Please don't shed a tear. I'm spending my Christmas with Jesus this year. Love Always.'"

There was another inscription on the back of the ornament—Jimmy's full name and his birth and death dates.

The entire family was in awe. "It's like a miracle," someone exclaimed. "Where did it come from?"

"Let's open the others." And they did.

They each contained the identical ornament with the same message on the front. The back sides, however, were inscribed with the names and birth and death dates of Olivia, Jonathan, and myself.

"Who's Jonathan?" one little girl with curly blonde hair asked. After all, Jonathan had died long before she was born.

"He was a wonderful little boy whom we all loved dearly," Veronica replied softly. "Aunt Bella's son, and…and your Grandpa Jimmy was like a father to him."

As the children hung the new ornaments on the tree, Veronica settled into a chair, looking like she might faint.

"What the hell just happened here?" Melanie shook her head.

"I don't know, but I think your Aunt Bella may have had something to do with it," Veronica replied. "She always believed in things like this; and who knows...she may be right."

I was so proud, I couldn't quit smiling. I'd done it, just as Jonathan told me I could.

"What a wonderful gift," Jimmy sighed as he drew me into his arms. "Thank you, Sa Bella."

As we turned our attention back to the family, I began to psych myself up once more for the grand finale.

"Merry Christmas from Heaven," the children sang out as they danced around the tree. "Merry Christmas from Heaven!"

Veronica suddenly gasped, her eyes wide.

"What is it? Are you all right?" Her children closed in around her.

"I'm fine. Better than I think I've been in a very long time. But...do you feel anything strange in this room?"

The children suddenly stopped in their tracks, a look of amazement spreading across their faces. Their parents also appeared to be in shock as a wave of love and peace seemed to swirl through the room, into their hearts and souls.

A gust of wind suddenly blew the front door open. The wave drifted out into the night as the bells on the Christmas tree began to ring once more.

The family resumed their Christmas celebration, recognizing that something profound had happened. Something had opened their hearts to a newfound sense of peace, joy, and love.

The words, "Merry Christmas from Heaven" would be with them always.

YOU AND I
Rumi
A moment of happiness,
You and I sitting on the verandah,
Apparently two,
But one in soul,
You and I.
We feel the flowing water of life here,
With the garden's beauty and the birds' singing.
The stars will be watching us,
And we will show them what it is to be
A thin crescent moon.
You and I, unselfed,
Will be together,
Indifferent to idle speculation,
You and I.
The parrots of heaven will be cracking sugar
As we laugh together,
You and I.
In one form upon this earth,
And in another form in a timeless sweet land.

Janet Kay, Author

Janet Kay lives and writes on a lake in the woods of Northwest Wisconsin. Drawn to nature since she was a child, she sees it as a source of renewal, reflection and connection with something greater than oneself. She's also strongly drawn to the Victorian era and its fascinating history, themes which are reflected in her writing.

She began writing, and decided to become an author, at the age of 8. Her early ventures included short stories and a neighborhood newspaper that she wrote by hand and sold to her neighbors for a nickel. Her dreams of becoming an author were interrupted temporarily while raising her three children and becoming the grandmother of ten amazing grandchildren.

She has previously published two novels, WATERS OF THE DANCING SKY and AMELIA 1868. Both novels have earned excellent reviews:

"Janet Kay is a gifted storyteller who enthralls her readers with her brilliant imagination and alluring plots." Stacie Theis, Beachbound Book Review

Her work can best be described as a blend of paranormal, historical, fantasy, romance, spiritual and visionary fiction. Her mission is to make a difference in people's lives by expanding their horizons above and beyond the confines of this world and this lifetime.

Janet Kay's lifelong passions include creative writing, travel, photography and spending time with family and friends. She frequently combines these interests as she explores new and exciting destinations to set her novels. *Waters of the Dancing Sky* is set on the wilderness islands of Rainy Lake along the Minnesota/Canadian international border. *Amelia 1868* is set in the old western ghost town of Virginia City, Montana.

Her latest work, THE SISTERS, takes place on the historic, haunted Galveston Island in Texas.

For more information, check out her website at www.novelsbyjanetkay.com; or her Facebook page – www.facebook.com/Janet-Kay-Author.

CPSIA information can be obtained
at www.ICGtesting.com
Printed in the USA
FFOW02n0246260418
46347021-47970FF